Almost Dangerous
Copyright © 2020 Joseph W. Bebo
Published by Joseph W. Bebo
(An imprint of Joseph W.M. Bebo Books Publishing)

Joseph W. Bebo
Hudson, MA, 01749
Email: joewbebobooks@gmail.com
Editor: James Oliveri
Cover Design: Elyse Zielinski
Proof Reader: Paul Kelloway

Library of Congress Cataloging in – Publication Data
Joseph W. Bebo
Almost Dangerous /Joseph Bebo – First Edition

ISBN: 978-1-7339308-5-7
Fiction, Crime Drama

This book is dedicated to Paul, a first avid reader of this story, who has read all twelve versions of it. May this be the last.

Prologue

He sat in the cramped darkness of the closet, still as stone, silently watching them at their sex play through a sliver of light. While they gyrated frantically on the bed before him, his mind wandered to his boyhood, when he would disappear for hours in the forest behind his grandfather's house with his only companion, his hunting knife. He loved to hunt the small, wary wildlife that made their homes in the woods. Their hardwired patterns made them easy prey, as if they were born to die at his hands, as if his hands were made to kill.

He had been watching them far longer than these past few hours, waiting far longer than the two weeks he'd been stalking them. He had been waiting all his life. For as long as he could remember, he had been pulled taut as an arrow in a high-powered bow. A lifetime of pain was about to be unleashed in an instant. The hours of watching and waiting were about to end.

He practiced deep-breathing exercises as he sat in the tiny space planning his move. They were ancient techniques taught to him long ago when he was an initiate in the art of silent death. His moves would be flawless. His query would be bagged. The end was a foregone conclusion.

Quickly becoming acquainted with their routines and habit, he formed his plan. Everything fell into place as if it were a script already written. Now all he had to do was act and all his suffering would be rewarded.

He watched and waited as the lovers satiated each other's lust. Now they were lying together on the bed, their passions spent for the moment. Their eyes were heavy-lidded with alcohol and drugs.

Mrs. Alice Stienman rolled back on top of her young lover. Bobby Dolan had those dark good looks that many women, including Alice Stienman, found appealing. It didn't hurt that his family owned a good portion of the town. He leaned up to kiss her pert, smiling mouth. His manhood was already starting to come to life again. Touching the soft downy skin of her buttocks and feeling her firm tight belly against his, he found it hard to believe she was the mother of two young children. But then Alice spent a large portion of her time and money in heath clubs and salons. She prided herself on her *supple, shapely body. Even so, she would probably not have kept her new lover interested for long. For the moment, however, she held his total rapt attention.*

Imperceptibly, the stalker started moving his hands and feet, ever so slowly. Tightening his grip around the dark-grained handle of 'Jim', his trusty Bowie knife, he readied himself for the lunge. The wide, tapering blade quivered in the darkness like a living thing. It could cut through bone like most knives could cut through twigs.

The world was filled with dirt. He would cleanse it.

A moan from the woman brought him out of his reverie. It was time to die.

Slowly getting his hands in place, he tensed his muscles. Then quickly snapping the sliding door of the closet open with a bang, he jumped out of the darkness and leaped like a cat across the few feet of floor to the bed. The blade of his Bowie knife flashed in the darkness.

As the couple struggled in their death throes, the killer lost all sense of time and his surroundings. He saw only his vision-guide, who had come to him long ago in his hour of need. It was to Him that he owed his every allegiance, his very life.

Chapter 1

Summer, 1990, Upstate New York

Day 1

It was Thursday night when I first heard about the murder. It was the first of a long series of events so incredible I still can't believe it really happened. It sounds even more unbelievable when I try to write it down. Write it down I must, however, even though no one is likely to believe a word of it.

The year was 1990, only a year ago. It seems like another lifetime. It was the first night of the band's second week at the Pontiac Club, a small nightclub on the south side of town. It's on the highway that runs along the lake. If you follow that highway south far enough it will take you all the way to the 'Big Apple', New York City. In my youth I traveled that road many times in my mind, always in one direction, south out of town. In all my wild imaginings I never saw myself ever traveling back. Well, I was sorely mistaken.

It was a week-night. The place was virtually deserted by the time we started our last set. That was just as well with me. We weren't playing all that good and I had to get up early to put in a long day investigating insurance scams.

Yep, there I was, mister almost-made-it, a born loser, master of unfulfilled dreams, finally back where I started, with a life full of failure and regret. Going nowhere fast, now you see him, now you don't. That about summed up my life at that point.

The last set of the evening dragged on. The dance floor was as empty as a church pew on Saturday night. I started to space-off, remembering the dismal road that led me back here. I daydreamed myself into a half-trance, while I mechanically got through the night, one slow song after another. My whole life paraded before me like the long, tedious march of a defeated army.

One of the things I always wanted to be was an FBI guy, like my favorite TV hero, Elliot Ness. By the time I was ready for college I pretty much knew what I wanted to do. I applied and was accepted into Northeastern University's criminology degree program.

I guess you could say I was a prime candidate for a career in law enforcement. I couldn't figure out what was wrong with people to make them want to take dope. Even Coca-Cola and aspirin stuck in my craw. I also had kind of a chip on my shoulder, partly because of my size, partly for other reasons. I found it physically impossible to take crap from anyone. Needless to say, this made life difficult at school and at home. As far as I could tell, FBI guys didn't have to take shit from anyone either, except maybe J. Edgar himself, and that suited me just fine.

Things went along smoothly enough, at least at first. I applied myself to my school work without distraction - since I couldn't get a date to save my life - and did well. I liked the curriculum, learning about the fundamentals of criminal investigation, law, sociology, and the psychology of the criminal mind. Although I didn't know it at the time, this was to be the high point of my miserable life. That was as good as it was going to get.

I had planned to go right on to graduate school after four years, and work for my masters in criminology. The summer before my senior year my father lined-up an interview in Washington, DC to discuss my enrollment in the FBI Academy and the prospects of future employment. I was headed for a career as one of the 'Untouchables'! I ended up an untouchable all right, but more like one of those sleeping in the streets of Calcutta than the one portrayed by Robert Stack on TV.

Like everything in the life of mister 'almost-made-it', it was not to be. Seems I have this behavior flaw, an inherent inconsistency with everything I do. I'll be going along fine, everything running smooth as a fine-tuned engine, almost tasting success. Then before you know it, I blow it, like stumbling in a foot race at the finish line. One minute I'm performing with the best of them, the next I'm scuffling along just barely able to keep afloat.

It was soon after my interview, in the summer before my senior year when my life finally came tumbling down like a house-of-cards. I had met a girl down at the Commons. It was at one of those 'happenings' that used to take place a lot in Boston at the time, in the early eighties. One thing led to another and we made a date to meet that night at a party.

If I had wanted to start my career in law enforcement off with a bang, I couldn't have picked a better place to be, only not as a guest. The place was filled with hippy wannabes and dropouts, all ingesting illicit drugs of one sort or another. There was pot and hash, LSD and coke. It was a regular cornucopia of narcotics, all the stuff I had read about in class. Now here I was, surrounded by it. I grabbed a beer and tried to get my date doped-up enough to let me in her pants. I was getting nowhere. Then there was a knock on the door. Before anyone knew what was happening there were enough cops in the place to form a parade.

"What's this?" one of them said, snooping around and picking up a bag full of grass. Duran Duran was playing, 'Hungry Like a Wolf' on the stereo in the background. With that I knew my future in the FBI had just gone up in a puff of smoke. The whole place was busted. The drugs weren't mine and it wasn't my apartment, but I did most of the talking, being the only one not totally zonked out of his mind. I should have kept my big mouth shut. I was the only one they handcuffed! I was lucky to get off with a year probation and Community Service, along with six weeks of drug rehabilitation. And I don't even take the stuff. Quite a price to pay for one measly date!

That spelled the end of my career in law enforcement. They tend to frown on drug felonies in the FBI. My father had been paying my tuition. He resented how I had thrown away the career he had worked so hard to insure for me, and refused to foot the bill for another semester. Not that it mattered. I was thrown out of school because of the bust. With a criminal record and no degree, I was lucky to get a job as a night watchman in a K-Mart, let alone in the Federal Bureau of Investigation.

It's amazing how fast things can change, how you can be riding high one minute, and crashing and burning the next. Although my father had paid my tuition, I had been supporting myself with odd jobs and music gigs since my second year. Now my future seemed bleak. The whole affair knocked the stuffing out of me. I stumbled on for a while, like a wounded buck with a bullet in its side, before I fell, but in the end my failure was complete. It was as if someone had pulled the plug and I was being sucked down the drain with the rest of the garbage. Finally, I got a job as a night watchman at the Prudential Center. Hey, I knew those three years of law enforcement would come in handy someday.

There followed a string of more meaningless jobs that seemed to get harder to keep the worse they got. Soon I was having trouble keeping even the most menial of work, night watchman, repo-man, fast food waiter, bus boy, one failure after another. The occasional music gigs I picked up helped – I had played drums since I was a kid - but they were too few and far between to support myself on. I started to drink heavily, at one point doing a good imitation of an alcoholic. Then

I got into the martial arts and kicked the booze, well, pretty much. I survived like this for a couple more years before things bottomed out. I came back home like a cur with my tail between my legs, licked and skittish from too many defeats and backhands from life.

So there I was back in this dead-end town, after a short life of long failures. I guess it could have been worse. It could always be worse. At least that's what I kept telling myself, but it seemed hard to imagine how.

Situated in the northeastern-most corner of New York State, my hometown is tucked between the Canadian boarder, Lake Champlain, and the Adirondack Mountains. Considered by some to be a scenic vacation spot, I always thought of it as the end of the earth. Now here I was again.

When I came back home my dad let me move into the old homestead. He pulled in some favors and helped get me a job as an investigator for a local insurance agency. In a town this size there's really not much need for insurance investigators, not that there's not a lot going on of one sort or another that needs investigating.

There's quite a bit happening for a small town. It has an active Strategic Air Command base. Although with the fall of the Soviet Union, who can tell for how long it will remain. There's also a good-size state college, and carloads of Canadians that come down in the summer. And it has a constant flow of strangers and transients passing through to cause trouble. Not to mention its own local breed of genetically inferior, inbred, social mutants. For a place its size, it boasts one of the highest crime rates per capita in the country. Unfortunately, there's not much in the way of insurance fraud, except for an occasional car torching or two.

I was fortunate enough to hook-up with a group of local musicians when I returned home. One of them, the guitarist, George Austin, I had played with when I was in high school. When George heard I was back in town, he let the kid who was playing drums with him go, and hired me on the spot.

The other members of the band were a husband and wife team from the Buffalo area, who taught music in the local high schools. Our little combo was starting to sound pretty good and beginning to work steady, making the rounds of Holiday Inns and other local clubs. With the extra money I was making with the band, I was able to get my own place, a small efficiency apartment, down near the beach.

Things were not as bad as they could've been. Yeah, I was home again, a failure at everything I had tried, but the situation was passable. I was getting by, at least for the time being.

So there I was, mechanically getting through the last set, wishing the song would end so I could pack up and go home to bed, when my girl Mary walked in. She sat at the bar and eyed me like a hungry bird. Suddenly I wasn't tired anymore.

I'd been home about six months, when I hooked up with the town's only female mortician. Mary Cascia was a misplaced Brooklynite, a fading blonde in her early forties just going overripe. Even though she was a decade and a half older than me, she kept herself in good shape, riding horses and dancing among other things. She sure looked great in a sweater.

I remember the first night I met her. She was wearing one of her tight sweaters, and talked about her work, how she loved making her clients as presentable and life-like as possible, especially the men. It was an art to her. We'd been seeing each other pretty steady ever since.

Finally, the set ended. Mary and the group wanted to go out for a late-night snack. I was persuaded to go along. It was that or face the likelihood of George, for whom absolutely no female was taboo, hitting on Mary in my absence. As it turned out, I would have been better off had I gone home after the gig and let Mary take her chances with George alone.

I hated going out after the gig. By the end of the night I was usually sick and tired of whiskey-smelling drunks. That evening my stomach was doing push-ups of bile-tasting acid to the tune of six per minute. It was the tradition, however, and the others, who also had to get up in the morning, felt like going for some after-hours chow.

We were in one of the rear booths of the Pancake House, a concession to me, since it was out of the way of most of the smoke. The late-night crowd was the usual assortment of can't get enough, burnt out partygoers and general undesirables. It also included a mixture of truck drivers, guys on break from the nightshift at the paper mill, and local law enforcement personnel.

Marge had just taken our orders. The last thing I felt like doing was eating. I ended up ordering French toast in the hope it might settle my stomach until I could get home to my antacids. George ordered enough food for the Royal Highlanders. With his six-foot-two frame, he could get away with it. I forget what they were talking about, but being in a generally sour mood, I piped in with my usual cynical comments. George just ignored me.

"Why do you have to be so negative all the time, Jay?" asked Denise, the piano player and singer in the group.

"Yeah, Lawless," chimed in Paul, her bass-playing husband, laughing. "You're a real pain in the ass."

"Bite me," I retorted.

"Hey, Mary," said Paul, grinning at my mortician girlfriend. "Why don't you cork him up with some of that embalming fluid of yours."

Everyone laughed at his lame joke but me. I sat back and sulked until the chow came. When Marge came back with our tray, she told us the news. The two cops sitting in the booth by the door had told her. It seems earlier that evening, Bobby Dolan, the son of one of the town's wealthiest merchants, was murdered in the sack with the wife of some officer from the air base. They had apparently been killed while having sex. The cops had told her all the gruesome details and she looked like she was in a minor state of shock.

Everybody knew Bobby Dolan. He was the town's most eligible young bachelor, the boy most females wanted to live next door to. Just graduated cum laude from a prestigious law school - much better than the shyster school my brother Tony went to - Bobby had a bright future in law and politics ahead of him. That future had been cut short in a most brutal way this very night.

Mary sounded especially shocked. She had just seen him earlier that evening at his dad's restaurant.

"What a terrible waste," she said. "I just saw him. I can't believe that poor boy has been cut down like that in the prime of life. My God, what a tragedy. It's just so terrible!"

Marge, the waitress, looked like she was ready to cry and hurried off, forgetting to get my maple syrup.

"Sounds like he got himself in the wrong place at the wrong time," I observed. "Hopping in the sack with another man's wife does not lead to a long life expectancy."

George speculated that drugs might be involved. He'd heard that Bobby was dealing. I thought the husband probably did it. After all, he had the best motive. Mary knew one of the cops, so went over to get more information. When she came back she said that it sounded like a sex crime or a crime of passion. They were both stabbed repeatedly while in the act. Mary confirmed that the police had taken the husband of the murdered woman in for questioning.

"They always suspect the husband," Paul stated flatly. "That's why I haven't bumped Denise off yet."

"You haven't bumped me off yet because I'd get you first," she said, giving him a shot to the arm. "And besides, you'd be lost without me. Who would cook lasagna for you?"

Mary wondered who would be doing the funeral arrangements. Talk about your ghouls, the bodies weren't even cold yet and she wanted to work on them.

The whole conversation had the effect of completely ruining my appetite. I looked at my French toast. It looked back at me like a flank of dead flesh. My stomach was doing back flips now. I needed my antacids and slumber in the worse way.

Later that night, as I lay in bed tossing and turning, trying to sleep, the news of the murders kept creeping into my thoughts like an uninvited house-pest. All I could think about was those two ill-fated lovers, just trying to have some fun, now lying dead in the morgue.

Chapter 2

Day 2

The next morning I managed by a superhuman effort to get to the office by ten. As I slunk in, Suzie, the secretary, eyed me knowingly.

"Boy, you look terrible," she observed. "What happened, stay up all night playing with that undertaker friend of yours? You're starting to look like one of her stiffs."

Suzie is a cute, five-foot-two, wisecracking redhead with stunning blue eyes and a girlish figure. Exchanging quips with Suzie is often the only mental stimulation I get during the otherwise boring day.

"I didn't get much sleep," I replied. "Late night. We're gigging at the Pontiac Club this week. You should come by sometime and hear the band. Bring your friend, Clark Kent, along."

She smiled at me under her thick, red mop of hair.

"His name is Neil and at least he works for a living, which is more than I can say for you."

"Yeah, but under his three-piece suit I'll bet you'll find superman pajamas."

I was starting to feel better, although my head ached and I was still tired. My verbal exchanges with Suzie always seemed to cheer me up, though I seldom had the last word.

"Mister Majerka wants to see you as soon as you get in."

She still called him Mister Majerka, even though she had worked for him for ten years. She called me Clyde. Don't ask me why. I called her 'Spritzer', after the guy in the old Federal Express ads.

"Oh, did you hear about Bobby Dolan?" she asked as I headed toward Majerka's office. Her eyes widened with excitement or shock, I couldn't quite decide. "Can you believe it, a sex murder right here in our town?"

"I can believe anything about our town. I thought the police suspected the husband."

"I don't know. I only know what I read in the morning papers about it. God, isn't it awful? Poor guy. He was such a hunk too."

Hearing her go on about the dead guy was starting to depress me, so I headed for the restroom to freshen up a bit.

"Yeah, you'd better straighten yourself up before you go in to see Mr. Majerka," she called after me "You look like garbage warmed over. Don't you have a mirror at home?"

"You already told me how I look. I don't need no stinking mirrors. I don't have to look at myself, you do."

I splashed some cold water on my face and looked at myself in the mirror. I did look bad. I stared at the pathetic creature looking back at me. My eyes were red-rimmed with deep purple bags under them. I couldn't seem to find my comb, so I tried to force my hair into place with my hands. There must be a ground-fill somewhere in New Jersey full of my lost non-biodegradable combs. The more I tried, the more hopeless my hair became. I had on my last clean shirt, but it was wrinkled and already streaked with sweat.

I left the bathroom and went to see the boss. It didn't really matter what I looked like, the guy thought I was crud. He was always telling me how he only hired me as a favor to my Dad. Said he owed him, but he never told me why. I made a note to ask my father about it next time I saw him.

I rapped on Majerka's office door and let myself in. He was talking on the phone. He waved me in with his free hand, smoke trailing like a steam engine from the cigarette he was holding. I sat down across from his old-fashioned, paper-strewn metal desk. As I did, I noticed the morning paper, with headlines about the murder and a recent picture of the deceased Bobby Dolan.

Dick Majerka was a red-faced little man with balding black hair, colored and slicked across his wide forehead. He chain-smoked incessantly and had beady eyes like a rodent's, set in thick black-framed glasses. He looked more like a seedy theatrical agent than an insurance man. A social climber, he was always trying to improve his standing in the community by entertaining the correct people, and being seen at the right places.

Dick finally got off the phone.

"That dumb schmuck. Lets his insurance payments lapse and then expects us to cover his ass. What's wrong with people these days? Everybody wants something for nothing," he complained.

I started to reply, but he went on.

"Did you see today's paper? What a mess. The son of Dan Dolan and some Air Force broad murdered. What a mess."

"Yeah, I heard about it last night."

I was starting to get my acid stomach back. At least I had the foresight to bring my antacids to work.

Dick went on.

"Dan Dolan is a close and personal friend of mine. Christ, we just had him and the missus over to the house last month. Dan's one of our best customers. He knows the value of security for his loved ones. He had a policy taken out on Bobby shortly after he left for college."

"If my dad did that, I'd start looking over my shoulder."

"This is not a joking matter, Jay," he said. "After all the money he invested in his son's education and future, I guess he felt the need to protect his investment."

"What do you want me to do?" I asked.

I felt drained and less energetic by the minute. I had all I could do to focus on what he was saying. He kept fading out like a dying radio station on a mountain highway as he explained my involvement.

"The policy he took out on his son covered him in case of accidental death, including murder, but not suicide or if the cause of death was drug related. It's just the usual, standard stuff. I want you to determine if drugs were involved in the Dolan kid's murder. There's a lot at stake here. Check it out, but keep it quiet. I want to see everything you come up with first, before you show anyone else. I'll decide what to do then, OK? Any questions?" he concluded.

"What about the Spindle case I've been working on?" I asked laconically.

"Don't worry about that. It can wait," he replied. "This takes precedence. I want it cleared up as soon as possible. I only hired you as a favor to your dad. He speaks so highly of you, always bragging about what a good martial artist you are, and what a good musician you are. Anyway, I don't really need a full-time investigator. Now I have something important for you to do. Don't let me down. It could make a big difference all the way around, if you know what I mean."

I had no idea what he meant. I could barely follow him.

"Yeah, I'll give it my best shot," I told him. "I'll talk to the police and a few of the people I know in the coroner's office. I'll check out the drug angle, don't worry. If you get any more info for me, let me know."

I tried to sound confident, but I didn't feel the least bit motivated. I couldn't seem to get the cobwebs out of my brain. I stood up from the desk.

"Dan insisted his kid was never into drugs," Majerka told me as he waved his cigarette smoke around the room.

"Yeah, the parents are always the last to know," I replied.

"Speaking of drugs," he said as I turned to leave. "You look like you have a drug hangover. Can't you at least shave and comb your hair when you come to the office? You'd better get it together, Jay, or it'll be you we're reading about on the front page."

Great, fatherly advice from *this* toad.

"I should be so lucky," I answered. "At least he got himself laid before he died."

"Real nice," he responded, with a look of disgust wrinkling his pointed little nose. "Never mind the wisecracks. Just help me clear up this case. And remember. Pass every bit of information by me first. Got that?"

"Sure, Dick," I said, leaving the smoke-filled office with an audible sigh of relief.

I dragged myself back to the dingy little hole-in-the-wall that served as my headquarters, a converted broom closet at the rear of the building. Luckily, Suzie was busy on the phone, laughing and chatting. Her attention was totally focused on her nails, which she filed vigorously with a small brown object that resembled a tongue-depressor. I didn't feel up to parrying her verbal jabs at the moment.

I flopped down in my creaking chair and stared at the battered, peeling piece of furniture that passed for my desk. It was cluttered with papers and empty Coke cans. The one miserable filing cabinet I had was full of old case records. It hadn't been opened since the agency automated three years before. This left me with a single desk drawer to keep my bulging case files in. The cabinet held my fan, which I flipped on. It was the third week of June, and summer had arrived in upstate New York with a vengeance.

I sat back, with my feet up, daydreaming. The erotic thoughts lying just beneath the surface of my mind filtered into consciousness like hungry fish. Apparently, my brain wanted to think about anything except the case.

I resented being involved with the whole sordid affair, some twisted love triangle of the bored and overly stimulated. I knew I was in a losing situation. Being accustomed to failure, I had an intuitive feel for it. If I couldn't see any obvious signs, I could certainly feel the subtle hints - the shift in the wind, the sinking feeling in the pit of my stomach that warned of impending doom.

Forcing myself into activity, I made of list of people to talk to and places to go. The first name on my list was my old friend, Jerry

LaGrand. Jerry was on the local police force and sure to be in the know.

Even though it was early, I left the office and walked down the street to the 'greasy spoon'. This is where the local boys in blue hung out, and there was a good chance Jerry would be there having a late breakfast.

Jerry used to live next door to us when we were kids, in a big, white farmhouse with his ten brothers and sisters. Jerry's wide forehead, big ears, and freckles gave him a decidedly Alfred E. Newman appearance. This was especially true when he smiled his 'what me worry' grin. Tall and slim, with light, reddish-brown hair, he usually dressed in plain white shirts and blue-jeans when not on duty.

Jerry had joined the local police force as an auxiliary cop right out of high school. He persisted and worked hard, completing his training and getting his badge. Afterward, he attended courses and continued to advance. Now he was bucking for lieutenant. If he made captain he'd become totally worthless, but for now he was well worth the cost of a cup a coffee.

He was sitting at the counter alone. A few plain-clothes guys were in a corner booth. I sat down next to him and ordered lunch. Luigy spooned up some of his famous bubonic meatballs and sauce on a plate of cold spaghetti, and slid it down the counter. I gave my stomach the challenge and washed it down with a Coke.

"So, buddy, how are things going?" I asked.

"OK. What's up with you?"

"Nothing. How's the family?"

"Good. Janice is taking the kids to the beach today."

"Hey, I was hoping you could tell me what you guys have on the Dolan murder. Was it the husband?"

"You know I can't talk to you about official police business."

"I was wondering if they were doing an autopsy or found out anything."

"Dr. Sharp did the autopsies this morning. Why don't you talk to him yourself?"

"You know Chief McNeil doesn't care for me all that much."

"That's an understatement if there ever was one," Jerry replied.

"He wouldn't like me asking his man questions."

"The coroner is not chief McNeil's man," he responded. "You're just a lazy chicken-shit".

"I have a need to know. I'm working on the case for the insurance company. Dolan had a big policy on his kid. I can get a letter if you need one. Want to see my license? Don't forget how I saved you from getting your butt kicked by Freddy Higgens when we were kids."

"The hell you did, Lawless. I just didn't want to fight, that's all."

"He was ready to kick your ass until I stepped in. You owe me."

"You're never going to let me forget that, are you? It was just that one time. I'd like to see him try that now."

"Me too. You'd shoot him."

We laughed.

"Will you help me?" I pleaded. "I trust you to be on the level with me. You're not like the other townies. You're not one of them."

"You sound like there's a conspiracy or something. You're getting paranoid, Jay. I'm not working on that case, but I'll see what I can find out."

"Why don't you come over to my dad's house later?" I asked. I was always trying to get him into the martial arts. "I'm holding a test tonight. I've got a good group. You might learn something useful."

"I'm trained. I don't need all that kung-fuey."

"OK, but you might find yourself without your gun someday. Then where would you be?"

"I'm never without my Magnum," Jerry said amiably in his slight North Country accent. "Anyway, I'm busy with the family tonight. Why don't you come over to dinner sometime?"

I told him I'd consider the offer and tried to pick his brain some more, to see what he might have learned.

"So what's the scoop? Did the husband do it?" I asked again.

"I don't know, but both victims were nude, obviously killed while having sex. The woman was the wife of a Major John Stienman, a bomber pilot at the base. Cause of death for Mrs. Stienman was strangulation. The male, Bobby Dolan, was stabbed in the abdomen just above the navel. It must have taken him several minutes to die. Both victims were stabbed repeatedly after they were dead. Whoever did it must be a pretty sick puppy."

"Were there any drugs present at the scene of the crime?" I asked.

"Yes, a small quantity of cocaine, but they're not sure if it was Bobby's or Mrs. Stienman's. The guys on the case are being unusually tightlipped about this one. There's apparently a lot of pressure from above to get it settled quickly. Right now they have no suspects. The husband had the strongest motive, but he seems to have a good alibi.

He was on duty somewhere in a B-52 over Greenland. A drug or sex motive has not been ruled out yet either."

I couldn't get much more out of him. The detectives in the booth were giving us a look, so I thanked Jerry and left five bucks on the table for him. As I was leaving the diner, I used the payphone to call Dan Dolan's office to make an appointment to see him. As usual, what I thought was going to be a very simple task, turned out to be a hassle.

"The family is in mourning. I'm sorry, but you'll have to wait until after the funeral to talk to Mr. Dolan," the secretary told me in a smug, condescending voice.

"Could you tell me when that might me?" I asked.

"No, I don't know."

I wasn't exactly in the mood to put up with any crapola from some snobby secretary, but I kept my temper.

"I realize the grief the family must be going through right now. I only want to expedite the matter of the insurance claim in the most discreet way possible. If I have to wait or pursue some alternative method of getting the information I need, it could cause quite a lot of embarrassment for Mr. Dolan. I suggest you get in touch with him as soon as possible and tell him that Mr. Jay Lawless of Majerka's Insurance Agency would like to set up an appointment for the earliest convenient moment."

She seemed to get the message.

It was a little after noon. I decided to go to the scene of the crime and dig around.

I had a strong hunch how this one was going to turn out, in the worse possible way for me, of course. If I could show that it was a drug motivated crime, our company would not have to pay. In that case, Dickey's old and influential friend might be pretty peeved that he didn't get to collect on his son's policy. I would probably be offered as a sacrifice to assuage the poor father's grief. On the other hand, if it was shown that drugs were not involved, our parent company would end up paying in a big way. I was sure to be the scapegoat in that scenario as well. So either way my prospects appeared grim.

These thoughts oppressed me as I made my way to the apartment complex where Bobby Dolan had lived and died.

The apartment building where Bobby and his babe bit the big one was on the west end of town, a row of brand spanking new townhouses for the almost rich and perfectly unknown. I talked to the manager and a next door neighbor, but didn't learn much I didn't already know or couldn't guess. The guy had girls coming in and out of his apartment like there was no tomorrow, which in his case, there wasn't. It sounded like Bobby Dolan was a very popular guy. It also sounded like he was involved with drugs in a more than casual way. In fact, it seemed to be pretty common knowledge around the neighborhood.

I learned that another girlfriend of Bobby's came by later in the evening for an impromptu liaison and found the murdered couple. Gee, two in one night, not a bad life. Too bad he couldn't keep it. The poor girl had to be sedated and taken to the hospital for shock.

The police had been there all day and luckily for me had just left. They'd be back, I informed the manager. They never get it right the first time. I asked if I could see the apartment, but was told it was sealed under police orders.

After talking to a couple more of Bobby's neighbors, two buxom ladies named Marsha and Stephanie, who lived in the adjoining townhouse, I went back to the office. They told me all about Bobby Dolan's sexual endowments and stamina in relation to the numerous other men they had bedded, but little about the murder itself.

Back at the office, I spent a few more desultory hours trying to work on the case. I was getting nowhere fast, constantly slipping off into bizarre sexual fantasies of Marsha and Stephanie. Eventually my thoughts rested on the unfortunate couple. I imagined their last minutes together, and how their pleasure had been turned to sudden terror.

After a few minutes of this, to get my mind off these morbid thoughts, I turned my attention to Mrs. Spindle's case. The poor old woman was being sued by the drunk driver of the car that killed Mr. Spindle and their son Josh. I ask you, is there no justice in the world? The insurance company of the drunk driver didn't have a case to spit on. Their client had already been convicted of vehicular homicide. What they were doing amounted to cruel mental harassment. It was just a desperate, futile attempt to avoid paying on the claim as long as possible. But then my company could be in that boat soon itself. In any event, I was doing my best to make sure she got to enjoy what, by all rights, was due her.

I was about to leave for the evening when Dan Dolan's answering service called to say that I could see him the next morning for twenty minutes at his downtown office. She gave me the address and had the nerve to tell me not to be late.

On the way out, I bumped into Dick Majerka. He was waiting for me, and pounced out of his office as if he'd caught me stealing. Suzie had gone for the day. I was trapped.

"What have you found out?" he asked. "Got anything for me? Were drugs involved or not?"

"I'm working on it, Dick," I replied. "I need more time. Could be a random sex murder for all the police know. Or it could be the husband. There's no indication at this point that drugs were the cause."

I didn't bother informing him that Dolan might have been dealing drugs. I didn't want to brighten his day with hope.

"I need an answer by the end of the day tomorrow. It's an easy question. I'm counting on you, Jay."

With that I left the office. I needed to work out some aggression.

Chapter 3

Day 2 (p.m.)

A couple nights a week I got together with a few guys to practice karate in the basement of my father's house. I don't charge them much, but that together with what I pick up playing drums and the minimum wage Majerka pays me, enabled me to get my own place and still have enough left over to keep me in burgers and pasta.

I decided to get an early start on the evening, and hurried home to collect some dirty clothes from my skimpy, all but depleted wardrobe. I planned to wash these at my dad's while we worked out.

I've been into the martial arts for several years. I started shortly after my involuntary departure from Northeastern. I needed some form of physical exercise to counteract my couch-potato existence. I also figured it might help me get security jobs.

I had always been something of a scrapper, in spite of my size, or maybe because of it. Many bullies looking for an easy target got a rude surprise when they tried picking on me. Not that I wasn't scared of bigger kids. It was just that once they hit me I sort of went berserk. I was more indignant that they would do such a thing than I was mad. Whatever it was, I saw red. I would pounce on my attacker with my tight little fists flying windmill fashion, aimed at the nose. It usually did the trick. At the worst, I would land four or five punches to one of my larger opponent's. But I really didn't know how to fight, and was not big enough to survive many blow for blow encounters with a really determined adversary.

I studied Chinese Kenpo karate with a guy on Revere Beach, where I used to go in the summer to cool off. Len was a black dude, and looked like a linebacker. He also taught Aikido, tai-chi, and weapons training. I figured it all might come in handy some day.

In spite of his ferocity on the floor, Len instilled in us the true spirit of the martial arts, the spirit of peace and oneness. The martial artist comes to every situation with peace in his or her heart, like a lamb. Should she or he be attacked without provocation, however, they become like a tiger, a tiger behind bamboo. By the time you know it's there, it's too late.

Each style of martial art is unique and stresses a different aspect of self-defense. Chinese Kenpo, the 'Old Pine Tree' style that Len taught us, is a Japanese form of Chinese kung fu as taught by an Okinawan master, Professor Kwai Sun Chow, in Hawaii. It stresses speed and precision to weak areas of the body. The theory is that no matter how big and strong an opponent is they will have places where they are vulnerable. The trick is to learn how to hit these spots quickly with accuracy.

This approach mixes hard and soft techniques, and borrows from both northern and southern Chinese styles. Kenpo embodies a multitude of kicks and hand-strikes, using just about every part of the body as a weapon. It was called the 'Old Pine Tree' method because it has many branches or styles, borrowed from different Shoulin schools – tiger, dragon, crane, mantis, snake, and so on – as well as jujitsu.

Like many other types of karate, Kenpo endeavors to condition the body so that a person's weaknesses become their strengths. Practicing karate also teaches one how vulnerable the human body is, and all the terrible things that can happen to it. Crushed and broken bones, ruptured and punctured organs, ripped cartilage and concussions, black-and-blue skin and bloody contusions, and these are some of the nicer things.

The moves practiced hours on end in the dojo build up synapses in the brain. These are patterns of brain-cell to nerve-cell firings or connections, which become second nature to the practitioner. Without thought, mechanically as it were, from any position or stance, one has an arsenal of things to do to defend oneself.

It was only after I had progressed to a high level in these things that Len began to broaden my training with aikido and tai-chi, to build power and inner strength.

Aikido stresses locks and throws, and like judo, teaches how to use the other person's momentum or force against them. By applying locks on pressure points, the aikido expert can cause excruciating pain and control their opponent. Although it looks gentle compared to karate, there was nothing gentle about the way Len threw us around. When he put an aikido lock on you, you felt it for days.

Tai-chi exercises were meant to develop the chi. This is the inner life-force that we are all supposed to have, but which few know how to control and use. I don't know if it was the chi or not that gave Len his power, but he could send you flying through the air with just the flick of his wrist. It was as if he had picked you up with both hands and flung you. He never seemed to exert himself.

I practiced Kenpo religiously for several years. Because I had a lot of free time, I was able to work out four or five hours a day. After three years of this, I got my black belt and helped Len run the school. Unfortunately, when he moved to the West Coast the dojo closed down. I took on a few of his students part-time, but between the hassle of finding a place to work out and setting up their ever-changing schedules, I bailed out on them like I did with most things.

My dad was always bragging about his son the karate champion - I have two cheap trophies from my competitive days - so when I came home he already had a couple of students lined up for me. He set up the basement of his house for us to work out in. He even hung a heavy bag.

My first students were the sons of a good friend of his, the oldest of whom was leaving for the Navy Seals at the first of the year. The younger brother was still in high school. I also picked up a couple of air force guys who had gotten on the wrong side of the base instructor. They were also brothers, 'soul brothers' that is.

My dad wasn't home. I threw my dirty laundry into the washing machine, then changed into my workout clothes and stretched out until my four students arrived. They were all chatting excitedly about the recent murders when they came in.

This was a special night. Tonight I was giving them their first test. The test was meant to push them beyond their comfort zones, to stretch them further than they were used to going. I intended to make them do more than they thought they could do. It was no more business as usual. They were all in for a rude awakening. Len's first test had been terrifying. I thought I was going to die. I ran my tests the same way.

I started the class with some meditation. Sitting on their knees, breathing deeply, in through the nose, out through the mouth, I had them clear their minds of everything except what they were about to do.

The patient, helpful, considerate instructor – yours truly - was about to turn maniacal.

I ran them through their basics, fast and hard, yelling at them at the top of my lungs to go faster and harder.

"You guys look like a bunch of candy-asses," I growled, looking at them menacingly. "You better hope you never have to defend yourselves on the street. You'd get your butts kicked. Faster! Harder!"

I screamed at them as I ran them through the various kicks and hand strikes.

I made them do 400 punches as hard and fast as I could give the command.

"I want to see power. Front two-knuckle punch, face, midsection, groin!"

I barked the command louder and faster.

"Up and down the body, let's see some precision. Snap those punches. Keep those shoulders back. Straighten up your stances!"

I paced back and forth in front of them, glaring at them as if I was mad.

"Front ball kick!" I yelled. "Groin! Solar Plexus! Face! Drive those kicks. That's it. Faster! Higher!" I demanded.

I walked up and down the line of students, randomly taking them down to the floor with vicious leg-hawks and sweeps. When they got up and back in their stance, I struck their midsections with well-aimed punches.

They had all been taught how to fall without being hurt, slapping the floor with their palm and forearm. They knew how to yell or kiai when hit in the solar plexus, to expel air and prevent the wind from getting knocked out of them. But none of them were quite prepared for the onslaught of abuse that rained down upon them that night. I was being careful not to hurt anyone, but they didn't know that. I'm sure they thought they were getting murdered. Not more than ten minutes had gone by and they were already sweating profusely, more from fear and stress than exertion.

Testing their knowledge, I yelled out the different hand strikes in rapid succession.

"Hand-sword to the collar bone...to the neck...ridge-hand to the floating ribs...palm-heel to the nose...spear-hand to the throat...trigger-fingers to the eyes...leopard's-paw to the heart."

I tested their stances to make sure they were strong and well-balanced. If not, I'd push them back or yank them forward.

If someone slipped up, I made them do pushups. If someone froze, I stopped the whole class and berated the culprit an inch from their nose like a drill sergeant. Then I'd sweep them off their feet and make them do fifty.

I knew they could execute the material and techniques I had taught them. I saw them do it in class every night. But could they do it under pressure, in a stressful situation, when their system was pumped full of adrenaline with fear and anxiety? Only practice under these conditions will teach you how to function under them. This is what the test was for. Much of military and police training attempts to do the same thing, but my students must have thought I had gone stark raving mad.

I had them pair-off and do their punch techniques and combinations, block and counter exercises with a variety of hand strikes and kicks, usually leaving the attacker on the ground with a leg-hawk or sweep.

I was making them move fast. I expected the man being taken down to get up quickly. If not, I bounced them off the floor even harder. I also tested their control as they worked with each other. I wanted to see if they could do the techniques without hurting one another, which was just as important to me as whether they could perform under pressure. The more dangerous the techniques I would teach them moving forward, the more important their control became.

"Watch your control, Conners!" I yelled when one of the defenders hit his attacker a little too hard in the midsection. I kicked him in the solar-plexus and was glad to see he kiai'd and maintained his stance.

"No contact!" I shouted to the whole class. "You guys aren't ready for that yet. Just show it. Like you mean it! Kiai! Good!"

As it was, the test was brutal by any standard, especially for a first one, but that's the way I had been taught – old school.

At the end of the session I had them stay in push-up position with a ten-pound weight on their backs. If anyone came off it they failed the test. Of course, I wasn't going to let anyone fail, but I wanted to see how much they wanted it. So I kept them in push-up position, their arms shaking and sweat pouring off their foreheads.

"Concentrate on a point on the wall and your breathing," I told them as they fought to stay in position, when every fiber of their being was crying out to give up and drop. Just as the first of them was about to give out, I yelled, "Up!" and it was over. They had their belts.

I doubt many of them slept that night, filled with elation and aftershock. It was something they would never forget, and hopefully, something that would help them in a bind. They all came back. None of my students would get caught on the street with their pants down.

Later that evening at the club things were jumping. The band sounded great. Everything seemed to be clicking. Everyone was 'on'. As tired as I was, I played effortlessly, hands and feet working together in perfect synchronization. But then that was how it always was with me. One night I'd be as good as the best of them, the next, I'd be scuffling. I'd have all I could do just to get through. Mister inconsistent, that was me all over.

The crowd was lively. They talked and laughed during the tunes, and yelled for more, clapping, afterward. Nothing like a double homicide to get the locals' juices flowing.

My girl, Mary, arrived just before the last break of the evening, and slipped onto a barstool.

"Where you been?" I asked, going over to her after we finished the final tune of the set. "The night's almost over. You missed our best set."

"I was over at Brandy's. They've got a new band playing there. They're from Montreal, and boy, are they hot! They play all the latest tunes. Real cute, too," she said matter-of-factly.

"So much for loyalty," I replied, feeling instantly dejected.

Brandy's was one of the hotter nightspots in the 'burgh'. Located south of town near the base, it was always jammed with jostling bodies of young people, frantically seeking a few hours of fun in their otherwise boring lives. Live music featuring some of the better-known rock bands in the North Country and Montreal drew large crowds from the base, the college, and the surrounding area, not to mention Canadians during the summer. On weekends there were usually long lines at the door waiting to get in, and at least one fight or accident in the crowded parking lot. It was not a place I frequented.

"Hey, I was having a good time. I left and came here just to see you," Mary reminded me.

The rest of the group came over and we all went into the dining area at the back of the club. It was after eleven so the dining room was closed, but when it was busy the crowd would spill over into this area. We found a booth at the rear. George went into the kitchen to see if he could scrape up some food, and soon came back with a plate of hot chicken wings. George always maintained close relationships with the kitchen staff of the clubs we played.

As soon as we were seated, Mary started talking about the autopsies performed earlier that day on Bobby Dolan and Alice Stienman. I knew she wouldn't spare any details now that she had an audience.

"They performed the autopsies this morning, both at the same time. Doctor Sharp did not let me attend. It seems there was some Air Force doctor present who objected. But I was able to talk to the medical examiner afterward."

I told her what I had found out from Jerry earlier that day. She confirmed his information, and filled in considerable grisly details in her usual lurid way.

"From what the coroner told me, they were engaged in heavy sex just before or during the attack. The woman was found on top, with Bobby pinned under her. I guess they had quite a time getting them apart because of the rigor mortis."

"I hate it when that happens," I said. No one smiled at my attempted joke.

Mary went on unaware of the effect her story was having on her audience. Paul turned pale. Denise sat wide-eyed, with tears in her eyes.

"The doc said there were high levels of alcohol and cocaine in their blood."

"Sounds like they were having one hell of a good time," I observed, with a sick grin.

"Both bodies were stabbed repeatedly, all over. Most of the wounds were inflicted after death."

"Yeah, that's what Jerry said," I confirmed

"Sick!" moaned Denise. Paul got paler.

"Sounds like a real wacko, all right," I said. All of a sudden I didn't feel much like playing the last set.

"Mrs. Stienman was active in the community, a mother of two and the wife of a Panama War hero."

"Yeah, I'll say she was active in the community," I quipped. Mary just ignored me.

"The whole base is in shock, as you can imagine. I'll be preparing Bobby's body. There's going to be a wake tomorrow, with the funeral on Sunday. They expect a large turnout. Poor Bobby, what a terrible tragedy."

She was starting to get on my nerves.

"I saw them laid out after the autopsy. Not very pretty the way they opened them up, but he's still the best specimen I've seen in a long time. Better than most of the live ones I see around here."

"Gee, thanks," I responded.

"Present company excluded," she said too late. "It's just all so sad. It makes me want to cry."

She paused for a moment. Denise was almost in tears herself. Paul looked sick. We sat there in stony silence like gray tombstones.

"He's going to be beautiful when I get done with him," she said finally.

I found myself getting jealous of the dead guy. If Mary lavished half the attention on me she was going to lavish on the deceased Bobby Dolan, we'd have been married by then.

Paul looked like he was going to get sick. Denise looked about to faint. George finished his wings, licking his fingers clean noisily, not the least bit affected by the gruesome conversation.

We started the last set. Despite the enthusiasm of the crowd, everything seemed hollow and empty. No matter how lively we tried to play, it felt like we were playing underwater. To make matters worse, my stomach was splashing my esophagus with a bile-tasting acid that made each swallow a test. It was the longest set I could remember playing. All I could think about was how death had descended so swiftly and cruelly upon our little town.

Interlude

11:40 p.m., Same Evening, Brandy's

Eighteen-year-old Marshall Gurny watched his date, seventeen-year-old Kathy Riley, waiting for his chance. Kathy had been dancing with just about every airman in the club, all at least two years older than him and outweighing him by fifty pounds.

He had brought her here to Brandy's to listen to the new band from Montreal, even though she was underage. He had intended to take her to a movie, but she had insisted and would have gone alone anyway, so he acquiesced.

The place was mobbed. Smoke hung in the air like mountain fog. Kathy was drunk out of her mind. The way she was dressed meant she got plenty of attention, in a short, white sweater that showed her belly and emphasized her nubile, young breasts, and black slacks so tight you could see her crack. He had long since given up trying to control her.

Marshall could do nothing but bide his time and look for the first opportunity to hustle her out of the club and get her home. He was honor bound to have her home by midnight. That's what he had told her father, Captain Jack Riley of the U.S. Strategic Air Command, and he always kept his word, especially to the captain.

His pop had warned him about the fathers of young women. How you'd be better off caught between a mother bear and her cubs, than to mess with some man's daughter. The way it was going, however, there was no way he was going to get her home in time. It was almost midnight and she showed no sign of letting up.

Finally, the band finished the last song of the set with a resounding crescendo. The dancers moved back to their tables. Marshall saw his opportunity. Kathy was headed for the ladies room. She would have to walk right past the club entrance.

As she wobbled by the door, Marshall took her arm and swiftly guided her out of the building. Catching her off-guard, he had her in the parking lot before she could stop his momentum. She put up a half-hearted resistance for awhile, but he finally got her headed in the right direction.

Tonight they were on foot. Fortunately, Brandy's was not far from that part of the base where Kathy lived, about a quarter of a mile up the road, in a section of identical split-level brick homes built for the officers and their families. The only way you were supposed to enter was through the main gate, where an Air Police sentry stood guard. But the local kids had several places along the perimeter of the six-foot high wire fence that skirted the highway, where they could slip through, under, or over, undetected.

They left the noisy parking lot. It was jammed with young partygoers cooling off and letting off steam. They did not notice the lurking figure stalking them in the shadows. The follower knew instinctively just when to move, just when to freeze. He knew how to melt into the shadows and be part of the scene. It was all second nature to him, hardwired into his brain, like a shark mindlessly stalks its wary prey.

Kathy and Marshall made their way along the highway toward her home. The road was bordered by large pine trees and dense shrubs. The few street lamps were too widely spaced to shed much light along the path they walked. Despite his great bulk, the figure that followed them was virtually invisible in the darkness.

The walk to Kathy's house was interminable. Marshall half dragged, half carried his inebriated girlfriend as he tried to herd her in the right direction. As they staggered along at a snail's pace, she mumbled strings of obscenities into his ear. It was quarter past twelve, not too bad. He could still get her home in time enough to avoid facing the wrath of an irate Captain Riley.

They came to an auxiliary road leading to an unmanned gate that was closed and locked most of the time. The wire fence marched along the side of that street from the highway back to the gate. It was along this road, between two old pine trees, that there was a hidden break in the fence. Kathy and Marshall headed toward it.

As he followed them in the night, the stalker thought of his youth and those times on warm summer evenings just like this one, when he'd steal down the road and up into the wooded hills to hunt.

He had just gotten his first hunting knife. It had a four-inch blade of tempered steel with a white elk-bone handle. A sharp, saw-tooth edge ran halfway up the length of it. It was on his tenth birthday. That same day, he had chased down and killed his first dog.

He killed it in a heart pounding frenzy of pent-up anger and bloodlust, slashing at the animal with his small knife long after it had ceased to move. His grandfather spoke to him as he bandaged his grandson's bite wounds.

"Anyone can kill something with a gun. That takes no great skill or courage. But to chase down an animal and kill it with your bare hands, with just a knife, that is exceptional. That is the way of a warrior."

Soon that was how he began to think of himself, as a warrior. It didn't take long before he had killed every stray dog in town and most of the cats too.

It wasn't long after that that he killed his first human. It was the summer of his twelfth year. It was early in the morning. The sun was just asserting itself. No one was about yet on the quiet, sleepy streets. His grandfather and he were crossing over the bridge that spanned the canal, on their way to fish for their breakfast. As they were crossing, they met another boy coming in the opposite direction, a large sullen kid with red hair and freckles. Our little warrior was big for his age, but he was slightly smaller than the boy coming toward them, who was probably a few years older as well. Their paths led them face to face, where they met in the middle of the bridge. The red-head ruffian refused to give way, but stood staring at him. When he moved out of the way to let the other boy pass, his grandfather derided him scornfully.

"Sissy," he yelled. "Are you always going to let other people push you around? Go back and teach that punk a lesson. Chase him down like a dog and give him a good whipping."

So he did, in fact he did much more.

The young warrior turned and ran back across the bridge. Jumping the redheaded kid from behind, he beat him on the back with his fists. The surprised boy swung his arm up and out, and knocked the little warrior back on his ass. He sat there bruised and shaken.

At this point, his grandfather began yelling at him to get up, hurling vicious curses at him. In his confused, lonely state, the words stung him like a cat o' nine tails.

He slowly got to his feet. Snarling like a wild animal and squinting his eyes in rage, he advanced on the bigger boy. As he did, he pulled the boned-handled hunting knife from its leather sheath.

The redheaded boy's eyes widened in fright at the sight of the sharp, four-inch blade. Turning, he fled back across the bridge

toward the other side of the canal. He looked back just in time to see
the blur of the knife as it slashed down at his back. Panic stricken, in
pain, he screamed as he reached the end of the bridge, and
stumbled. Rolling down the grassy embankment that ran along the
canal and under the overpass, he cowered in terror.

This is just like killing dogs, thought the hunter, as he followed
his victim down to the edge of the steep embankment. In his
confusion and terror, the other boy tried to crawl away under the
bridge. What followed was hidden from view. Not that it mattered.
No one was about that morning on the canal to hear the freckled
boy's terrified screams as the knife plunged into him again and
again.

Without being told, he slid the dead youth's body into the water.
It would eventually be found, just another homeless waif, who had
fallen into the canal and been cut to pieces by the propeller of some
large tanker. To our young warrior, it was a moment he would never
forget. It replayed over and over in the dark cavern of his mind.

And so it went, day after day, year after year. Brought up by his
brutal grandfather, for his special purpose, he grew up in solitude,
shunned and alone, with nothing but his dark thoughts and his trusty
knife to keep him company.

The killer snapped back to the here and now with an almost
audible click of awareness as he silently closed the distance between
himself and the unsuspecting couple.

Kathy and Marshall had just slipped between the hidden opening
in the fence, into the airbase housing area. They were in a field, dotted
with large pines and maples, which separated the fence from the first of
many quiet streets. Kathy Riley lay down on the long grass, stretching
out luxuriously.

She looked appealing in the pale moonlight. Marshall lay down
next to her, trying to kiss her and fondle her breasts. If they were going
to get into trouble, he might as well make it worth his while. She
pushed him off, got up, and staggered behind a tree to take a leak.

"Can't you wait?" he said petulantly. "We're almost at your house!
Your dad's going to kill me if I bring you home any later."

"Ah, who gives a crap what he thinks," she slurred.

When she came from behind the tree her pants were unzipped. She walked toward Marshall seductively, taking him by the shoulders. When he went to kiss her, she moved her head to the side and sank her teeth in his shoulder. He tried to dislodge her, but the more he attempted to push her head away, the harder she bit. It was excruciating, more pain than he had ever felt in his life. What was she trying to do? This would be the last time he'd ever take her out again, he thought. He didn't know how right he was.

Finally, unable to bear the pain any longer, he grabbed her by the hair and slapped her sharply across the face, splitting her lip. That loosened her up enough for him to remove her teeth from his shoulder.

"You crazy bitch!" he cried. "What are you trying to do, give me rabies? You can walk yourself home. I hope your father kicks your ass."

She only laughed at him as he walked away. Then she headed across the field in the direction of her house.

Marshall let himself back out through the fence and started walking homeward, nursing his shoulder and swearing under his breath. He didn't see the large figure slip from the trees and through the fence, right where he had just left.

The killer moved quickly and quietly across the silent lawns and sidewalks to head Kathy Riley off. It was after 1:00 a.m., the night overcast and dark. No one was about. A strong wind rustled the trees.

He caught her from behind, just ten feet from her front door. Grabbing her across the throat, he thrust the large bowie knife into her narrow back so far the blade almost protruded from her chest

Without allowing her to fall, he carried his victim back to the hole in the fence, and up the auxiliary road toward the highway. Staying in the shadow of the trees, he went virtually unseen.

Standing her against the chain-link fence, he took a roll of wire from his pocket. He then proceeded to wrap this around her, tying her to the fence like a small, limp ragdoll. When he had finished his grisly work, he made his way through the shadows, back up the deserted highway, where his car was parked. Getting in, he drove westward out of town to the cabin.

It was almost two in the morning. He drove toward the mountains. He wasn't alone. He had a passenger, a Captain Jack Riley, late of the U.S. Air Force. He was comfortably stuffed in the car's trunk, dressed in boxer shorts, t-shirt, and black socks. He had been dead for several hours, his throat slashed from ear to ear, another trophy bagged and tagged in the grisly game of death.

The terror was about to begin.

Chapter 4

Day 3

I woke-up about eight, soaked with sweat and feeling like I hadn't slept a wink all night. Taking a long shower, I tried to shake the cobwebs out.

My interview with Dan Dolan was at ten. Putting on some shorts, I sat out on the sandbox that passes for the beach at the one star motel I live in. Drinking several oversized cups of java, I tried to gear up to talk to Dolan. But I could barely keep my eyes open, despite the strong brew.

Around nine, I went back inside to get ready. I took out my best shirt and pants, along with my only tie, and threw a towel on the floor. Getting out my travel iron, I did the best I could with the shirt. It would be OK as long as I kept my jacket on. Unfortunately, the only presentable one I owned was corduroy, not exactly designed for a summer heat wave.

Just as I was getting ready to head over to Dolan's office, there was a knock on the door. It was Jerry from the police station. He was in uniform.

"Hey, I tried your office but they said you hadn't come in yet. Jeez, Jay, you've really got cushy hours there, eh."

"Late night last night. Couldn't get to sleep. Got an interview with Dan Dolan this morning. Since when do real investigators keep straight hours? Not like you 9-to-5 cops."

I was trying to be witty, but at this time of the morning all I could manage was to sound defensive.

"While you've been sleeping your life away, things have been happening. There was another murder last night. Young girl at the base, she was stabbed just like the others."

"Oh? What the hell's going on around here?"

"I don't know," Jerry admitted. "It looks like we may have a serial killer on our hands. They're talking to the kid that was last seen with her. He's pretty shook up. Hasn't got an alibi. He might have a motive, though. Seems they'd been fighting. He admits to splitting her lip."

"Where was it?" I asked, popping one of my antacids.

"She was strung up on the fence that runs along Route 9, out by the base there. He used wire. She was found early this morning by an elderly couple. The old woman turned just in time to see the victim as they drove past. She thought the young girl was hitchhiking at first. Thought it funny she was standing off the road like that, against the fence. In any case, there was something peculiar about the way it looked, so she got her old man to stop the car and turn around. When they saw what it really was, they pretty near had a coronary right there on the spot. They found a pay phone and called the station. This one was also stabbed repeatedly, almost thirty times. Looks like the cause of death was a deep knife wound in the back that practically sliced her heart in two. From the wounds it looks like the same weapon and MO as in the Bobby Dolan case."

"Was there any evidence of drugs?" I asked, trying to establish some kind of connection.

"No, not that I've heard," Jerry responded. "She wasn't one of the people we've been watching. There doesn't seem to be any obvious connection with the other murdered people, except the other woman, Mrs. Stienman, was also from the base."

"Have you notified the next of kin?"

"No. The father is a divorcee, a Captain Riley. He lives on the base only a block from where the girl was found. Seems he wasn't home. When they went in to check it out, they found the TV on with a half bottle of beer opened in front of it. No sign of a struggle or forced entry. They found what might be a few drops of blood under the kitchen table. They're checking it now. The neighbors didn't see anything suspicious, although the captain kept pretty much to himself since the missus left. Not really what you'd call sociable from the sound of it. I guess that part of the base is kind of wooded, and the houses fairly wide apart. It would have been easy for someone to go unseen, especially after dark."

"Sounds like some bad shit happening around here. I hope you find this guy and quick. Let me know if anything else develops, will you? I've got to go talk to Dan Dolan."

"OK, let me know what you find out. This is still a police investigation, you know."

"I know. Thanks for stopping by with the info, Jer'. I owe you."

"Yeah, just remember that. Maybe you can get that band of yours to play some of my songs."

"Hey, don't ask for too much. I'll see if I can't get George to play a Patsy Cline tune for you so you can cry in your beer."

I left the apartment and headed for the downtown area, where Dan Dolan had his office. Dan Dolan is Upstate New York's version of 'Daddy Warbucks'. He owns a good portion of the city's real estate, as well as several of the town's more prosperous businesses. The father of the dead Bobby Dolan was one of the most powerful men in the community.

Dan Dolan's office was located on the main street of town, above what some considered the burgh's best restaurant, the Carriage House, also owned by Dan Dolan. I walked up the plush carpeted steps leading to the offices on the second floor. I could smell the aroma of fine food coming from the restaurant below. I decided to splurge and have lunch there after the interview.

I walked into the reception area. The secretary said I could go right in, Mister Dolan was expecting me. It was already getting too hot for the heavy jacket I was wearing. I started to perspire and I hadn't even begun the interview yet.

Dan Dolan sat behind a massive mahogany desk in a high-backed, green leather chair. On his desk were all the trappings of a successful company ECO - large impressive glass and bronze paper weights, an expensive set of gold pens that looked like they had never been used, gilded-framed pictures of his family, including the now deceased Bobby Dolan.

The walls were covered with awards and pictures of him with all the local bigwigs, including the mayor and the governor of the state, all richly framed. Everything in the room was meant to impress and imply wealth, like a posh private club.

He asked me to sit down, and pointed to what turned out to be one of the most deep-cushioned and comfortable leather chairs I've ever rested my behind in. He offered me a cigar from a leather-bound case, which I turned down. Lucky for me he didn't light one himself. The way I felt, in that heavy, warm jacket and stuffy room, I probably would have passed out.

"How is your dad?" he inquired politely.

"Good, thanks" I answered.

"I wish we had worked together more. He's a good man, your dad."

"I know. He speaks highly of you, too, Mister Dolan. First let me express my condolences, and thank you for seeing me. This is just a simple formality. I won't take much of your time. We'll try to settle this whole thing as quickly as possible. Have the police talked to you?"

38

"Yes, they have," he responded. "They gave me all the details of my son's death."

He looked on the verge of tears, but too proud to show his emotions. I hadn't given much thought to what I was going to ask him before now. My lack of preparation was causing me some physical discomfort, making me perspire even more, which further fogged my brain. I had started the interview off smoothly enough, but it was all downhill from there.

"Did you know your son was seeing a married woman?" I asked, shooting my question out from the hip.

"Now wait a minute, Mister Lawless. I don't see what that has to do with anything. I agreed to talk to you regarding the insurance policy I took out on my son. I've answered all the questions I'm going to regarding that for the police. Do you understand?" He talked in a low, tightly controlled, monotone, almost like a growl.

"I understand, Mister Dolan. I'm only trying to help. You must realize that the policy you took out on your son expressly states non-payment in the event drugs are found to be a contributing factor in the death. The police seem to think drugs were involved in more than a casual way with this crime. Any information you give me may help in disproving this connection. Did you know your son was involved with drugs?"

"No! Absolutely not! Bobby would never have had anything to do with drugs!"

His voice became shrill. He looked close to coming apart at the seams, so I plunged on.

"They had drugs and alcohol in their blood. It seems pretty common knowledge around town that Bobby was dealing drugs."

"That's rubbish! That's just hearsay, vicious rumors from jealous know-nothings. If he had any drugs in his system, that woman he was with or someone else put them there. He was framed, I tell you."

"Do you know something? Was the Stienman woman dealing drugs?"

"No, I don't know anything about that. This is all crazy!"

I could tell this line of questioning was getting nowhere, so I tried a different tack.

"Can you think of anyone who would want to harm Bobby, anyone who held a grudge against him? Someone he knew who might have had drug connections?"

"No, his friends are all upstanding people. No one would want to hurt Bobby. Everyone loved him."

I wondered who Dolan was talking about. It certainly wasn't the Bobby Dolan I knew and had heard about. The old guy was living in a fantasy world. And we wonder why things are so messed up, with people seeing only what they want to see and ignoring the ugly truth staring them in the face every day.

I continued with the usual round of questions.

"When did you see him last?"

"That night at the restaurant here. He had dinner alone around six, and stopped by the office on his way out to say hi. I was working late."

"Did he seem preoccupied, worried about anything?"

"No," Dolan answered. "He was on top of the world. He had everything to live for."

I changed topics and asked him about the life insurance policy.

"Dick Majerka suggested it to me a few years ago after learning of the considerable investments I had made in Bobby's future. At the time, the drug clause that Dick insisted on seemed normal enough, despite the hefty premiums I was paying. If I had known how much trouble it was going to cause, I never would have agreed to it."

At that moment I realized that the whole policy thing was that slime-ball, Majerka's, idea. It figured.

I told Dolan we'd have everything settled for him as soon as possible. That didn't seem to placate him. He insisted on an answer as to exactly when he would have his money. I told him he'd have to talk to Dick Majerka about that, but that I would have my investigation finished by the beginning of next week.

I then asked him if he had heard about the latest murder. He said he had, but didn't see any connection between it and his son's.

I told him that the new murder seemed to point to the same killer.

"We may have a serial killer on our hands, some kind of maniac running loose. Or maybe it's just a jealous husband, but all the evidence points away from a drug related crime. This is all very favorable for your cause."

He said nothing. He appeared to be on the verge of an emotional collapse.

"Mr. Majerka will get in touch with you early next week," I informed him. "In the meantime, I'll be gathering evidence to support your case. It looks good."

I tried to sound optimistic, even though I had serious doubts about anything good coming out of this one, especially for me.

As I got up to leave, Dolan began speaking, almost as if talking to himself.

"I invested so much in Bobby. It wasn't supposed to end this way. He was all I had. How could this have happened?"

I turned at the door.

"If there is anything we at the agency can do, please don't hesitate to call."

He ignored me and kept talking in a desultory way as I showed myself out of his office, a broken man with shattered dreams. Well, I could relate to that. After all, it was the story of my life.

It was almost 11:30 by the time I left Dolan's office. I hadn't had breakfast, but didn't feel much like eating. For some reason I had lost my appetite again. At least working on this case was keeping my weight down.

I was soaked to the bone with perspiration, so I stopped home and changed. I spent the rest of the day musing on the latest events.

Judging from the description of the wounds that Jerry had given me, there was obviously a connection between the murders. It sounded like some sex maniac was on the loose, someone even more messed-up than the usual run-of-the-mill, inbred misfits we find up here. Then there was the base connection. Maybe Major Stienman was the murderer after all, and killed the Riley girl to throw the police off the track. Or perhaps she had something on him. Maybe he was screwing her on the side. And what had happened to Captain Riley? Where could he have gone? Had he been abducted?

All these thoughts were playing around in my mind, careening off each other like billiard balls. Though it was too early to be sure, there seemed to be minimal evidence pointing toward drugs being the cause of Bobby Dolan's murder. The mere presence of drugs at the scene did not invalidate the policy. Only where drugs could be proven to be a direct factor in the death is the policy voided.

The more I thought about it, the more I became convinced that it was the work of a deranged mind, or someone wanting to look that way. I wondered if the cops had any more leads, but decided not to call Jerry until later. I didn't want to overuse my one and only source of information prematurely.

I finished writing my notes. Then I got a call from Majerka. He wanted me to come down to the office. I was about to complain. Even though the agency was open on Saturdays, it was my day off, but he promised to pay me overtime. He said it was important, so I agreed to go in.

"What'd ya got for me, Jay?" he asked, as I knocked and let myself into his office.

"There was another murder late last night," I informed him. "The police think it's the same MO. The evidence, at least at this point, indicates drugs were not a factor in the Dolan murder. I think suicide can also be safely ruled out as well. Looks like the company may have to pay on this one."

"You let me worry about who has to pay. My sources downtown tell me drugs were involved. You should be able to confirm that in your report. Get it to me as soon as possible and don't speculate."

Before I could reply, he went on.

"Dan Dolan called, said you'd been by. Said you were rude and offensive. Is that any way to treat one of our best customers?"

Dick was waving his cigarette carelessly in the air as he talked, continually dropping ashes all over his desk like so much napalm from a dive-bomber.

"That's not true, Dick," I said. "I was only asking some questions. I thought he might have some insight into what happened, who Bobby's friends were, stuff like that. I may have pushed a little, but he wouldn't tell me anything. I assure you I wasn't rude or impolite."

"Well, can you blame him for being a little upset? He must be totally devastated. You should have been more sensitive, Jay, but don't worry about it. Just leave your report with me as soon as it's finished. When will it be ready?"

"I should have it for you by next Tuesday. I want to have one more follow-up meeting with my police contact. I also want to interview Major Stienman, the husband of the first murdered woman."

"Why him?" Majerka asked.

"There are still plenty of loose-ends. I'd like to check him out, check his alibi. He might know something about his wife's extra-curricular activities."

"Just be careful and make sure you keep your mouth shut. Don't go blabbing about this case to anyone, not even your friend at the police station. I'll handle it all from here. Just make sure you give me your report as soon as it's finished."

I told him not to worry, but he was already shuffling papers around his desk and ignored me as if I was already gone. As I left his smoke-filled office, I could barely suppress the urge to turn and call him a blazing a-hole, but my better judgment prevailed for a change. I couldn't afford to lose this job, but then that had never stopped me before.

It was almost 4:30. I hadn't had anything to eat all day except a donut, a Coke, and a Snickers bar for lunch. My stomach was growling an out of tune cello sonata, so I decided to grab an early supper.

As I was leaving the office Suzie came in from her rounds at the registry.

"Hey, Clyde, what brings you in today? Isn't this your day off?"

"Murjurka asked me to come in. I'm working on an important case for him. I have to go out and pound the pavement for a living, not like some people I know who can sit around all day and talk on the phone."

I wasn't going to let her get the last word. I may have to take Majerka's abuse, but that didn't mean I had to take it from his secretary.

"That's not all I'll bet you're pounding, Clyde," she quipped. "Did you hear, there was another murder last night?"

"Yeah, how did you know?"

"Oh, it's all over the papers. Some girl from the base. I'm scared. Maybe we have a sex murderer in town. I could be next." She shuddered.

"You'd better get Clark Kent to change into super nerd and protect you. Anyway, I hear the killer doesn't go after redheads, they're too weird."

"Yeah, look who's talking, the king of the weirdoes himself."

"Well, it's been nice talking to you, but I have no one to blame but myself," I said, leaving her with one of my overused Groucho lines.

Nothing like exchanging quips with Suzie to get the juices flowing.

Chapter 5

Day 3 (p.m.)

After scarfing down a couple of burgers at the 'Spoon', I headed over to my dad's house. I hadn't talked to him in awhile and thought he might have some insight into what was going on in town.

It was around 5:30 p.m. when I arrived. I went in through the back door and called his name. There was no answer. His car was in the garage, which meant he was either sleeping or visiting next door. I had a class at six, so decided to work out a little as I waited. I had plenty of time before I had to get ready for the gig.

Going down to the basement, I changed into my gi pants and a t-shirt, and started to stretch out. I worked on my thigh and calf muscles, pulling and working each muscle group in turn. I could feel the heat build with the familiar pain. I worked my back and sides. I practiced deep breathing, in through the nose, out through the mouth. Doing a few quick calisthenics, I then ran through some kata. These are prearranged patterns of kicks and punches that simulate fighting multiple opponents. I finished off with some slow tai-chi.

Working out always took my mind off my problems. No matter where I was, or what was happening around me, I could always escape into the mysterious world of the martial arts. Man against himself, that's the true spirit of the arts, not one man against another as so often depicted in the movies. But then again, in a pinch, it didn't hurt to known how to defend oneself.

I decided to work on the heavy bag until my students arrived. There's nothing like a seventy-five pound bag to work out your aggressions. I started slowly, with a few tentative kicks and hand strikes, working up to a flurry of straight, hard punches and spinning-wheel kicks that sent the heavy bag jumping and jangling on its chain. After a few minutes of this my father came down. He had been taking a nap.

"Jesus, Jay, you're shaking the whole house!" He looked like he was still half asleep. "I didn't know you were down here."

"Sorry, Dad. Didn't know you were sleeping. Guess I kind of got carried away. I told you a heavy bag would shake your house up."

I was breathing hard, out of breath from the exertion.

"Do you have to hit it so hard? You'll knock the house down."

"Don't worry. Those kicks aren't the ones you have to worry about. These are the one's you have to watch out for."

I backed away from the bag, then cross-stepped into it with a full-power side-thrust kick, throwing my hip, and therefore my whole bodyweight, into it. The bag swung toward the ceiling with a shudder. As it descended downward again, back toward me, I spun around on it with a back kick. The force of the spinning kick meeting the seventy-five pound swinging bag shook the house like an earthquake.

"Jesus!" he yelled. "What do you think you're doing?"

"I thought you liked this stuff," I panted, out of breath. "It was your idea to put up the bag in the first place."

I liked showing off in front of my Dad, although I was still breathing heavily. He was impressed with this new-fangled fighting, as he called it. Dad had seen his share of street fights and brawls. He was an ex-marine, and knew about hand-to-hand combat and jujitsu from his days in the service. But he had never seen anything like the combination of hand and foot strikes a good martial artist can throw.

"Why are you huffing and puffing like that? You sound like an old man," he said derisively.

"You try throwing some punches and kicks at this bag and see how hard you're breathing."

Well, so much for trying to impress him. Now he was getting on my nerves.

"Hey, I'm an old man. You're the one that's supposed to be in shape. What are you, smoking pot?"

He was a master at keeping me off balance and distracted in our verbal exchanges. God knew he'd had enough practice.

"I don't care if you were in your prime or not. Three minutes with this bag and you'd be out on your feet." I was finally getting my wind back.

"Why, in my prime I could have gone with that bag of yours all day and all night and not broken a sweat. And remember, the bag doesn't hit back."

"Yeah, talk's cheap," I jabbed back, punching the bag with a straight left. "So I got a little winded, big deal. I could still go six rounds if I had to. You're welcome to go a few with me. I'll show you how out of shape I am."

"No thanks, chump," he laughed. "I wouldn't want to hurt you."

"You hear what's been going on around town?" I asked, changing the subject to what I wanted to discuss. "I mean the murders?"

"Yes, real shame about Dan Dolan's son. Young kid like that, why, he had everything going for him. A millionaire at twenty-four, he had a great future in front of him. What a tragic waste." He pretty much summed it all up in his inimitable way. "Probably drug related. Damned drugs are ruining the country."

"Dad, our elected officials are ruining the country, not drugs. Drug abuse is just the symptom of some deeper ill. Anyway, the cops don't think drugs were directly involved in this one."

To change the subject, I asked him what he knew about the chain of command at the base.

"Well, let's see," he said thoughtfully. "I know a few of the top brass there. The base commander is a full colonel, Colonel Michael Dene. He's been there forever. What a crab he is. I've never met a more sour man. They used to have a one star general as base commander, but in recent years, with the cutbacks, that's no longer the case. Then there's your wing commander, in charge of all the pilot squadrons. He's a full colonel, too, a Negro, Hugh Fitzgerald. Nicest guy you'd ever want to meet. I've played golf with him once or twice. After that there are your squadron commanders, usually lieutenant-colonels or majors. They're in charge of the various fighter and bomber squadrons."

"Isn't that a bit odd?" I asked, hearing something of interest, "Dene being there for so long. I thought they changed those guys around so they don't get too comfortable in one place."

"I don't know," answered my father. "He must be good at what he does. Say, they're burying Bobby Dolan tomorrow. You should go to the funeral."

"I didn't even know the guy," I said, tossing the excuse over my shoulder as I went up the cellar stairs to answer the door bell. My students had arrived. "Besides, funerals depress me, and I'm depressed enough already as it is."

"You always were a spoiled, selfish kid, you know that?" he called after me as I went to the door.

Things were slow that evening at the Pontiac club, especially for a Saturday night. Mickey, the owner, walked by during one of our breaks and complained.

"How come Brandy's is doing so well tonight and this place is empty?" he asked.

"It's early, the adults aren't out yet," I replied.

"Brandy's has them lined up all the way down the street waiting to get in," he answered. "I'm going to change over to rock. I can't keep paying expensive groups to play music nobody wants to listen to."

"The local funeral parlors are probably stealing some of your business," I observed

"It doesn't seem to be affecting Brandy's business," he responded.

"Their business is good because that Riley girl, the one who was killed last night, was dancing there just before she was murdered," I told him. "They're all just morbid thrill seekers."

That didn't appear to placate Mickey. He eyed the room, looking for someone to sacrifice to the gods of a quick buck. The conversation boded ill for my future, which hadn't looked that promising to begin with.

"I told you we needed some new songs," I said to George, who just grunted and went back to the bandstand to start the next set.

Mickey must have hit a nerve, because George picked things up. The group sounded good that night and I was having fun. My girl, Mary, showed up for the last set. By that time the place had started to fill up with a late crowd. Mickey was actually smiling behind the bar.

During the break, Mary and I speculated about the murders.

"The police have that kid, Marshall Gurny, in custody," I told her. "But I doubt he could kill a flea. I think there's a connection between the two murders. They all appear to have been killed with the same weapon, in the same manner."

"Yes, that's what the coroner said," Mary confirmed.

"I wonder if there's something going on at the base."

"Like what?" Mary asked.

"I don't know, but the two female victims lived there, not far from each other."

"I think a deranged serial killer is stalking the town," suggested Denise, who had joined us with the others.

"I'd love to meet him and shove that knife up his anus," I said.

"You'd probably run," replied George.

"You're probably right. I'd run and find a weapon of my own."

I went home that night feeling vaguely troubled, but didn't know why. Maybe I was worried about what Mickey had said. I needed the gig. If I had any dreams, they were lost in mindless oblivion. Unbeknownst to me, the ride I was on was rapidly picking up speed, heading toward disaster.

Chapter 6

Day 4 (a.m.)

I gave my friend Jerry a call the next morning, reminding him about the insurance claim I was investigating and the drug clause.

"Do you think I could get a written statement from your guys that drugs have been ruled out as a motive for the Dolan murder?" I asked hopefully. "It would really help the agency."

"Sure, Jay, I'll see what I can do. No sweat," he replied.

Jerry fed me more information spiced with a fair amount of speculation.

"Mrs. Stienman's funeral was held yesterday afternoon. They didn't waste any time putting her in the ground, eh? She was cremated. The ceremony was held on the base. She was survived by her husband and two young children. The ceremony was closed to everyone except the immediate family and a few close friends. The base has been very quiet about the whole thing, if you ask me."

"Do they think her husband did it?" I asked.

"I don't know. They're trying to confirm his alibi. I've probably said too much already. I really don't know what to think," he confessed, telling me the Riley girl was still at the base morgue until her father could be located.

We speculated back and forth for a few more minutes, going around in circles with no results. Finally, just before our conversation ended, he added a disturbing piece of information. As brutal as the murders had been - and they were gruesome by any standards - there was absolutely no evidence found at the crime scenes, no fingerprints, no footprints, no body hairs, no cloth fibers, nothing. It was as if some demon had popped out of another dimension, did its grisly work, then disappeared back into the stinking void that spawned it without a trace. People were beginning to get scared. I thanked him and hung up.

I spent the rest of the morning staring out my window into the motel's mostly empty parking lot, trying to fit all the pieces of the jigsaw together. I gave Major Stienman, the husband of the first murdered woman, a call around noon. I had a funny feeling about him. I wanted to ask him a few questions, see if I could find out something that would help make sense of the whole mess. There was no answer, so I hung up after the tenth ring. He was obviously not taking any calls. I couldn't really blame the guy.

I felt that my report, with the official police statement, was sure to result in the speedy settlement of Dan Dolan's policy. Even though he didn't need the money, a principle had been upheld. Though I couldn't help feeling some concern over how Majerka would react, and saw myself as a potential scapegoat.

I tried to get in touch with the Major again a short time later, but again there was no answer. After trying unsuccessfully several more times, on an impulse, I decided to go down to the base and see him in person. I called Mary and asked if she would accompany me, not telling her exactly where I was going. There's nothing like a friendly female face to help make the guard at the main gate more cooperative. She would be a reassuring presence if I got to see the Major, like a squaw with a party of warriors means peace.

I picked Mary up at her place and drove the short distance to the base.

"Are you expected?" asked the guard at the main gate of the housing area.

"No, not really," I answered. "I've been trying to get in touch with Major Stienman for two days. I'm investigating a case for a local insurance agency and need some additional information that only the Major can provide."

The guard tried to phone him, but like me, received no answer.

"Major Stienman is not home," he informed me.

When I asked him if the major was on duty, or if there was any record of him leaving the base, he declined to answer, saying only that he had not seen him that day.

"I'll inform the Major that you were asking for him and have him contact you," he said.

I thanked him, left my card, and drove off.

It was mid-afternoon, almost two. Bobby Dolan's funeral was taking place across town. Mary wanted to go, but I had other ideas. I figured she had seen enough of the dead Bobby Dolan.

"Let's take a walk. I need some air," I said as I drove toward the boat docks below town.

The officers' homes bordered the lake. Although this was fenced off like all the other areas of the base, I remembered places where you could easily get in through a hole in the fence. I used to date a girl who lived there. We snuck in and out all the time.

I drove down behind town. There's a little dirt road that runs along the lake, parallel to the train tracks from the nearby station. I drove down this road a bit then parked the car where it comes to an end. It is only a short distance from there to the section of the base housing the officers and their families.

We walked along the deserted shoreline, strewn with rocks and driftwood, for about ten minutes. The ground rose gradually on our right to form wooded slopes of oak and pine, along which the railroad tracks ran. The six-foot high chain link fence that separated the base from the civilian world ran through these woods. So far, my plan was going smoothly. Mary had no idea of what I had in mind.

I headed up the embankment, across the tracks to a spot I remembered from those years of my misspent youth long ago. Mary followed reluctantly, not sure where we were going. Lo' and behold, there it was, the same spot where the fence had fallen into disrepair long ago. The hole in the chain-link was still gaping after all these years.

Mary had come along this far unsuspecting and uncomplaining. When she realized what I was up to she started to object.

"What's wrong? Got cold feet?" I teased.

"We can't just break into the base like that. Isn't it a federal offense or something?" she asked.

"Only if you get caught," I answered as I crawled through the hole in the fence.

I was intent on talking to Major Stienman, one way or another. I wasn't sure exactly what I was going to say to him, or whether he'd have me thrown off the base or arrested. I hoped that if I could convince him that I could help find his wife's murderer, he might open up to me. Then again, he could be the killer, in which case I might be able to get him to tip his hand. It was worth the risk. I didn't really have much to lose and everything to gain. Solving a big murder case might be my ticket out of this dead-end town.

I figured the cops hadn't had a chance to talk to Stienman yet. I knew the base people. They tended to stick together against the local authorities. I doubted much information would be forthcoming through official channels.

"Well, are you coming?" I asked, holding the gap in the fence wide for her. "Even if you don't come you'll be an accessory. That is unless you turn me in. So you might as well join me."

She stood there a moment in indecision. "Ah, what the heck," she said finally, and followed me through the hole in the fence.

The sun penetrated the pinewoods in bright, spiked rays of light. It grew hotter as it moved higher across the sky.

"You're going to see Stienman, aren't you? How do you know where to go?" she asked, breathing hard behind me as we walked up the steep, wooded slope.

"I got his address from the base phone book. I know the area from when I was a kid. I'm pretty sure I can find his house."

We headed along a path in the general direction I thought the Major's house should be. We walked in silence for awhile, along a well-worn trail carpeted with pine needles. It was the same path my girlfriend and I had walked those many years before. I was fifteen, with all my possibilities, all my dreams and unsuspected failures, still before me.

Mary had regained her voice and was softly trying to get me to turn around and go back. I had come too far to stop now. I reassured her with lies. It more or less worked.

The path came out near the very house where my old girlfriend used to live. There was the same backyard I had snuck across in my pursuit of sex, back when it was all a new discovery.

We left the covering of the woods and cut across a street that appeared to go in the right direction. It was lined with trees, and single-level, two-family brick dwellings fronted by small, well-tended lawns.

It was after two. Most people were in town or in the country, or preparing for Sunday dinner. The street was empty. We could hear kids playing on the next block. A dog barked in the distance. Even though I hadn't been there in years, I remembered my way around fairly well. We soon located the Stienman residence.

By all appearances the place was deserted. Wanting to stay out of sight as much as possible, we went around to the back. I knocked at the rear entrance several times and waited. There was no response. I tried the door. It was open, just my luck.

I stuck my head in and called out.

"Hello, Major Stienman? Is anybody home? Hello?" There was no response. I pushed open the door and walked in. I had a sneaky feeling we shouldn't have come. I ignored it.

Mary stayed by the rear door, while I entered the small carpeted living area. There was an upright piano against the wall, with a worn but comfortable looking sofa next to it. A low, mahogany table sat in front of the sofa, which faced a cabinet with a combination television/Hi-Fi system.

I walked slowly down the hallway toward the rear of the house, calling as I went.

The first door I came to was slightly ajar. I peered in. The room was empty. There were model planes and toy soldiers scattered across the floor and small play tables. A train set sat in the corner. The small track twisted and turned in a complex array of figure-eights and loops.

Mary called from the living room.

"Jay, is everything all right? What's going on there? Jay, let's get out of here!" I could hear the slight quiver of fear in her voice, the strain of anxiety building rapidly to panic.

I answered reassuringly, trying to calm her, and continued down the hall to another empty room. The bed was covered with raggedy dolls and stuffed animals. A tidy, well-stocked vanity table sat opposite the bed. The walls were covered with pictures of bare-chested, longhaired rock stars, which contrasted sharply with the picture of innocence denoted by the stuffed animals and dolls.

The last two doors stood closed. Cautiously, I opened the one on my right. It led to the master bedroom. The drapes were drawn, the room dark and quiet. I called out and walked in, squinting in the half-light as my eyes adjusted to the gloom. I did not expect anyone to be there. I was mistaken.

There hanging by the neck just a few feet in front of me in the middle of the room was Major John Stienman, of the U.S. Air Force. I stopped dead in my tracks, frozen at the sight. His silk pajama tops were knotted around his neck in an ingenious form of noose. The other end was tied to a hook that had been screwed into a ceiling beam. The plant that had previously hung on the hook was dumped on the floor, along with the chair he must have been standing on to hoist himself up. The slim, slightly balding major was still wearing his pajama bottoms, and looked quite dead. The bulging front of his PJs was stained with something dark and wet.

I stood gaping, trying to catch my breath, while adrenaline flooded my system in a rush. My knees were weak. My heart was beating wildly. My mind was stuck in freeze-frame. At that moment, Mary came to the bedroom door and looked in. When she saw the dead man, she screamed.

"Oh, my God! No! Is he dead? Is he dead? Help him!" Her first thought was to help him, even though it was obvious from the stiff way he was dangling there that this guy was long beyond saving.

She rushed in and tried to get him down, lifting him around the waist from behind in a bear hug, to relieve the pressure on his neck. She yelled frantically for me to help. I finally started to move, as if in a dream. As she held the cold body against her, I stood on the chair, which I righted, and tried to untie the silk noose around his neck. It seemed to take forever. It was so tight it had cut into the dead man's flesh. Finally, I succeeded in tearing it loose, and we lowered him to the floor.

Even to a non-medically trained person like me it was obvious Stienman had been dead for awhile. His skin was sallow and gray, his eyes partly open. His swollen tongue was sticking out. He was stiff as an ironing board and cold as a frozen fish, his bare chest fully expanded in a last inhalation.

"Oh, no, he's dead!" gasped Mary, stating the obvious.

"Look's like he's been dead for hours," I said, looking at the corpse lying between us. "Now what do we do?"

I was shaken. I still couldn't believe this was really happening. It was just my dumb luck. I suppose, had I given some thought to the consequences of my actions, I would have foreseen trouble, but sometimes seeing it doesn't always help you avoid it. It seemed obvious what had happened.

"It looks like the Major did himself in. I wonder, was it guilt or grief? We better get out of here and call the authorities. Maybe we can leave an anonymous tip or something."

I gazed about the room looking for any hint of what might have happened, a note, a clue, anything. Except for the overturned flowerpot and chair, nothing was out of place.

Suddenly, Mary, who had been leaning over the dead man examining him, straightened up and looked at me in alarm.

"Oh God, what about his children?" she exclaimed. "He has two kids. Where are they?"

We both looked in the direction of the closed door at the end of the hall. It obviously led to the bathroom. I told her to stay where she was, and moved quickly to the door.

Expecting the worst, I flung it open. It banged against the tile wall. To my relief, the children were alive. They were sitting hogtied and gagged in the empty tub, their eyes stained with tears. Mary and I were untying them when I heard a vehicle drive up to the house. Two doors slammed shut and heavy footsteps came up to the front entrance. The base police had arrived. They stormed into the house and arrested us at gunpoint.

Chapter 7

Day 4 (p.m.)

I was sitting in one of the interrogation rooms at what appeared to be a base compound. We had been brought here in the back of a military jeep by a group of hard-eyed MPs at gunpoint. These guys looked like they would just as soon shoot me as look at me. I kept my mouth shut and did as I was told, a rarity for me.

I repeated my story to at least three people, each succeeding interrogator a higher ranking and more ignorant moron than the preceding one. I was not much impressed with the military ranking system. I thought the first guy I talked to, a young lieutenant, the brighter of the three, and made a point of telling that to the other two. They were not amused, and asked me if I was aware of the gravity of the situation. I responded that I sure as hell fucking was. That 'smart' mouth that had gotten me into so much trouble with authority when I was a kid had apparently raised its ugly head again after many years of lying dormant. Losing my patience, I asked them if they knew where their brains were.

I had been stewing in the interrogation room ever since. As I sat there, I went over my sorry excuse for a life, wondering where I had gone wrong.

My mom died during my senior year in high school. It was quite a shock and probably accounts for a lot of the anger I carry around inside me. One day off to the hospital for a hysterectomy, the next day dead. It was all extremely sad, but I didn't shed a tear. I knew I'd miss her terribly, that I was being robbed of a tremendous treasure, but I also knew there was nothing I could do. She was gone and I'd just have to accept it. She was at peace. I kept my pain hidden, but showed my anger like a badge. Nothing seemed able to assuage the terrible rage I felt at her loss. After awhile, things kind of cooled down on their own.

Dad carried on the best he could. In a way, I think he stopped caring about anything after mom died. Oh, he went through the motions for our sake, but it was empty, you could see it in his eyes. There was no feeling, no joy behind anything he did.

My older brother by two years, Tony, was away at school. He was always the best at everything he did, the smartest, the best looking, the best athlete. He always got the prettiest girls. God, how I envied him! Now he's a big-shot lawyer. Thinks he's so cool, Mister 'Big Man'.

What a stiff he turned out to be! My younger brother Billy turned out even worse than I did, living in the streets of St. Petersburg, Florida, preying off the old and feebleminded. It seems that each successive child got less and less of the good genes. By the time Billy was born, the gene pool had plumb run out.

I had been reviewing my life in this desultory manner for about forty minutes, when in walked the chief of the city's police force, Ed McNeil. He was accompanied by my latest interrogator, the dim-witted major.

Eddie McNeil was only a year or two old than I, but looked in his forties, pot bellied and graying. Dressed even worse than I was, he had on an over-worn, wrinkled, brown polyester suit that looked a size too small for his bulging frame. He stood there with his hands on his chubby hips, with a stare that was intended to intimidate me, but which only made me want to laugh.

I had known him since we were kids. He was an a-hole and a bully then, and he was even more so now. His father had been Chief of Police and had used the authority of his office to get his way and push people around. No wonder his kid turned out to be such a jerk.

Eddie used to taunt the other kids. He'd call them names and insult their parents, or make fun of their clothes. If they were small enough, he'd pick fights with them. He used to get everyone real mad, but there was nothing they could do about it because his father was the chief of police. Now Eddie was the head cop and even worse than his father.

As far as Eddie was concerned, I was the scum of the earth, right down there with your child molesters and drug dealers. He knew that I had majored in criminology and had wanted to get into the FBI, and that I had been kicked out of college for drug possession. He never lost an opportunity to throw it in my face. I guess he held a grudge. I'm not sure why. I never picked on him. As a matter of fact, I stuck up for him one time when three of my friends wanted to beat him up. He actually taunted them after I stepped in to stop them. Whatever the reason, Eddy McNeil disliked me intensely. To Eddie I represented everything that was dirty and undesirable in the town, everything that needed to be cleaned up and disposed of. By the way, he hated jazz like a puritan hates the can-can.

"Well, you stupid bastard, you've really done it this time," he said as he entered the room. "You're finally going to get what's coming to you. You're going to burn for this one." He leered at me like I was a monkey in a cage.

"Hey, I didn't..."

"Shut up!" he yelled. "You've had it in this town, Lawless, trespassing on government property, murder."

"I didn't do anything! We just walked in through a hole in the fence. I had to talk to the major for a case I'm working on for the agency. He was already dead when we got there."

I knew my rights.

"Are you going to charge me or what?" I asked him. "I've told you everything I know. Check my story if you don't believe me. If you ask me, Stienman must have killed himself, possibly from guilt."

"I'm not asking you, smart ass," he growled. "I'm not interested in your opinion. Why don't you just keep your mouth shut? I've got a good mind to let these military boys have their way with you. They'd probably love to get their hands on a troublemaking, dope smoking mama's boy like you."

Seeing he had struck a nerve with the mention of my deceased mother, he dug at the sore spot with sadistic glee.

"My dad always said you'd end up no good," he told me. "Just the product of a seedy, know-it-all politician, and a woman who dressed like a whore."

With the insult to my dead mother I was out of my chair, across the table, and on him before anyone could react. I don't know, I'm usually in better control than that, even with someone like Eddie McNeil. It must have been the strain of seeing the dead Major Stienman, together with the long hours of grilling by people who acted like robots on auto-pilot. It all just finally got to me and I snapped.

"You keep my mother out of this, you little shit! You can't go running to daddy now, you dick!"

I said this as I delivered a series of rapid backhands and slaps, knocking him into a straight-backed, wooden chair, and from there onto the wastepaper basket next to it.

Two MP's and the major pulled me back. One of them looked like he was about to unleash his billy club on my noggin. Eddie had sprawled out on the floor with the contents of the can, yelling in a high-pitched voice like he used to when we were kids.

"He tried to kill me! You saw it! He assaulted me!" he said with a red face, as he got to his feet. "He's a maniac! You just assaulted a police officer, you stupid bastard. You'll pay for that!"

The two MP's sat me down roughly and stood over me. They eyed me menacingly as they repeatedly beat the shafts of their clubs into their large, meaty hands. The major escorted Eddie out of the interrogation room, trying his best to calm the irate chief of police down.

Well, I thought, you've really done it this time. Bad enough you got mixed up in this mess, now you had to assault the Chief of Police. You must have the brain of a four-year-old, and he was glad to get rid of it! Yeah, I had a Groucho line for every occasion, even my own funeral. I figured at this point, they'd just lock me up and throw away the key. I'd be lucky if my next of kin ever found out what happened to me.

I sat there for about twenty more minutes before the major and Chief McNeil came back in. Apparently the major had succeeded in calming McNeil down. He just looked at me sullenly with bulging, pink-rimmed eyes.

"Lock him up," said the major to the MP guards.

"What's the big idea?" I objected. "I didn't do anything!"

"How's trespassing on a military facility sound for starters? McNeil said. "Would you like to go for assaulting a police officer? Just say another word, asshole!"

They led me out of the interrogation room through a series of thick doors deeper into the building. Each door had a single, square window reinforced with wire, and clicked lock behind me. They put me in a holding cell, and locked me up like a common criminal. I asked for a blanket and lay on the small cot with the blanket over my head, trying to block the whole thing out. Now I know what an ostrich feels like. One of the guards was a little taken aback by my strange behavior, and asked if I was all right. I responded with a grunt. I just wanted to be left alone. I didn't have long to stew. After about half an hour, my big-shot brother, Tony, came in. Mary must have called him.

"Are you crazy, Jay?" he began before I could even say hi. "What were you thinking, sneaking onto the base like that? And into a major's house! A war hero whose wife was just murdered! Are you out of your mind? You're taking this investigating thing too far. I told you it was a lousy idea years ago."

"Nice to see you, too, Tony. Now I know why it's been so long."

"Fine, after I leave a perfectly good dinner party to come and bail you out of jail. You're welcome."

"Thanks, I owe you, bro'. Now get me out of here."

Talking to my older brother Tony is like talking to the district attorney. He never let's up for a moment. The interrogations of a few hours before were nothing compared to the inquisition Tony gave me.

"Tell me what happened. I'll have you out of here in no time, don't worry."

I repeated my story for the eleventh time, this time to the biggest moron of them all, my brother. I told him what I told the authorities to convince them I couldn't have had anything to do with the death of Stienman.

"Stienman must have been dead at least twelve hours, probably more," I told him. "At least that's what Mary said. Our whereabouts can be accounted for at the most probable time of death. If it hadn't been for me, those poor kids would still be hogtied and gagged in the bathtub. It's more than likely a suicide."

I had to endure a continuous barrage of Tony's questions and accusations, while I waited for them to unlock me. Finally, just when I thought I would reach through the bars and strangle the pompous fool, an MP came in and let me out.

As I was leaving, the major told me that I was never to step foot on the base again. That suited me just fine. If I didn't visit the place for another fifty years, it would be too soon. I was also told to make myself available for a court appearance in the near future. I told them not to worry, I wasn't going anywhere. I asked about Mary and was told she had been released several hours ago. I had to sign a form before I could leave, stating I would not discuss the events of the evening with anyone, under penalty of imprisonment and fine. I lied.

I was on my way out when Eddie McNeil called after me.

"You were lucky this time, Lawless. These gentlemen are civilized. But you better stay out of my way! If you stick your nose in police business again, I'll make you sorry your mother ever hatched you. Got it?"

I flipped him a mental 'bird' and let myself be led away and off the base. I was lucky to be getting off so lightly, and wondered why. My brother Tony certainly didn't have any pull. Perhaps Dad pulled in a favor, maybe his friend, the second in command at the base. I made a point to ask him next time I saw him.

By the time I got home it was after nine p.m. The band wasn't working that night. I called my dad and told him what happened. He told me he hadn't eaten yet. So we decided to meet for a late dinner out at the Depot.

The Depot is a diner, located at the truck stop on the highway that runs north out of town toward the Canadian border thirty miles away. It's a plain square building filled with plain tables and chairs, where plain looking people sit and eat plain home-cooked food. They serve hot meals for a good price twenty-four hours a day. My dad ate there at least twice a week, when they served all-you-can-eat buffet dinners for $6.99.

We ate pretty much in silence. He didn't know about the incident at the base yet, so he couldn't have had any part in my release. He was obviously disturbed when I told him about it. He listened to my story with an undisguised expression of disgust. How could I be so stupid as to go trespassing on base property?

"You could have been shot!" he said.

I told him I was working on the Dolan case for the agency. I had wanted to ask the husband of the murdered woman some questions that might have a bearing on the insurance claim. He was avoiding me, so I decided to pay him a visit. How was I to know he had hog-tied his two children in the tub and squeeze-stretched his neck with his own pajama tops.

I began to muse out loud about the events of recent days. Was it possible that Stienman had been the murderer all along? How did the killing of the Riley girl fit into this? Could Stienman have been balling the teenager on the side, or was that the work of the skinny nerd, Marshall Gurny? Or was something else going on? Then again, there just might be a good old-fashioned sex maniac on the loose.

My father's advice was to mind my own business and keep out of it. He told me I was lucky I wasn't in chains in some federal prison. I reminded him it was my business, and that he had sent me to school to learn how to investigate crime.

"Don't remind me of that," he replied. "I've been trying to forget that little episode of your life."

"Good, I'm trying to forget my whole life!" I retorted. I was getting miffed at the lack of support. To change the subject, I asked him a question about the bomber runs at the base.

"Do they still fly those missions to Russia?" I asked. "You know, the B-52s carrying H-bombs toward Moscow, and then turning around just before entering their airspace and coming home?"

The B-52 Stratofortress had been our main nuclear deterrent from the mid-50s to that time. I remember as a kid hearing the loud roar of the huge, long-range bombers as they warmed up their engines. They flew over our house constantly on their strategic missions at all hours of the day and night.

"No, I think they stopped doing that just a few months ago," he answered. "With what's going on in Russia these days they probably figured there's no need. Though I don't trust those Ruskies now any more than I did when they were commies."

"I wonder if Stienman and the missing Captain Riley knew each other?" I said, changing the subject.

He looked at me disapprovingly.

"Put it to rest, Jay."

We finished our meal in silence. Later, he drove me home. I told him I'd see him Tuesday night after my workout session. As we were pulling up to my apartment, I remembered something.

"Hey, Dad, what did you do for Majerka to get him to hire me? He's always saying how he doesn't need an investigator and only hired me as a favor to you. What'd you do, buy a huge policy from him or something?"

"No, it was nothing. He was having a few problems awhile back. I leant him some money, that's all. It was no big deal. Why?"

"Oh, I was just wondering. He said he only hired me as a favor to you in return for something you did for him once."

"Well, I knew you wanted something in that line of work. It seemed like a good fit. He thought so too. He never said he didn't need an investigator. Are you sure you're working hard?"

"Why bust my ass for that dead-end job?"

"That's a lousy attitude. How do you expect to get ahead like that?"

"Dad, there really isn't any work to speak of there. That is until now, and all it's getting me is trouble."

"Well, try to do the best you can. You never know, maybe it will lead to something else. I'll see you Tuesday."

He dropped me off at my motel, driving off in his Cadillac Seville, the picture of success. I crawled into my meager efficiency room, the epitome of failure.

It was after eleven when I got home. I was too keyed-up from the day's events to sleep, so I worked on my notes for Dick Majerka. As I worked, I finished off the bottle of Crown Royal I had been nursing for the last few weeks. My report concluded that there was no evidence of drugs being a factor in the death of Bobby Dolan.

I sat on the couch, with my notes spread around me, watching an old Ronald Reagan movie and waiting to get tired enough to go to sleep. I thought about all the sudden death visited upon our town recently. The more I thought about it, the less convinced I became that Stienman was the murderer. He could have had any number of reasons for killing himself. After all, his wife had just been murdered in bed with another man. If that's not a good reason for suicide, I don't know what is. It's certainly just as likely a motive as guilt. Then again, maybe it really was a serial killer? I was having trouble coming up with anything that added up.

I didn't have much faith in the local police solving the crime. The whole affair was becoming personal. I had gotten involved with something I didn't understand, something deadly. That made me more determined than ever to get to the bottom of it. But I was going to need help.

I needed access to information only computers could provide, computers I couldn't hope to get access to. I decided to call my friend, John Rothburg, to see if I could get him to help. John was the head radio astronomer at the university's observatory, located on the top of one of the local mountains. John is not only an astronomer. He's also a computer wizard. If anyone could help me get access to computer files, he could.

I had quite a buzz by the time I staggered to bed at 1:30. I slept like a dead man that night, and don't remember a thing after lying down. I woke in the exact position I fell asleep in. I don't think I moved an inch all night.

Chapter 8

Day 5

Monday morning I had the inevitable headache and that other unmentionable problem that always flared up after one of my drinking binges. It was getting pretty bad when I couldn't even tie one on without suffering humiliating physical infirmities. I splashed some cold water on my face, gargled some mouthwash, and threw on the first available items of clothing I could find. Grabbing a can of soda from the fridge, I headed for work. It was about ten. I felt slightly nauseous and was in no mood to face Suzie's jibes. She was waiting for me when I came in.

She looked up from the newspaper she was reading.

"Boy, oh boy, you really did it this time, Clyde," she said loudly. "Got your name right on the front page, you did. Say's here, 'Local man held last night for questioning in connection with the discovery Sunday of the body of Major John Stienman.' How do you do it? And I thought you were goofing off all this time."

She went on to say the police were theorizing that Major Stienman killed his wife and Bobby Dolan when he found them in bed together. Then in a fit of guilt he went crazy, tied-up his son and daughter, and hung himself. Gee, that had a familiar ring to it.

Marshall Gurny, the eighteen year old boyfriend of the murdered teenage girl, was being held for further questioning regarding her death. Her father, Captain Riley, was still missing and was presumed dead. Up to this point, no murder weapon had been found. A possible connection between the first murders and the Riley girl's was mentioned in passing. It looked like everything was going to be tied up in a nice neat bundle.

"How convenient," I said. "That's about what I'd expect from our local boys in blue." I was still smarting and bitter over my treatment at the hands of the local authorities, and took the opportunity to snipe at them. "They'd be lucky if they could find a snowflake in a blizzard."

"So did you really find the body?" she asked. "What was it like?"

"Oh, it was just dandy. I'll be lucky if I sleep again in a year. If it weren't for my snooping around, those kids would still be sitting in that tub hogtied. Hey, will you be needing the word-processor today?" I asked, changing the subject. "I want to type up my report for Dick."

"No, be my guest. So, what do you think happened, Jay?" she inquired.

"I don't know, Spritzer. The police would like to believe it's solved all nice and tidy like, but I doubt it. They certainly shouldn't close the case."

I went over to the word-processor and typed up my report on the Dolan case. It took me all morning and most of the afternoon with my hunt-and-peck technique. I knew I should have taken typing in high school instead of that extra music course. Suzie brought me a tuna sandwich at noon. Normally I hate tuna, but I was so hungry this one tasted good. I made a mental note to do something nice for her. I'd think of something.

My report stated that there was no indication of drugs contributing directly to the death of Bobby Dolan. His death could instead be attributed to an act of violence perpetrated by a jealous husband, or an unknown and probably mentally ill assailant. I included the letter that Jerry had obtained for me from the investigating officers, stating as much. By all rights, our company was legally responsible for paying the claim as stated in the policy.

When I finished, I gave the report to Suzie. I didn't have the intestinal fortitude at the moment to stomach the sight of Dick Majerka. She laid it on the desk without looking at it, and continued gossiping on the phone with her friend at the registry. I went into my cramped, miserable excuse for an office and shut the door. The first thing I did was call John Rothburg at the observatory.

When I initially got back to town, one of the first people I looked up was John. His friendship during those first few depressing months fresh from failure and unemployment helped me keep my sanity, or at least some facsimile of it. We used to get together quite regularly. I'd go to his place or he'd come to mine to play chess and drink wine. Sometimes he'd take me up to the observatory and show me around.

I met John while I was a senior in high school. He, too, was a frustrated musician, playing a little blues guitar in his spare time. He had just arrived at the college here on his first teaching assignment after graduating from MIT with PhD's in mathematics and astrophysics. Some mutual friends at the college, who knew about our common interest in music, introduced us. We jammed together a few times and became good friends despite the age difference. Now that I think of it, he was the older brother I wished I'd had, rather than the Cro-Magnon cave dweller I got for an elder sibling. When I was going away to college, John had some good advice about living in Boston. Later, during my years at Northeastern, we would get together during vacations. Sometimes John would come down to Bean Town to visit.

Short and squat, he has long hairy arms that give him a distinctly simian appearance. His head of massive, wiry, black hair stands straight out like a solar flare. You will invariably find him dressed in t-shirts and jeans, or threadbare sweaters and corduroys. He can talk endlessly about astronomy and how the stars hold the secrets of the universe and life itself.

We hadn't gotten together for quite awhile, so I was looking forward to seeing him. He answered after the fourth ring, but his voice was so garbled I could hardly understand him.

"Hello, John. Is that you? You OK? You sound like you're choking. This is Jay."

"Hi, Lawless," he answered, clearing his throat several times before he could get the words out intelligibly. "Where you been keeping yourself lately?"

"Here and there. Been playing at the Pontiac Club. You should stop by some night and sit in. Preferably a slow night when there's no one there."

"Screw you," he fired back.

"What's wrong with your voice, you sound terrible?"

"Nothing a little shot of tequila wouldn't cure," he said laughing. This caused a coughing fit. It took him some time to recover. "You just woke me up that's all, you moron," he continued finally.

"Well, wake up and join the human race. It's almost three o'clock in the afternoon. Sounds like you're keeping musician's hours."

"Yeah, I'm afraid that's about as close as I'm going to get to being a musician. I haven't touched my ax in ages. My chops must really suck by now," he lamented.

"Your chops always sucked," I told him. After all, what are friends for if not to rib and insult each other mercilessly?

"Eat me, Lawless! Them's fight'n words. I challenge you to a duel on the field of dishonor, and may the best queen win."

"Sounds good. Whose field did you have in mind?"

When talking to John, you always had to go through the obligatory amount of banter before you could get anything serious out of him.

"How about the observatory?" he replied. "I've got a lot of work to do up there. There's a lot going on these days. I was up all night working with the telescopes."

John was always talking about his work, how some cloud drifting in deep space is made up of so many parts hydrogen, so many parts helium, nitrogen, and silicon, all determined by the characteristic patterns of the radio waves bounced back from space. But what I had in mind for John was much more down to earth.

"Fine, the observatory it is," I replied. "Hey, before I forget, I called you for a reason."

"That figures. You wanted something or you wouldn't have called your old buddy John."

"Would you be able to give me advice on getting access to some computer files?" I asked hopefully. "It's for a case I'm working on for Majerka."

"What do you have in mind, the Bank of America or the CIA?"

"I need information on certain individuals. Personnel files from the base would be helpful. Any information you could get me from city files, like the Registry or Telephone Company, would be good."

"Gee, you're not asking for much. Why don't I just transfer their bank funds while I'm at it."

"Nothing that complicated. Wasn't it you who once said there wasn't a computer in the country you couldn't break into?"

"No, that wasn't me. I said there wasn't a bar in the county I couldn't break out of. I bet you could find the information you want in your agency's computer files. You know those nosy son-of-a-bitch insurance companies have enough information on most people to fill an encyclopedia. No offense."

Despite his usual rough gibes, I knew I could count on John to help. I could tell he was intrigued. I could almost hear the gears in his brain turning. I sensed his curiosity starting to peak. He was hooked. I started reeling him in slowly.

"I wouldn't know how to begin looking," I complained. "I've reached a dead end, but then so have the cops. I'd appreciate any help you could give me on this one, John. It's a really important case. It could mean my job."

"If it's for a case, why don't you use official channels?" he asked.

"Official channels are closed to me. That's why I'm calling you. You know the local authorities and I don't exactly see eye to eye."

"Yeah, that's an understatement. You don't seem to see eye to eye with anybody in authority."

"Do you think you can help?" I pleaded. "I don't know much, but I'll fill you in on everything I do know. I think you'll find it interesting."

"Well, we've been awful busy at the observatory lately. You know the new super-nova I've been telling you about? It's keeping me damned busy."

In 1986 a super-nova exploded right next to our very own galaxy, the closest event of its kind in recorded history. The exploding star flooded the instruments of every stellar observatory on earth with an incredible amount of data, data that would take years to digest into knowledge.

"I've been working on some of the new data that's been coming in," he told me. Things are jumping in the cosmos these days, but I'll see what I can do. Sounds like it might be interesting. Nothing like a little detective work to get the juices flowing."

"I knew I could count on you, John. Thanks!"

I gave him a brief summary of what I knew, along with a list of names - Major Stienman, his wife, Alice Stienman, Captain Riley and his daughter, Kathy Riley, and Bobby Dolan. He made a loud exclamation when he heard the names. Even John, the absent-minded professor lost in the depths of space, had heard about the recent murders.

"So you're involved in that stuff? You should have said that in the first place. I'll have to make this a top priority."

I felt better after talking to John. With his help, I had a real chance of making some headway on the case that was rapidly becoming an obsession. If he couldn't get the information I needed, no one could. When it came to breaking into computers, John was the best in the west.

That afternoon I drove back toward the beach to see Mary. She lives in a new, fancy apartment building, much better than the dump I reside in. When she answered the door and realized who it was, there was a long silence. For a minute I thought she wasn't going to open it.

"Hi, it's me, Jay," I repeated, trying to elicit a response. The door opened a crack and she peered out. The chain was still latched as if I was a stranger and it was late at night

"Hi, are you going to let me in?" I asked politely.

"I don't want to talk to you," she informed me.

"I'm sorry," I replied. "How was I to know what was going to happen? It wasn't all my fault."

"You and your snooping," she said forcibly. "Always have to do things your way. Can't you ever do anything right?"

She was obviously still upset over the whole affair. Who could blame her?

"Are you all right?" I asked with concern. "How did it go in interrogation?"

"Oh, I'm just fine. I had a grand time with you yesterday, finding dead people, getting arrested for trespassing, getting my name plastered in the papers. Who could ask for anything more?" The anger in her voice rose with each phrase. "I didn't get a wink of sleep last night thinking about that poor man!"

"I know, Mary. Is there anything I can do? Want me to come in?"

"No, I don't want you to come in. I'm not sure I ever want to see you again."

"Fine," I said, getting angry. "That suits me just fine. When you make up your mind give me a call."

I really didn't want to blow the only relationship I had managed to have since coming back to town, not without a fight.

"Look," I said before she could close the door. "I don't blame you for being upset with me, but can't we still be friends? I thought we had a good thing going. You can't tell me we haven't had fun." I tried to sound convincing.

"I'm sorry," she replied. "But it was all so horrible. If it hadn't been for your nosing around, I wouldn't have had to go through it. It's all your fault, Jay. You're so damned pushy. Why'd you have to drag me there? I can't sleep. I can't eat. I can't work. I'm so upset, I'm sick. And on top of it all, my reputation has been ruined."

I didn't want to tell her that as far as the town was concerned, her reputation had been ruined long before.

"I know, babe. Don't worry. Everything will turn out OK, you'll see. Try not to think about it. Take care. I'm sorry. Bye."

She closed the door abruptly in my face before I was finished apologizing.

As I drove away I was overcome with an acute sense of loss. I knew it was all over with Mary. I guess I should have seen it coming. Our relationship was never that solid to begin with, but I was taken by surprise anyway. Once again I was cast alone onto the sea of life, rejected and scorned, with no one to share my troubles and joys with. I had gone and done it again, lost another one for the 'Gipper'. Everything seemed to slip through my fingers like a greased up pigskin at the one yard line. My miserable life began to look bleaker by the minute. How had I gotten myself into this mess?

As I drove by the diner in town where the cops hang out, I saw Jerry coming out. I pulled into a parking space across the street and went to head him off as he walked to his truck.

"Hi, Jer'," I yelled crossing the road.

He pretended not to see me. I had to run up to him as he was getting into his vehicle.

"Hey, Jer', I'm glad I bumped into you. Can you talk for a minute?"

"I don't know, Jay. I've got to get back to the station," he said. "I really can't talk to you about police business. I don't have any information other than what was in the papers."

He seemed uncharacteristically abrupt, as if he didn't want to be seen with me.

"What I read in the papers is bull," I told him as he got into the truck.

"Sorry, Jay, I can't help you. I shouldn't even be talking to you after what you did. I've never seen McNeil so mad."

"Afraid of the chief, eh?"

"Yeah, and you should be, too."

"I don't think Stienman is the murderer," I told him. "I thought he had an alibi for the time his wife and Dolan were murdered? Wasn't he on a flight to Greenland or something?"

"They were unable to locate the flight logs for the trip he was supposed to be on, so his alibi was never confirmed," Jerry answered.

"But it contradicts the evidence. The same person killed all three victims. You read the coroner's report."

"The second murder was a copycat killing. The Gurny kid probably read about the first murder in the papers and copied it when he murdered his girlfriend to throw us off the trail. The Dolan case is being closed. Gurny admitted having a fight with the Riley girl. Her teeth marks are still in his shoulder. The drop of blood found under Riley's kitchen table was the same type as the captain's. They think the kid may have killed him, too, and hid the body, but he still insists he knows nothing about it."

"I believe him," I said. "There's no way that skinny eighteen-year-old could have killed anyone. Why? Why would he do something like that? It doesn't make sense."

"That may be, but you can never tell with these psycho types. They're still trying to get the kid to crack and admit to the girl's murder."

"Have they found a murder weapon?" I asked.

"No, no sign of a murder weapon, although the homes of the victims and the surrounding area of the base have been thoroughly searched."

"Then what are they basing their case on? Have they found any hard evidence linking Stienman to his wife's murder, except him hanging himself? Have they even verified that it was suicide, that someone else didn't hang him?"

"You'll have to ask the coroner, Jay. As far as we're concerned the matter is closed. I really can't help you. It's against regulations."

I figured the chief had gotten to him, so I didn't press him. The Chief knew we were friends and that he supplied me with information from time to time. I imagined he was under some pressure not to associate with me. I thanked him, and left more depressed than ever.

I was less sure about the whole thing than the cops seemed to be. I couldn't help feeling there was more to it than met the eye. Something was going on. I felt it in my bones. But what was the connection? As I entered the office, I noticed my report was no longer on Suzie's desk.

"Did Dick pick-up that report yet?" I asked her. "I worked my little fingers to the bone typing that."

"Yes, Mr. Majerka picked it up on his way out of the office. He said he'd look at it later this evening at home. He was busy on the phone most of the day and asked me to see that he wasn't disturbed. He also said he wanted to see you first thing in the morning."

She acted formal and stiff, like she was upset about something. She even looked as if she might have been crying. Majerka had probably browbeaten her. Not that I thought of Suzie as being that defenseless. However, Majerka had a nasty talent for finding peoples' vulnerable points and a tongue that could lash like a whip to go with it.

"First thing in the morning, that's about ten, right?" I asked facetiously.

"No, that's 8:30, first thing, when most normal people get to work," she said without smiling.

"Thank goodness I'm not normal," I replied.

"You can say that again!" she snapped without humor as I headed for the door.

"Thank goodness I'm not normal!" I yelled over my shoulder.

Chapter 9

Day 6

The following morning I got to work early, 8:15. This was something of a milestone for me. I was anxious to show my report to Majerka. I had worked hard on it, using much of what I learned in criminology to support my conclusion. I was proud of it, and thought Majerka would be impressed, even though the company had to pay.

No one was at the office yet, so I waited until Dick arrived to let me in at exactly 8:35. I knew the time because I had waited in the damp, humid air for twenty minutes and already felt sweat-soaked. He looked in a dour mood, and didn't say much as we entered the office.

"Did you read my report?" I asked expectantly.

"Yes, I had a chance to skim through it last night. That's what I wanted to talk about this morning. Why don't you get a cup of coffee and join me in my office."

He took out a cigarette and lit it up, looking for an ashtray to throw the match into. Finding none, he threw it on Suzie's desk.

There was no coffee made, and I wasn't about to make it. I said nothing and followed him into his office, trying to breathe as little of his secondhand smoke as possible. I had an uneasy premonition, but passed it off. I was certain that my report had been well-written and accurate.

He sat down behind his cheap metal desk and got right to the point.

"By my reading of the police reports and my own talks with Chief McNeil, I'm more convinced than ever that drugs were a major contributing factor in the death of Bobby Dolan. He had the stuff up his nose and in his blood. A large amount of drugs were found at the scene of the crime, and he was under investigation for drug dealing. All this leads me to conclude that there is a reasonable likelihood that drugs were one of the primary factors in the cause of death."

"What about the police report? They think the husband, Major Stienman, killed them in a jealous rage and then committed suicide. How does that imply a drug related crime?" I asked incredulously.

"When that amount of drugs is found at a crime scene like that, it's considered drug related, no matter what the police may have said to news reporters or in some semi-official report. The fact that Stienman committed suicide could have nothing to do with it. As far as the insurance company is concerned, the Dolan case is drug related. Until proven otherwise, I'm afraid we are going to have to go under the assumption that the killing was drug motivated."

From his tone and manner I knew there was no use arguing.

"Fine with me," I muttered. "No skin off my nose."

"But I'm afraid it is. I'm going to have to let you go."

He sounded both sorry and satisfied at the same time.

"What!" I yelled. "What's the big idea? I worked hard on that report. I got the facts straight. I met the deadline. You didn't ask me to speculate or base my report on conjecture. You can't just fire me like that for no reason."

I felt totally confused. Had I missed something so obvious as this? I began to doubt myself. I knew that some amount of cocaine had been found at the murder scene and Jerry had mentioned Dolan being under investigation. Nothing he or anyone else had said, however, made me seriously consider it to be a drug related crime.

I looked at him hard, my eyes burning into him. Why did this situation feel so familiar, like I've been here before?

"Your report was flawed. You failed to reach the right conclusion. It's a good thing no one else read it or our credibility would have been ruined."

"Yeah right," I snarled. I figured at this point I had nothing to lose. "You have no credibility. It's obvious what you're up to. Everyone's going to see it for what it is, an attempt by the company to welsh out on yet another legitimate claim. You can't get away with this," I said, leaning forward in my chair.

"Look, I took you on as a favor to your father, who I've known for many years," he said. "I gave you a chance, even though I really didn't need an investigator. But you've failed to earn your keep, Jay. You haven't saved me a cent. Now you try to stab me in the back. You have the wrong attitude for this kind of work. If you had your way I'd be paying every schmuck who ever signed a policy. And that fiasco out at the base was the last straw. It's the worst possible publicity we could have for our firm. Look at you. You look like you're on drugs or something. Your eyes are bloodshot. You haven't shaved. Your hair's not combed. You're a mess."

I stared at him darkly for several moments, completely baffled. I felt that old familiar sinking feeling. Something was terribly wrong with this picture, but I couldn't figure out what it was.

"Fine," I said finally. "I'll be cleared out by the end of the week. I wish I could say it's been good working with you, but it hasn't."

"That's about the gratitude I expected from you. Don't worry about coming in this week. You can leave as soon as you get your things together, today."

"Don't worry," he added quickly, reading my reaction. "You'll get paid for this week and next."

I didn't say anything as I sulked out of his office, not bothering to close the door. What did I care about this stinking job, anyway? It was only a stopgap, only a temporary detour on the road to my real destiny. What that destiny was, I didn't have the foggiest idea, but there was an excellent chance it wasn't going to be very good.

A wave of depression and self-pity descended on me as I cleared out my measly belongings from what used to be my excuse for an office. As I did so, I realized that as crummy as this job was, it was the closest I had gotten to my dream of being a criminal investigator. It gave me a certain amount of freedom and respectability, and with this last case, a feeling of satisfaction. A stupid job for a half-rate insurance agency and I couldn't even keep that.

Luckily Suzie wasn't in yet. I don't think I could have faced her. I felt too embarrassed. A big-time, small-town, tin-plated loser, rapidly on my way to becoming one of those poor unfortunates begging on our city's streets.

I drove to my apartment, dejected and wondering what I was going to do now. I thought about starting my own private-eye business in the 'burgh'. That was so funny that as depressed as I was, I laughed at the sheer absurdity of it. The band was working steady. That would hopefully get me through until I could find something. Maybe I could get them to work more nights, or maybe I could get more karate students. If worse came to worst, I could always move back home again. But that thought was almost enough to make me play chicken with the trees.

As I drove in numbed silence I began to wonder about Dick Majerka's proper place in the scheme of things. I couldn't help feeling he was somehow involved. He was the one most responsible for the policy on Bobby Dolan in the first place, and his recent behavior was highly suspicious. Now that I thought about it, there was nothing standard about the drug clause Majerka had insisted on. Of course, he wouldn't want the insurance company to pay, but he seemed to be more than casually involved in the whole affair. I might just start my new investigating business by investigating Dickey's business. That thought made me feel better, so I clung to it, like a drowning man on a raft.

Later that day, I gave John Rothburg a call. He said he was making progress on the computer files, but needed a little more time. He asked me to come up to the observatory the next morning instead of that evening. I told him that was fine with me and asked him to add another name to his list - Dick Majerka. I also gave him the password to our agency's computer for good measure.

Interlude

The small cabin cruiser pulled into the sheltered alcove, just as it was getting dark. The shallow bay was protected from the open lake by a tree-clad finger of land. Jutting out from the shore, it ran parallel to it for about 200 yards, forming a long narrow pool. It offered a perfect anchorage for the night, protected from the rough waves of the lake, which was at its widest at this point.

The boat was a 25-foot Cris-Craft. It was quick and quiet, perfect for his needs. He stayed in it often, on those warm summer nights when his cabin in the woods was too hot to tolerate. He kept it moored at the city boat docks, behind the train station, in the old part of town.

He had staked-out the local yacht clubs and marinas, waiting and watching. Stalking his prey, he bided his time, until his single-minded patience paid off and he found his quarry.

Ever since he had received the phone call exactly one month ago, he had been freed from his shackles. The moment had come. The time of terror was at hand. That for which he had been destined was about to be realized. It was just as his spirit guide had said.

Before that call he had been living a nomad's life, driving his rig across the country, picking up work wherever he could. Then his grandfather phoned him. It was out of the blue. He had not heard from him in almost ten years. He didn't know how the old man had tracked him down, but he had, and he had spoken the long expected words.

There was only one other boat in the small bay. He had followed it earlier that evening from the yacht club. There were bigger boats on the lake than the 82-foot custom-built Motor Yacht, but not many.

The sleek, white pleasure craft bobbed peacefully in the half-light of the fading day. There was loud music coming from it. It rushed across the calm water of the bay to splash across the stalker's eardrums, irritating him.

As soon as it was dark, he put on his wet suit. Quietly slipping unobserved over the side of his small boat, he started swimming toward the yacht anchored a hundred feet away.

The large boat belonged to Claude Laplace. Claude and a few friends were enjoying the fruits of his illicit business in the local drug trade. Whoever said crime doesn't pay hadn't looked at Claude's bankbook lately. Claude was no dummy. Far from it, and was always three steps ahead of the local authorities.

Besides himself and his girlfriend, there were two other couples onboard, along with his brother, Gene. The three girls pranced around the aft deck in their tiny French bikinis. All of them were wiggling to the music blaring out of the four stereo speakers situated at each corner of the deck. The guys lounged on the gray velour settee watching. Claude was at the wet bar mixing drinks. Everybody was feeling good. The liquor was flowing and they had plenty of drugs. It was going to be a hot time in the old tub tonight.

As it got dark, they moved from the sun deck to the main salon. Then the party began. Claude's girl leaned over a low, glass-topped table covered with lines of white powder, and sucked some up her nose.

Gene, Claude's brother, had stayed on deck after the others went in, smoking a cigarette in the warm evening air. He was horny and frustrated from watching the half-naked women carousing on the sundeck. He missed his girlfriend, Andrea, who was not into drugs and disapproved of his brother, Claude.

He had been momentarily perturbed when the other boat showed up in the quiet bay to disturb their private party. But it stayed a discreet distance away. No one even showed their head. After awhile he was able to forget about it. His thoughts drifted back to the cute brunette who was sitting on his brother's lap in the salon. He cursed his luck for not being able to get a date. As it turned out, he would have more to curse about this night.

Slowly and silently, the killer swam toward the twinkling lights of the large pleasure craft. Loud music and laughter drifted over the calm, still water of the bay as he slid through it like a giant squid toward its unsuspecting prey. The multicolored party lights strung from the antenna tower to the bow, sparkled like a Christmas tree in the mirror reflection of the water. It was a perfect night to die, he thought with grim satisfaction. The distance between him and the yacht steadily decreased.

As he slowly approached the large craft, the cold water snapped his mind back to his childhood. He was no longer swimming in the lake, but struggling to stay afloat in the canal behind his grandfather's house.

He had been thrown off the dock into the canal. He sank deeper and deeper, the cold dark water engulfing him. His hands and feet thrashed about desperately as he tried to touch bottom, but there was only more dark deep water beneath him. His mind panicked. Suffocating in fear, he fought to hold his breath and stay above the liquid surface. Then, there was no more air, no more strength, no more will to struggle on. Just when he thought he was going to die, his grandfather pulled him up by the rope he had tied around his waist. Another moment longer and he would have drowned.

"You look like a drowned rat," his grandfather said, laughing as he held his little grandchild at the end of the rope. The boy splashed and choked, half-in, half-out of the canal. "You'd better learn to swim like I told ya', or I'll untie this rope and let ya' drown, you good for nothing little shit."

The boy learned to swim in that one harrowing afternoon.

Ever since he was a young child, his grandfather had been training him in the art of survival and hand-to-hand combat. The old man's way of teaching him to fight was to do the techniques for real, knocking him senseless across the room every time the boy made a mistake.

From his earliest years, he had been subjected to extreme deprivation and physical abuse. The worst of this early trauma he blocked out of his conscious memory, like the pit, a four-by-four hole in the ground, three feet deep. His grandfather put him in it for hours, covered with a plywood board and cinder-blocks.

Then there were the beatings, the almost nightly, almost routine beatings. Sometimes it would be with a birch rod, sometimes with a belt or strap. Often it would be with bare hands, but always there were beatings. He would still wake from a half-sleep, warding off the dream-blows from his grandfather's large hands. Worse, there was never any rhyme or reason to it, never any warning. One minute everything would be fine, almost jovial, and the next, wham upside the head with the back of a hand.

His grandfather hit him and deprived him continuously, to the point where his spirit was completely broken. Then, when he was totally malleable to the old man's will, he slowly started to rehabilitate him. He taught him more and more, only using the beating and deprivations to punish some infraction of the many rules. Through this regimen of alternating mistreatment and *instruction, kindness and abuse, the old man kept his grandson at a fever pitch. Until he became a confused, seething mass of suppressed anger, hatred, and fear - the perfect assassin.*

He became accustomed to extreme discomfort and pain. His grandfather showed him exercises to condition his body. He trained him to endure punishment without physical ill effect, to control his breathing in a yoga-like fashion, to slow or speed up his metabolism at will. He was also taught how to withdraw his consciousness from pain and discomfort through meditation. It allowed the boy to endure that which would make most grown men whimper and pass out.

Because of all this, he was impervious to physical suffering. He also developed a total disregard for the pain and suffering of others. He could withstand extremes of hot or cold, go days without food or water, sleep on the ground without a blanket, suffer beatings without a sound. In his young life he had to endure all this and more. The sad part was he could just as easily inflict it on others.

As quickly as his mind flashed back to another time, it snapped forward to the present again. While images of the past had flooded his brain, he hadn't missed a stroke. When he looked up, however, the yacht was much closer than he expected. He stopped swimming and let himself float silently toward his target. As he approached, he swam wide. Circling the craft completely, he checked and made sure he knew where all the occupants were. Then he quietly swam to the stern of the boat. The blare of the stereo would drown out any noise he might make.

He could see a lone figure sitting on the sundeck. The red ash of his cigarette flared brightly as he puffed on it at intervals. The killer swam toward the tiny red glow in the darkness.

At the rear of the yacht was a grated-metal diving platform just at the water level. Attached to it was a ladder that led up to the stern deck. A small dinghy was tied to the platform. The killer floated just out of range of the reflecting lights, virtually invisible in his black wetsuit.

He watched and listened for several minutes, waiting for whoever was on deck to join the others inside. As long as someone remained outside, it would be difficult to get aboard the yacht unnoticed.

When the figure made no move to go in, the killer improvised. Slowly taking his trusty bowie knife from its black rubber sheath, he swam beneath the water to the metal platform, and started scraping his knife against it. The sound of metal grating on metal, made it seem as if the boat was rubbing against something.

Gene heard the sound, and becoming curious, went to investigate. Leaning out over the ladder, he peered down into the blackness. Seeing nothing, he climbed down to get a better look. He stood on the last metal rung, and holding the ladder by one arm, leaned over to see what was making the strange scraping noise.

Suddenly, out of the deep, like a shark grabbing an unwary seal, the killer lunged at the unsuspecting Gene LaPlace. Grabbing him by the hair, he yanked him down and jabbed him in the chest with the knife.

Pulling him under the water, the killer stabbed his victim repeatedly in the neck with a rapid sawing motion. Soon all that was left holding the head on the body was a few shredded pieces of cartilage and flesh-covered bone.

It was all over so quick that Gene had no time to think about his girlfriend Andrea, or his poor old mother back home, or even see his pitifully short life pass before him. He never even had time to wonder what was happening to him. He was dead before he hit the water and started to sink to the muddy, weed-strewn bottom. His blood mixed with the cold water of the lake. His last confused thoughts drifted into the eternal void.

The killer waited, listening. Floating in the inky blackness, he controlled his breathing. His senses were wide alert. No one appeared to have heard the brief life and death struggle. Quickly climbing up the aluminum ladder, he boarded the large pleasure craft.

Creeping along the sundeck toward the plexiglass sliding doors to the salon, he moved soundlessly. He was invisible in the shadows, barefooted in his wetsuit. The bright lights in the salon made the dark night outside even darker, a pitch-black curtain that blocked out all sight of the outside world. He knew there were six other people onboard, three men and three women. The women would be no problem. The men, doped-up and distracted, would be easily overcome. He'd finish all three of them off before they knew what hit them. One way or another, no one was getting off that boat alive.

He kneeled by the door to the salon and peeked inside, holding his twelve-inch bowie knife erect at his side. The sound of the rock music and noisy conversation drowned out all other sounds. One of the girls was dancing seductively with her back to him. Two men and a woman sat along a velour sofa watching. There was another couple sitting at a bar next to the door.

Inch by inch, the killer slowly began to slide open the salon door. Then, with a flick of his wrist, he snapped it open the rest of the way. Springing into the cabin, his knife flashing in front of him like a sheet of lightning, he looked like a demon from the void.

The screams echoed over the dark quiet water of the inlet for some time. They mingled with the latest hits from Claude's CD collection. Just outside the protection of the cove, where the waves and wind lashed against the shore, all sound was swallowed by the night.

Chapter 10

Day 7

The next morning was gorgeous, a bright clear sky, in the mid seventies. The trees shined and the grass sparkled with dew as I drove up the highway west toward the mountains. The twenty-mile drive to the observatory takes about thirty minutes, and gets more scenic the further you get up the mountains. I drove slowly, continuously rising above sea level with the land, as it rose to the foothills of the Adirondacks.

As the road enters the mountains it passes through the village of Dannemora, which hosts the state penitentiary. The massive concrete walls of the prison cast a noonday shadow on the main street of town. The road then abruptly begins to climb steeply, as it winds its way into the hills beyond.

Driving past the penitentiary and up into the mountains, I soon passed a large, bowl-shaped lake. It was surrounded on three sides by dark-green, tree-clad hills. The peak where the telescope was located was right behind it.

After going half-way around the lake, I turned off the highway onto a dirt road, which led into the woods. A number of small signs were nailed to the trees, one of which told me I was on the right path. Rutted grassy tracks just big enough for a vehicle led off the road I was on to various hunting camps. I stayed on the main track and followed the signs leading to the observatory.

The dirt road ended at a low, rustic log building, overgrown with ivy and weeds. Located at the base of the trail up the mountain, it was the main office and living quarters for the observatory. From here you have to trek another forty minutes and 2000 feet up to get to the observatory at the summit.

No one was around. I parked my maroon, seen-its-best-days, four-door, secondhand Ford next to John's beat-up, army-surplus jeep, grabbed the bottle of wine I had brought, and headed up the trail.

It was wide and well-kept at first, rising gradually through the woods. However, after twenty-minutes, it rose sharply and narrowed. It looked like a dry riverbed of broken rock and slag. I picked my way carefully up the steep incline. I walked deliberately and slowly, as if I were a Sherpa miles in the Himalayas, rather than a hiker a few thousand feet in the Adirondacks.

The view as I climbed was breathtaking, an ever-widening panorama. The bowl-shaped lake lay a thousand feet below me. The whole valley fell away behind it all the way back to my starting point twenty miles to the east, in the hazy distance.

It was getting hot, so I stopped for a rest. There was only a short distance left to go, through a stand of young pine trees, along a solid rock path. It was the steepest part of the trail. I decided to sprint up the last few yards to the summit.

By the time I reached the top, a broad, flat, grassy area, close to 4000 feet above sea level, I was breathing hard. I walked across the field toward the main observatory, which was to my right. The view to my left was so spectacular, however, it drew me over to the ledge. From where I stood, on the top of the mountain, at the northern most point of the Adirondacks, I could look south and see the whole mountain range in the clear distance below me. Moose Mountain, Loon Lake Mountain, Whiteface, Porter, Giant Mountain, and Mount Marcy, marched away like an army of giants.

I stood gazing out at the view. The steep drop in front of me made me momentarily dizzy. I was just starting to breathe normal again after the exertion of the climb when I heard a rush of sound behind me. I turned sharply, fearing I was about to be pushed head first off the cliff, but it was only John's dog, Trojan. He bounded up to me with his tail wagging and his tongue hanging out. John was right behind him.

"Hey, man, how you doin'?" he said in his usual excited way. "Long time no see. Glad you finally made it."

"Yeah, I bet you don't get many visitors up here," I observed. "I forgot what a tough climb it is. You've got to be a mountain goat to get here."

John would sometimes stay at the observatory for days. There were usually two or three other scientists or students in attendance, depending on what was going on. Today he had the whole place to himself. He liked to brag that he could make it up the mountain in less than ten minutes.

"And I thought you were supposed to be in shape. You climb like an old lady," he said, true to form.

"Watch it. I know plenty of old ladies who could make you eat those words. So what have you been up to?" I asked.

"There's all sorts of stuff happening, man," John replied, hardly able to contain his enthusiasm. "The newest data from SN1987A shows the pattern of decay of cobalt-56 to iron-56 we predicted. That confirms that our general theoretical models are correct, of which I may add, I'm a leading exponent."

"I'm happy for you, John," I said as we walked across the summit toward the main observatory building.

"You jest, Jay, but this is how life began, an explosion like this that spewed forth carbon, oxygen, and nitrogen, the basic building blocks of life. You and I wouldn't be here if it wasn't for expanding clouds of stellar debris like that from 1987A."

"Thanks for the lecture, Doc. You got any refreshments for those few souls hardy enough to come all the way up here to see you? I could use a nice cold brewsky. Then you can tell me all about it. And while you're at it, why don't you chill this for later." I handed him the brown paper bag containing the bottle of wine.

We walked into the observatory, a low rectangular, whitewashed building bustling with antennas and housing the observatory's equipment. Next to it was the giant, dish-shaped antenna of the radio telescope. It pointed straight up at the bright daytime sky. It took awhile for my eyes to adjust to the dim light after the glaring sunlight outside.

Inside, along the near wall, were the display panels of the radio telescope itself. They glowed incandescently in the half-light. Next to these were two large-screen workstations. One was on and displayed multiple windows full of graphs and spreadsheets. A glass-enclosed room contained an imposing mainframe computer with several terminals hooked up to it.

The area we were in was littered with papers and manuals. Empty beer cans and used paper plates filled the trashcans. A long metal table stood in the center of the room. Taking up the whole length of the table was a single large sheet of graph paper. It was covered with squiggling lines and dots. Enigmatic symbols and equations in red, black, and green ink annotated the chart, summarizing the results from the radio telescope.

I thought I was going to have to spend hours hearing about his newest project before we got to my business, but I was wrong. He sat down in front of the active workstation and hit the return key. It instantly came alive and prompted him for his name and password. He entered these then started typing in a blur of keystrokes, clicking away rhythmically like a Buddy Rich drum solo.

"It was a real bitch getting into the base computers," he informed me. "It took me awhile, but I finally lucked out. The city computers were a piece of cake."

"What did you do?" I asked eager to hear his results.

"I figured I'd start with the university computers and see what I could get to from there. It was easy breaking into the city machines. I've done it plenty of times before for one reason or another. The Telephone Company and Registry of Motor Vehicles are always good for a laugh. I helped some of the programmers who worked on them, and they left backdoors for easy access. Real thoughtful of them, wouldn't you say? It's amazing what you can pick up on somebody via their phone records and license number."

He was on a roll and I wasn't about to stop him. I stood there saying nothing, and watched him jab speedily at the keyboard, waiting for him to continue.

"Once I broke into a system, I sent little ferret programs to search the various files and databases for any reference to the names on your list. If they found a match, they'd copy that data back to my machine. Then I cross-referenced all the data I found, checking for any correlations or multiple references."

"That's ingenious," I muttered, only half understanding what he said.

"Not really," he replied. "Pretty standard stuff, but here comes the good part. I really needed to access the base computers. They're not on any of the networks I can get to. These machines are much more difficult to break into. They usually have multiple levels of security, and I had to figure out the access codes and passwords myself. But I have my ways. I'll tell you about them sometime. Suffice it to say their big mistake is only using six digit codes. My random number generator can crank out hundreds of thousands of these a minute."

He typed furiously on the keyboard as he talked, bringing up lists and tables of names and numbers with quick staccato keystrokes.

"I got onto the ATHENA network at MIT in Boston via the local link from the college here. From that link, I connected to the ARPR network on the West Coast. From there I attached to an administrative machine at the SAC training center in Colorado. As luck would have it, from there I was able to get to a computer right back here in the personnel department of our very own little old base."

As he finished his narrative, he looked up at me in triumph.

"Of course, I had a very small time window to operate in before their security systems sniffed me out and closed things up."

"That's absolutely amazing," I said in awe. "I can't believe you were able to do all that in such a short time."

"Ah, it's nothing. Like I said, I break into computers all the time just for fun. Working on a murder case just heightens the intrigue. But wait, I haven't got to the best part yet. I was able to run some analysis on the data I pulled. I listed all the names and numbers that I obtained from the different sources that referenced any of the names on your list. Then I ordered these by the number of times a given name was referenced. I ranked the ones with the most occurrences the highest. Then I cross-checked them against each other, to see if I could find things in common between any of the names, places, dates, numbers, and so on, that turned up. Finally, I created a scatter graph of the data to check for any positive correlations. This is what I found."

As he talked, he struck the keyboard with a final loud punctuating snap, bringing up a graphic display on the center workstation screen. It showed the original names on my list, with lines going to sub-lists of other names and items. In the upper right-hand corner of the workstation display, a second small window appeared showing another graph. It was related to the first, and showed a cluster of dots moving lazily, but uniformly, in an upward direction. A red line intersected the scattered dots, and rose at a 45-degree angle up the plot.

"This is a name correlation graph, with its corresponding scatter diagram," he informed me, pointing at the display.

"Looks like someone went crazy playing connect the dots," I joked, having trouble following his explanation.

"Nothing really out of the ordinary here, just the usual stuff, I guess. The base personnel records I accessed showed that both Major Stienman and Captain Riley flew in the same B-52 bomber squadron. They'd been together quite a few years, which is a little unusual. The military usually like to move people around more, no one staying in one place for more than two years, but not in this case. The only other name I found in the base files that correlated highly with these was a Lieutenant-Colonel Ed Tunny, the commander of their bomber squadron, who has been on the base even longer than they have. When I cross-referenced this list, I get about a half dozen other names that appear to be members of the flight or ground crew, or other pilots on the base. It's all pretty much what you'd expect."

"What about any connection between either of them and the Dolan kid?" I asked.

"Nothing I could find, except Stienman's wife being killed while in bed with him," John responded.

"How about anything in Stienman's record that might indicate violent behavior, or any hanky-panky with teenage girls?"

"Nothing, nada. The guy was as clean as a whistle, an upstanding family man and a Gulf War hero."

He brought up another screen, showing the same type of charts, but this time with phone numbers instead of names.

"I did the same analysis using telephone numbers and dates, but didn't find anything new. As a matter of fact," he said, turning around and looking at me. "I wasn't having much luck until you called last night and gave me the other name."

"Who? You mean Dick Majerka?" I asked, in disbelief. "You're kidding. How does he figure in all this?"

"He seems to be the missing link. I added his name to my analysis, went back over my sources and a couple of interesting things popped up."

He waited a little, looking up at me with that canary-eating grin of his for effect.

"Well?" I yelled, rising to the bait.

"First of all, I found a telephone number correlation between Bobby Dolan, Dick Majerka, and another number from the area. The same local number appears to correlate highly with Stienman and Riley. The correlation is a little too high statistically to be coincidental. Very interesting, eh? I checked the local number out. It's from Dannemora. It belongs to a counselor at the prison there, a guy named Barry Davids. Also seems Majerka has had recent contact with the head honcho on the base, Colonel Dean himself."

John smiled at me conspiratorially under his massive head of hair.

"Didn't you say you were working on a case involving an insurance policy for Bobby Dolan?" he asked, changing the subject.

"Yeah, why?"

"Well, I couldn't find any record of a policy under the name of Dolan in your agency's computer files. Kind of funny, don't you think?"

"Hmm, that is strange. Seems Majerka is up to his beady eyeballs in this."

"Not only that," John went on. "He's taking a vacation. He has a one-way ticket to St. Petersburg, Florida. Leaves tomorrow."

"I'll have to talk to Susie, his secretary. Maybe she knows something. Did you get any info on this Davids character?"

"Sure did. I ran a cross-check on his name, back through all the data sources I established. Didn't find much. Like I said, he's a counselor at the prison. His telephone records indicate a high number of calls throughout the northern part of the state, Massena, Malone, Buffalo, Glens Falls, the 'burgh', even Burlington and Montreal. This guy's quite the phone jockey. Here, I'll get you a printout of all this stuff."

He hit another key in front of him, magically causing a nearby printer to spring clattering to life.

John's feat of high-tech analysis totally amazed me. The way he accessed all those computers was pure magic. He made the miraculous sound merely mundane.

"Maybe I'll give this guy Barry Davids a visit," I said in my best John Wayne drawl.

"Well, you better not get him mad. He's an ex-special forces guy," John warned. "Here's all the information for you." He handed me the thick stack of printouts and Davids' picture.

"Thanks, partner. That's great," I said. "Hey, what about that brewsky you were going to get me?"

He jumped up from the chair and went to the cooler sitting on the floor under the table.

"Now we got the fun out of the way," he said, coming back with two cold-ones. "Why don't we get down to some serious business? How about a game or two?"

"Or three," I agreed, as I followed him over to his desk, where he had his chessboard set up ready for the slaughter.

As smart as John is, I still manage to hold my own against him playing chess. I won the first two out of three games. It was probably because he had his mind on so many other things. He only used a small portion of it on the game. I, on the other hand, concentrated my whole being into each move. What I lacked in brainpower I made up for in willpower. I wanted to beat him in the worst way. John probably didn't help his game by lighting up a fat joint, but I drank my share of beer and wine to compensate. I knew if I tried some of his smoke, I might never make it down the mountain, ever. So I refused his frequent offers to join him. The contact high was more than enough.

As we played, John pointed to the newspaper sitting by the table and told me about the murders out on Lake Champlain. When he mentioned one of the victims' names, a Claude Laplace, on a hunch, I asked him if he could add that name to the analysis.

"Check the Telephone Company files," I suggested.

He was pretty inebriated and high by this time, but went to the computer and did a search, plugging Laplace's name into the system and hitting the button. The name came up highly correlated with Barry Davids, the counselor at the prison. I decided to pay him a visit sooner than later.

It was late in the afternoon by the time I left the observatory. John walked down the mountain with me. Or rather he sprinted ahead, taking boulders two at a time. I followed, carefully trekking down the mountainside like a fully-laden Sherpa. I had things on my mind.

Chapter 11

Day 7 (p.m.)

On the way back to the 'burgh', I stopped at Ting's, a little diner in the village of Dannemora. As I ate my cheeseburger, I examined the dossier on Barry Davids that John prepared for me, which included his picture.

I looked across the street at the massive walls of the prison. It was almost 5:00 p.m., quitting time for the day shift. I had an idea.

Finishing my lunch in the car, I staked out the employee entrance of the prison. The shift was changing. Groups of men were passing through the gates. Perhaps I could spot Davids. He looked distinctive enough, a large man with a well-kept beard.

I got lucky after about twenty-minutes, when I spotted him leaving with several other workers. Waiting until he had driven out of the parking lot, I followed at a discreet distance. He drove through town, down a country road, and across the railroad tracks. After a couple of miles, he turned into a long driveway.

Davids' house was a well-built, two-story log cabin. Wide fields on both sides of the drive separated it from any neighbor. There were woods and thickets behind the house and across the street.

He got out of the truck, a new red pickup. It looked like a paramilitary vehicle, with flood lamps, official insignias, and flashing red lights on the cab. I immediately confronted him.

Now that I saw him up close, I understood John's warning. He resembled a first string tackle for the New York Giants. Broad shouldered, with biceps straining to escape the confines of his Van Heusen shirt, he had a bull-neck and a large forehead. Sporting short-cropped, black hair, he had a short, trimmed beard as well. He was a foot taller than me and outweighed me by at least a hundred pounds. As I looked him over, I was unable to find anything I would consider a weak spot. Not a guy I wanted to tangle with, but I didn't expect trouble.

He looked up as I approached with a steely-eyed glare. He probably had to be a pretty bad dude to counsel hard-assed prisoners. He made no pretense at being friendly. Just the opposite and he didn't even know who I was.

"What do you want?" he asked suspiciously.

"Hello, Mister Davids, my name is Jay Lawless. I work for an insurance company in the city. I wanted to talk to you about a case I'm working on. It involves the recent murders there."

"I don't know anything about that. I don't know what the hell I can tell you."

"I know, Mr. Davids, but my investigation indicates that you may have known Major Stienman and the missing father of the murdered girl, Captain Riley."

"So what? I know lots of people. What does that have to do with anything? Who did you say you represent? You're not a cop. Do you have any identification? How do I know you're who you say you are?"

I took out my wallet and handed him a card with my name and business phone number on it, along with the agency's address. I had paid for 150 cards out of my own pocket. Now I was finally getting a chance to use them. He didn't have to know I was no longer working there.

"I don't want to take up any more of your time than I have to," I continued rapidly, before he had time to speak. "As I said, my investigation into the death of Bobby Dolan and Mrs. Stienman involves a great deal of money. We need all the help we can get to make sure our client gets a just compensation for his loss. There were apparently several phone calls between you and Major Stienman shortly before their murder. I was hoping you could explain them and perhaps shed light on the situation. Your cooperation now will help us resolve the issue and save more hassles for you in the future in a court of law."

He stood glaring at me with evil intent, but said nothing.

"What was your relation with Stienman and Riley?" I asked, pushing on.

He thought a moment before answering.

"I used to take Stienman up to the mountains on hunting trips, him and some of his buddies. They heard I was a good hunting guide and always knew where to find the best game. He wanted to set up some hunting trips, that's all."

"How long have you known him?" I continued.

"Not long, a couple years maybe. We went on a hunting trip in the Adirondacks together last winter. That's when I met Captain Riley. We brought back a nice black bear."

"Do you know where I might find Captain Riley? I need to talk to him too."

"No," he answered as he began to move away toward his house.

"Do you know any of these people?" I asked, rattling off several names, including Colonel Tunny and Dick Majerka. He said he didn't, but laughed at the mention of Majerka's name.

"I have nothing more to say to you," he told me turning. "You'll have to leave. Get in your car there and get off my property."

He moved toward me menacingly. I stood my ground, though I was impressed with his size. He was not a man I wanted to tussle with, but I looked at him hard. Two could play this game. He stopped before he was within striking range.

"You must meet a lot of people in the prison, cons I mean," I said. "Do you keep in touch with them after they get out?"

"Get out of here!" he barked, taking a step closer.

I stepped back, but kept my hands down by my side and open, as if I was about to use them. I didn't want to appear on the defensive by assuming a stance.

"How about a con named Claude Laplace?" I asked, smiling.

He glared at me. A look of recognition flashed across his eyes. Then he turned and walked rapidly back to his truck.

I was afraid he might have a gun hanging on a rack in the back of the cab, so I ran toward him. I caught him just as he was opening the door and starting to reach inside.

"Hey, I just want to talk to you," I said loudly, holding the door. "I don't want any trouble."

He pulled open the door, sweeping me aside, and wheeled around on me with a crowbar in his hand.

"Well, you've got it," he snarled. "I told you to get out of here. You're trespassing on private property. Now I'm going to bust you up, motherfucker!"

He raised the crowbar to strike.

Before he could bring it down, while his arm was still outstretched, I stepped into him with a hard thrusting kick aimed at his solar plexus. I delivered the blow on target and with power, but it had minimal effect. It was just enough, however, to stop the crowbar in midair and knock him back a few steps. It was all I needed to gain the initiative.

Before he could recover, I followed-up with a double-front snapping kick to his groin and throat. The first kick brought his hands down. The second kick, delivered a split-second after without touching the ground, hit him under the chin full force. I was aiming at his throat. The kick snapped his half-opened mouth shut with a loud crack.

I'm not sure why I used such a risky move, leaving the ground with a jumping kick, and didn't just hit him in the balls like I tell my students to. I was scared and pumped with adrenaline. Before I knew it, I was in the air snapping a kick at his throat. The move took him by surprise. I had propelled myself forward, landing the kick with considerable power. It knocked him back against the truck, and made his mouth bleed.

I stepped quickly back out of the way as he swung the crowbar at my head. It looked like he was moving in slow motion. As his arm reached the bottom of its downward arc, I stepped in and grabbed it at the wrist and elbow in a lock, but his arms were too strong for me. Sweeping me back, he broke my hold and swung the crowbar at my head, missing it by inches. This time I did kick him in the groin, hard. As he bent over in pain, I snapped a second kick to his face. His downward motion hitting my rising foot sent him rocking back into the side panel of the truck.

Without giving him time to recover, I stepped in with a blade-kick to the side of his knee. Twisting around in agony, he went down on it. As he dropped, I slipped behind him and pulled his head back with my fingers dug into the tops of his eyeballs. Locking his throat with the ridge of my hand, I used my thumb to choke his windpipe.

I was standing braced, in a deep, wide stance. Davids was arched backward, with his full weight resting on my thigh as I held him in the throat lock. He struggled, but despite his size and strength, he had no place to go, and was rapidly running out of air.

In spite of his ominous appearance, Davids was not a trained man, and slow with his reactions. He was obviously in shape. I was surprised he had been that easy to subdue. I had never had to defend myself on the street. I guess all those hours in the dojo actually paid off. Still, I didn't underestimate him and wasn't about to give him a chance to recover.

I tightened the lock on his throat, using my cocked thumb to dig into his windpipe and completely cut off his air. The more he tried to squirm out, the tighter I made the lock. Soon he was completely still, probably seeing his life pass before him.

I loosened the choke hold and spoke softly in his ear.

"Now see what you've gone and made me do. All I wanted was talk to you. Are you satisfied, now?"

He choked and gagged, but for some reason couldn't seem to get the words out.

"What do you know about Bobby Dolan's murder and the missing Captain Riley? Why all the phone calls to Claude Laplace, the murdered drug dealer?"

"Nothing, I don't know what you're talking about," he managed to sputter out. "I don't have anything to do with that, if that's what this is about."

"Well, that's too bad, because I don't really give a crap any more. I just want to put some hurt on someone. It might just as well be you. Say goodnight, ass-hole."

I reapplied pressure on the throat, keeping it up for a count of twelve. I figured he would go under in fifteen or twenty seconds and probably be dead by sixty. Then again, one can never be too sure about that kind of thing. I had to be careful if I didn't want to kill him.

I released the lock with a smashing hammer strike to his face, busting his nose and driving him to the ground. Then I stepped over him and dropped my knee onto his chest. Another few pounds of pressure would have crushed his sternum. I knew I was taking a chance with this guy, but he hadn't left me much choice. I was pretty sure of my technique. Still, it was a chance. I was afraid of him and that made me almost dangerous. Besides, I could tell from his reactions that he knew something of what was going on. I aimed to find out, one way or another.

"If I could find the guy who's doing this, I might not have to take it out on you," I said in his bloodied, half-conscious face. "So what will it be?"

I dropped my knee on his chest again, this time with just a fraction more force. I followed that with a couple sharp blows to the side of his head, bouncing it back and forth like a punching bag. Kenpo may not always look pretty, but it can be very effective, at least the kind I was taught. He put up his hands.

"Stop!" he pleaded. "Leave me alone. You're assaulting a corrections officer." He tried to show me his badge.

"I'm not one of your prisoners," I said. "You had no call to come at me like that. I only wanted to ask you a few questions. I didn't want any trouble. You're the one who needs some correcting. So talk to me, Mister Davids. What's going on?"

"I don't know what you're talking about. I work with the prison to help rehabilitate the inmates."

"You're not doing a very good job," I told him. "Tell me something I don't know. Why all the phone calls to an ex-con dope dealer?"

"You have no idea what you're dealing with," Davids finally exclaimed.

"What do you mean?" I replied, pulling him to his feet. He leaned back against the truck, wobbly. "Enlighten me."

"Look, there's nothing you can do. It's too big. It goes all the way to the top. If you're smart, you can make this pay off for you."

"I appreciate your feeble attempt to buy me off, but I'm not quite that stupid, despite popular opinion. You, on the other hand, could do much to improve your situation by telling the police what you know."

"You're a dead man."

His words sent a chill up my spine. The feeling just made me madder.

"You're a dead man if you don't start talking!" I shouted. "What's going on?"

"Your boss, Dick Majerka, knows more than I do. Why don't you talk to him?"

"What?" I answered, not sure I heard him right. "What are you talking about?"

Suddenly, a large man dressed all in white, like an alpine ranger, appeared at the edge of the woods behind the house. Davids turned and followed my gaze.

"Now see what you've done!" he screamed.

Without warning, he pushed forward, shoving me with his forearms. I did a quick step back, but couldn't keep my balance and fell. Sitting on my heel, I rolled onto my back with my head tucked, letting my momentum rock me back up. But I failed in my attempt to spring to my feet. As I fell back, I bent my legs in a defensive position, ready to kick out in anticipation of an attack that never came. Instead, he quickly jumped into his truck and started the engine.

Getting to my feet, I reached the side of the cab as he was accelerating down the driveway in reverse. I ran after him as he backed into the road and was almost run over when he changed gears and sped away. By the time I got to my car and gave chase, he was already a quarter of a mile down the highway. He must have still been dazed because he swerved back and forth like a drunk driver.

He raced up the mountain with me in hot pursuit. I didn't want him to get away, though I didn't know exactly what I'd do if I caught him. He hadn't told me much, but what he did tell me was very troubling. I was definitely onto something, but what?

He knew the roads well and maintained his lead. As we sped along the side of the bulging mountain, I would lose sight of him for minutes at a time. Then I'd spot him again a little further ahead. We were going northwest, on a highway that would eventually take us to the Canadian boarder, over thirty miles away.

Soon we reached the highest point in the road, where it winds around a sharp corner and heads back down the other side. He hit the hairpin turn going too fast. He didn't see the car in front of him slow down as the driver gazed out at the spectacular view. As he swerved instinctively to avoid rear-ending them, he struck their right bumper and careened off onto the shoulder of the road. Going through the wooden guard rail, he went over the cliff, off into blue space. For an instant the car hung there, suspended in midair, part of the breathtaking view. Then it plunged down the mountainside, turning and crashing against the rocks and treetops, down three hundred feet. It crashed just out of sight with a fiery roar.

I stopped and mingled with the rest of the horrified onlookers, but left before the police arrived. There were enough eyewitnesses and nothing more I could do. No one seemed to notice my departure. After my run in with Chief McNeil, I had no desire to get involved with the local authorities if I could help it.

I drove home not a little shaken, well within the speed limit for the first time in days. Remembering what Davids had said, I began to feel threatened. I wondered if I should try to arm myself. Purchasing a firearm would be easy. Getting a license to carry one would be another matter, given my relationship with the Chief.

Not having a gun could be a distinct disadvantage in the situation I was rapidly finding myself enmeshed in. It would be especially so here in the middle of gun-toting rural America. Up here, everyone and his sister had at least two guns stashed in their desk or closets. I could always borrow one of my dad's hunting rifles if I had to. But that would lead the police right to his doorstep in the event it was ever necessary to use it. I definitely had an extreme case of paranoia.

What did it all mean? What did Davids imply when he said it went all the way to the top? The top of what? And who was the man in white?

Suddenly, everything that had happened in the past week, all the senseless killing, started to make sense. The murdered people on the yacht were involved with drugs. Was Bobby Dolan's death somehow related to those murders? If so, then Majerka had been right after all. It was a drug motivated crime. It figured that slime ball would be involved. No wonder he was leaving town

Was it some sort of power struggle, a drug war maybe? Whatever it was, it was spreading terror over the community. No one felt safe. Whoever was involved with the murders was ruthless. I couldn't believe what I had stumbled into. It had to be my luck to end up in this godforsaken town just when this insanity was taking place.

The stifling heat of the day and lack of sleep combined to make me drowsy. I had to fight to keep my eyes open at the wheel. It was a little after ten when I got home. Fortunately, I crashed on the sofa and not the highway.

Chapter 12

Day 8

I woke up on the couch a couple hours later and couldn't get back to sleep. My mind kept racing through the events of the past few days. When I finally did get to sleep, I'd jerk awake with a start, dreaming I'm sitting next to Barry Davids in his red pickup truck, plummeting into the rocky gorge below. I felt little refreshed from the night's slumber.

The morning news was screaming sex-crazed, mass-murdering maniac on the loose. With the recent killings taking place on the lake and off city limits, the state police had entered the case. However, authorities remained baffled and were being very tight-lipped. The news report indicated that the seven young people on the yacht had been killed by a large knife. I wondered if it was the same weapon used in the murders of Bobby Dolan, Alice Stienman, and the Riley girl. That case was being reopened. Too bad my only lead had taken a nose dive off a cliff.

I sat trying to put the whole thing together. Some fiend was running loose, wreaking havoc on the streets and lanes of our city. The slime and filth hiding just beneath the surface of this placid town had finally erupted like an overripe boil. Its poison was spilling out for the whole world to see, and I was right in the center of it.

I decided to visit Suzie at the agency to find out if Majerka had actually left town.

"Hi, Suzie," I said, walking into the office. "Surprise! I bet you thought you weren't going to see me today."

"Oh, Jay, I'm so sorry. I couldn't believe it when I heard that Mr. Majerka fired you. I tried to call you yesterday, but you were out all day."

"It's true. He didn't like the way I crossed my Ts. Said I did a lousy job on the Dolan report, and he really didn't need me anymore. And that's that."

"Well, I don't think it's fair. You worked so hard on that report. And what about Mrs. Spindle? You were the only one helping that poor old lady. It just isn't right!" she exclaimed.

"All's fair in love and the insurance business, but I appreciate you saying that. It's nice to see you. You've already cheered me up."

I was starting to feel depressed again. The sinking sensation in the pit of my stomach returned like a slow leak, with the reminder of my recent humiliating dismissal and bleak future.

"What would really cheer me up would be if you went to dinner with me some evening," I heard myself saying to my great surprise.

"I don't know, maybe. Give me a call sometime," she said, with no commitment, which didn't surprise me much. "I just want you to know I think it was awful the way Mr. Majerka fired you like that, for no good reason."

"What are you going to do, eh?" I replied lamely.

"Did you hear about the murders out on the lake?" she asked in a breathless voice, changing the topic on a dime. "Isn't it awful? Those poor people. What's going on, Jay?"

"I don't know, but I'm going to find out, job or no job," I said defiantly.

"My friend down at the registry says one of the cops told her that the bodies were all naked and mutilated. They were strung-up on the ship's riggings like flags. How horrible!" she said with an audible shudder. "One guy almost had his head sawed off! Can you imagine?"

"Sounds like a real sick-o," I answered.

I started to speculate out loud.

"I wonder how one person could have done all that, I mean overcome four armed men. But the cops seem to believe it was a lone assailant. Maybe he was trained."

"Oh, I almost forgot to tell you. Mr. Majerka got a phone call yesterday from some Colonel on the base. I think he said his name was Tunny. I could hear Mr. Majerka yelling on the phone. He sounded pretty upset. Then he came out of his office looking all nervous like, and told me he was leaving town for a few days. I was to tell anyone looking for him he would be back the end of next week sometime. Then he rushed out of the office. He didn't even take his briefcase and didn't come in today. What do you make of that, Jay? Real strange, heh?"

"Yeah, I'll say." There was an awkward silence as we both retreated to our private thoughts. "It's good to see you," I said again. "Let me know if I can do anything to help you out here while Dick's gone. I'll get in touch if I find out anything more about what he's up to. See you later. Take care."

"Are you going to be OK?" she asked. "Do you have unemployment?"

"That's a laugh," I answered with a snicker. "I'd be surprised if Majerka even pays taxes. I'll get by. I've still got the gig three nights a week and my karate students. Maybe I'll start advertising. With what's going on around town, more people might want to sign up for self-defense classes."

"Maybe you should check out the Y. They might let you give classes there too. I might even try it."

"Yeah, thanks, that's a good idea, but I don't think you need self-defense. You're already tough enough, Spritzer."

She laughed and threw a not half-bad front kick at me.

I kept up a good front, but the conversation with Suzie had totally depressed me. Not only was I reminded I no longer had a job, and that my meager income was about to become even more miserable. I had been soundly rejected in my feeble attempt to get a date. One humiliation heaped on another. Not only could I not keep a stupid-ass job, I couldn't get a measly date. I was nothing if not a failure. Even my half-hearted relationship with Mary had ended in ruins. I didn't know what I was going to do, but I had to think of something or I'd be out on the street. Despite what I told Suzie, without the agency job I would not be able to pay the rent.

I decided give Mary a call. Maybe we could still work things out. At a minimum I was hoping she would at least have sex with me. Her answering machine clicked in on the fourth ring. I felt certain she was there, listening, screening calls. I left a brief message in my most sincere voice asking her to call me.

I drove around town most of the afternoon, wondering who I could borrow money from. My dad had lent me a few hundred bucks when I first got back to town, which I had paid back. Perhaps I could hit him up for a few hundred more, just enough to get by for awhile. I'd have to swallow my pride, but I was good at that. I was without shame when it came to survival. I pulled up to the old split-level homestead and was gratified to see his pickup in the driveway. He was home.

I found him sitting in his recliner reading the paper when I walked in.

"Hey, Dad. Why aren't you on the golf course today? It's beautiful outside."

"Had to take care of some business. How are you doing? How's work?"

"That's what I wanted to talk to you about. I need to borrow a few dollars to get through the month. Majerka laid me off yesterday."

"What? What for? What'd you do?"

"I didn't do anything. He's been trying to get rid of me ever since he hired me. All he talks about is how he doesn't need an investigator. So much for that favor you did for him. First excuse he gets, he cans me."

"He must have had a reason. Did he give you some kind of severance? You have unemployment insurance, don't you?"

"Oh, he had a reason, all right. He's involved in some way with the murders. He promised me two-weeks pay when he fired me, but he's skipped town. I doubt we'll ever see him again. He must have had some kind of scam going with that insurance policy."

"What? What are you talking about? What scam? What do you mean, involved in the murders? How do you know this? It sounds pretty farfetched to me."

"It's farfetched, all right. You don't know the half of it. Anyway, I need a few bucks to get by."

"If you know something about the murders, you should tell the police."

"Don't worry, I will. Now, can you help me out?"

"OK, I may be able to help you," he informed me, much to my surprise. "I got a call from your younger brother, Billy, in Florida. He said he was in trouble and asked me to go down and help him. It seems he ran afoul of the law."

"So what else is new?"

"I was wondering if you could go down and get him, now that you're not working. I'll pay your way and expenses and give you a little something for your time."

"What about the police?" I said, coming up with my ace-in-the-hole excuse. "They told me not to leave town after that incident at the base."

"I can take care of that," he informed me. "You'll only be gone a couple days."

"I'll have to think about it," I said. The last thing I wanted to do was fly down to Florida and bail my brother Billy out of jail. Then I remember what John Rothburg had told me. Majerka had a one-way ticket to St. Petersburg, Florida.

"Do you want the money or don't you?" he asked finally. "You got nothing better to do. I'll pay you $250 for three days. You leave tomorrow."

"Make it $500 and you've got a deal," I replied. "But I can't go until Sunday. The band's playing at the Pontiac this week. I just can't leave them like that."

"You always were a selfish kid."

"Do you want me to go down and get Billy or not?"

Reluctantly, he agreed. Giving me $250 in advance, he told me he'd have the tickets the next day for a flight out on Sunday.

I was elated after leaving my father's place. Not only was I being paid half a grand for three days work, I'd have an opportunity to look for Majerka while I was there. I might even hit the beach.

I went to a park by the lake to do some form. The sun was just setting. I had my swords in the back seat of my car. While I studied with Len in Boston, I learned a number of nice sword kata. Len and I even developed some two-man sword forms for demonstrations. We'd get those blades whipping by each other's heads pretty fast. It was not only impressive. It was as close to real combat with a sword as you could get.

The long blade of my samurai flashed in the last rays of the sun. I visualized my foes before me as I slashed it this way and that, high and low, swirling and thrusting, in constant motion like a deadly dance.

Later that evening at the gig, all the stress and horror of the past few days dogged me like a persistent sore. The images of the past week kept recurring in my mind - Stienman hanging by his silk pajama tops, the lurid scene described by Jerry of Bobby Dolan and Alice Stienman's murder, the newspaper accounts of the killings on the lake. Then there was my conversation with Barry Davids and his words, "You're a dead man." Not to mention his dramatic death, and the guy in white. Whatever was going on, I was in over my head.

It was Friday night. The crowd moderate. The band played well that evening, in spite of me. People were dancing and digging the music.

After the gig, we sat around talking about some new songs we wanted to play. The place was deserted except for the band, Mickey, the club owner, and Dorothy, one of the waitresses he was currently sleeping with. Everyone was sorry to hear that I had been fired. George said he'd see if he could line up a few more gigs for us, but said we'd have to play more out-of-town jobs.

Paul, our bass player, Denise's husband, was loaning me his small portable keyboard for a few days. It was one of those wonders of modern technology that allowed a single person to sound like an entire orchestra with just the touch of a finger. I was looking forward to playing with it.

I gave Paul the keys to my car, and he went out to the parking lot to transfer it from his trunk.

We had been talking awhile when Denise wondered what was keeping Paul.

"He should be back by now," she observed.

"Ah, he's probably getting high," replied George.

"Not without me, he wouldn't," she said indignantly.

"I'll see what's keeping him," I volunteered, getting up and heading for the door.

It was a clear, balmy summer evening. The stars were out in full force. Crickets made a racket in the deep grass.

The parking lot was empty except for the few cars belonging to the band and club employees. I couldn't see Paul anywhere. Going over to my car, I noticed the trunk was open. Walking around to the rear of the vehicle, I heard a low moan. There on the ground was Paul. He was bleeding profusely from a bad head wound.

I yelled some obscenity. "What happened?"

It was a rhetorical question. I could see he wasn't going to be able to answer. He lay there moaning, semiconscious.

I kneeled down by his side. Stripping off my ruffled shirt, I tried to stem the tide of blood seeping from his skull.

"Don't move," I ordered, wrapping the shirt around his head like a turban. "You'll be OK. Just lie still. I'll get help."

I attempted to act calmly, but breathing became difficult. My hands were shaking. I ran back into the club bare-chested and covered with blood. Screaming for Mickey to call an ambulance, I ordered Dorothy to get clean towels and a blanket. It was the only thing I could think of.

At first they thought it was a sick prank. As soon as Denise realized I wasn't joking, however, she screamed and ran outside. Her rapid, staccato shrieks pierced the night when she found Paul. I ran back out, and tried to make sure she wouldn't do anything rash to make things worse. George and Dorothy were right behind me.

Denise was hysterical. Holding her head, she moaned, "Oh, God, Paul! Oh my God, the blood!"

Chapter 13

Day 9

Fortunately we were able to stop the bleeding, more or less. The ambulance arrived shortly after and took Paul to the city hospital. Thank God, he was going to be all right. He had a concussion, a few broken ribs, various facial contusions, and had lost a considerable amount of blood. It could have been much worse. The hospital would have to keep him for a few days. The doctor said he wouldn't be able to work again for at least two weeks. Now on top of everything else, we had lost our bass player and probably our gig.

Denise was in bad shape. I offered to drive her home. By the time I got her to her house, out on the north shore, the sun was just peeking over the mountains across the lake. The good news was I didn't have to be at work.

She was too upset to sleep. We sat in the kitchen and talked. She made some coffee and then started to cry. I went over and put my arm around her shoulder, and told her everything would be all right. She started to shake violently with sobs, so I put both arms around her and hugged her tight. The feeling of her ample breasts pushing against me, and the smell of her hair and skin, mingled with tears, were affecting my lower impulses. She seemed so vulnerable and helpless in my arms. It had been so long since they held a girl so soft and alluring.

I quickly let go of her. Getting some sleeping tablets from the medicine cabinet, I put her to bed like a good knight in shining armor. Resisting the urge to get in bed with her, I left the house, locking the door behind me.

I got back to my pad about seven a.m. I tried to sleep, but was too worked up. Lying in bed, despairing of slumber, I thought about what we had managed to find out from Paul before the police arrived. Two guys in leather jackets had come up behind him as he was moving the keyboard. One of them hit him with a lead pipe. The other one had brass knuckles. He remembered one of them saying, "Next time you go snooping around, it'll be for keeps." Then he passed out.

Had they mistaken Paul for me? Had I finally gotten to somebody? Did they want me off the case? The more I thought about it, the more my blood began to boil. Who had set this up? Did someone know about my meeting with Davids? Was it the man in white? There was too much going on, too fast. My head was spinning like I was the one who'd been mugged. Too bad it hadn't been me. Maybe I'd have stuck a pipe up somebody's anus! Well, that could still be arranged.

Being unable to sleep, and pumped up from my musings, I decided to take a walk on the beach. I sat and watched the sun come up over the mountains in Vermont, reflecting on my past, wondering about my future.

Dragging myself back to my room by the beach, I managed to nap a few hours before I was woken up by a loud knock on the door. I could tell by the sound that it was the police. I've heard that knock before. I opened it to see Jerry standing there in uniform with his sunglasses on.

I needed to confide in somebody. I had been considering calling him, but hadn't expected him to show up on my doorstep. I had to be careful not to implicate myself in Davids' death. Chief McNeil would like nothing better than to see my head skewered on a pike in front of City Hall. I didn't want to give him an excuse. Not only did I have no real idea of what was going on, whatever collaboration I had was splattered on the rocks at the foot of Lookout Gorge.

"I need to talk to you about last night at the Pontiac," he began. "What happened? What's going on?"

"I told your buddies everything last night. Why are you bothering me now? Read their report."

"I know you, Jay. What are you not telling us?" he said, putting his hand on his revolver. "If you have any information concerning the murders, you'd better come down to the station."

"Two goons attacked Paul, our bass player." I told him. "I'm not keeping anything from you. They beat him up pretty bad. It was probably just a random act by a couple of teenage hoods. Maybe they were after the keyboard."

"The Chief thinks it might have been drug related. He thinks you guys are dealing dope or something."

"He's a dope," I replied.

"Do you think they were after you and got your friend by mistake?"

"What makes you say that?" I asked, impressed at his astuteness. I decided to confide in him and tell him everything.

"I know you're not dealing drugs," he said. "I think it's tied to what's going on and your investigation."

"You're right, Jer'. They *were* after me. They told Paul they'd kill him if he kept snooping around. He's not the one snooping, I am. The day before last on a tip, I paid a visit to a guy called Barry Davids. He was a counselor at the prison in Dannemora. He knew Laplace, the drug dealer killed out on the lake. He knew Stienman and Riley too. I went to see if he knew anything about Bobby Dolan's murder. I just asked him a few simple questions. He got belligerent and I had to lean on him a little. He told me that whatever was going on went all the way to the top. He hinted that Majerka was involved, but wouldn't say much more. He tried to buy me off, and told me I was a dead man. I didn't take too kindly to that. A short time after I talked to him, Davids was killed in a car accident."

"Jee-zus, Jay! What are you involved in? You didn't kill that guy did you?"

"No way! While I was talking to him, somebody dressed all in white, in winter camouflage gear, appeared in the field next to his house. When Davids saw him, he spooked and ran."

"Who was he?" asked Jerry.

"I don't know, but he sure put a scare into Davids, and he was a scary looking dude. When I turned and looked back at the field, the guy in white was gone. Weird, eh?"

"I'll say. You've got to come down to the station and make a statement."

"You know I can't do that. The chief hates me. He told me in no uncertain terms to stay out of his sight. Anyway, I haven't got anything, except for what Davids hinted at, and he's gone. I just want your word you'll keep what I told you under your hat until I can get some more information. Maybe you can help me check out some leads. You could end up a hero, maybe even get a promotion. It'd be nice to have someone competent in charge for a change."

Although I was attempting to flatter him, I meant every word of it.

"Yeah, either that or get thrown in jail myself, and knowing you, Lawless, it's more likely to be the latter. But I know you wouldn't lie to me about a thing like this. What the heck, I'm game. All hell's broken out down at the station. Every spare man has been put on the case, including me. We still don't have any leads, except that someone likes to use a big knife in a very nasty way."

He also admitted that McNeil had it out for me and had warned everyone on the force to stay away from me unless it was to arrest or shoot me. Talk about your warm, cozy feelings. I was starting to feel like a hit-the-clown target at a carnival.

"You want a brew?" I asked, going to the fridge and pulling out a beer.

"I'm on duty," he replied.

"I'm not," I said, snapping off the lid.

"I think the murders are connected," I told him. "That includes Stienman's apparent suicide and the Riley girl's death. It's all related. Davids said it went all the way to the top, whatever that means. I think it's some kind of drug war."

"Oh? That's an interesting theory," Jerry mused. "Several of the murder victims out at the lake had been linked to local drug trafficking, but no one had anything solid on them. It was just the suspicions that come with an ex-con becoming ostentatiously wealthy overnight. One of them spent time in Dannemora Prison. Your information about that counselor will be very helpful. I'll follow-up on that."

"It sounds like the murders on the lake were rather bad."

"You should have seen them, Jay. It was awful, three men and three women, all nude and horribly mutilated. He strung them up on the riggings and along the sides of the yacht like gutted fish. It was the worse thing I've ever seen, and I've seen some pretty bad accidents. Remember the two car crash out on Route 9 that took those four teenagers and the newlyweds? That was pretty bad, but this was far worse. And there were drugs all over the place, including some smeared on the corpses. We found another body in the lake. He must have been on lookout. Real grisly. His head had almost been sawed off. There were just a few bits of cartilage and skin holding it on, a real bloody mess."

"It's all connected, but I need more time to unravel things."

"We'd have heard about that kind of drug war. If it were the Colombians or Jamaicans we'd know it. That kind of element would be very visible in this community. No, this looks more like the act of a demented sex maniac."

"Maybe, but what if they only wanted it to look like that? Maybe it's a professional hit man, the way he took care of all four of those guys on the yacht. Something must have happened. Someone decided to eliminate Bobby Dolan and the others, including any family members who happened to get in the way or knew too much. My guess is that Davids and Majerka were the middlemen, the contacts between the distributors and those smuggling the stuff into the country. How's it sound so far?"

"Crazy."

"Has anyone talked to Stienman's kids?" I asked.

"Yes, but they weren't much help. They said their father tied them up, told them it was a game."

"He must have been coerced somehow, perhaps with promises they wouldn't be harmed."

"We've got to tell someone," insisted Jerry. "You've got to come in."

"No. What if 'all the way to the top' means the mayor or your boss, or perhaps the base commander? Someone like that would have a lot of power. We have to be careful. We can't tell anyone. Dan Dolan may be involved. I know Dick Majerka is. He recently took an unannounced one-way trip to Florida. I think that case I was working on was a sham."

"This is all crazy. It's too serious to withhold evidence about."

"Who can we trust?" I asked him. "Anyway, I don't have any evidence."

I could tell by the way he was rocking his chair back and forth on its rear legs that the conversation was making him nervous.

"It sounds like someone's feverish nightmare," he observed, getting out of his chair and pacing the room.

"I have to go to Florida on Sunday to help my brother," I informed him. "Don't tell anyone. I'll be back in three days. Is there any way you can get a search warrant for Davids' house? You never know, it might turn up the murder weapon or something."

"I'll see what I can do, but without any hard evidence to go on it's not very likely. You should come down to the station and make a statement as soon as you get back. I shouldn't even let you leave."

"Jerry, I'm on to something, but we have to be careful. If what Davids told me is true, and I believe him, we don't know who's involved. We can't tell anyone. You've got to give me time."

I could tell he was unnerved by the whole thing. Still, he said he'd give me until I returned in three days. He'd try to help in the meantime. I hugged him, and breathed a sigh of relief when he left.

That evening at the club things reached an all-time low. George had found a young kid to fill in on bass. Only trouble was he didn't know any of our songs. It was a long night of bad notes and missed beats.

We sounded about as bad as a group of musicians can sound. The few people that came soon left. It was a disastrous Friday night. At the end of the evening Mickey told us he was sorry, but he couldn't afford one more weekend like this. He had hired another band to come in for the next night. A rock band, no less!

I flew into a rage.

"We signed up for three weeks and we're going to damn well play three weeks. If you think you can pull that crap on us, you're sorely mistaken. If another band shows up here tomorrow night they'd better be packing more than just musical instruments!"

Everyone looked shocked. Mickey appeared scared and backed away timidly, threatening to call the cops. There was really nothing we could do. We didn't have a contract, only a verbal agreement.

Denise and George calmed me down and did their best to smooth over the situation. The pimply-faced kid bassist looked scared and embarrassed. He was probably wondering if he'd get paid. You couldn't really blame Mickey. This wasn't the band he hired. We actually did sound terrible without Paul. The club had lost a lot of money these past two nights, not that it was entirely our fault.

By the time I got home I was in a foul mood, slamming things around my apartment as if they were punching bags. Every little inanimate object in the room seemed to conspire against me. Nothing functioned unless it was beaten into total bloody submission. My apartment looked like Hurricane Gilbert had slammed into it going 120 miles per hour.

And all the while, like a strong white noise in the background, the images and events of the past week kept hissing through my mind. That evening I slept in my bathroom on a cot, instead of in my bed. I don't know, maybe I was being paranoid, but the way bodies were piling up, I figured I couldn't be too careful.

Chapter 14

Day 11

Two days later I was in a small, twin-prop plane, flying over the lake on my way to Albany. From there I would take a 747 into Tampa Bay, Florida. On the trip down to the capital our plane flew through some bad turbulence. We were bumped up and down like a carnival ride. I wasn't particularly bothered, but the flight made several people quite nervous, including our inexperienced stewardess.

I fatalistically imagined the plane plunging down in a smoky plume into the steel-gray lake below. I could almost hear the sound of the engines whining in impotent defiance. I visualized the hard surface of the water rushing up to my window. I wondered what my last thoughts would be. Maybe I'd feel a few moments of pain. Maybe I'd pass out before we hit the ground. Contemplating my own demise came easily to me with years of practice. If it happened while flying in a small plane over the lake, so be it. There were a lot worse ways to die. They were happening all around me.

I tried calling Mary one last time from the airport before getting on the plane. She answered after the sixth ring. She must have forgotten to put her answering machine on to screen her calls. She was obviously still upset with me. I could tell from the venom in her voice when she heard who it was. I told her I was going to Florida for a few days, and asked if I could see her when I returned. She said she was busy and didn't know when she'd be free.

I looked at the lake below as the plane bounced us around like Mexican jumping beans. Was there really a Loch Ness monster down there like 'Champ', hidden beneath the deep, unfathomable waters, waiting for some unsuspecting angler to hook him? Like the monster who was slaying people here in our own small town. A monster who had probably been there all along, hidden beneath the facade of polite society, concealed by our inability to see the horror lying in the depths of a deranged human soul.

My plane arrived in Tampa exactly 1:30 Sunday afternoon. I rented a car at the airport and drove across the Tampa Bay Bridge to quaint St. Pete. I went to my hotel first, a big, pink, turreted place down on the beach. The literature in the lobby informed me it had been a naval hospital during the Second World War. From the looks of my room, with its small dimensions, creaky floors boards, old-fashioned door knobs, and small single bed, I could believe it. I planned to enjoy myself while I was here. I'd get my obligations out of the way as quickly as possible, and then hit the beach.

Freshening up, I put on my favorite blue Hawaiian shirt - the one that made me look like a short Magnum PI - and headed down to the police station, where my brother was being held. I thought it was hot when I left upstate New York, but it was positively broiling in downtown St. Petersburg. You could see the heat rising from the pavement. The sun's glare blinded me despite the cheap sunglasses I was wearing.

The police station was situated on Main Street and 1st Avenue North. I crossed the railroad tracks and pulled into the sun-drenched parking lot.

On entering I found myself in a glass-enclosed atrium, with corridors leading to the left and right. I headed toward the reception desk, where I was directed to the first office on my right.

Inside the room, behind a counter, was a uniformed officer with stripes on his arm. An IBM computer sat on the counter. It appeared more like the office of a bank than a police station, at least the ones I was used to seeing.

"Can I help you?" inquired the officer, looking up from his paperwork.

"Yes, I'm here regarding a prisoner I believe you're holding, a Bill Lawless," I answered formally. "I'm his brother, Jason Lawless. I believe my father has been in touch with you from New York."

"Wait just a moment, I'll check and see," he said, pecking out a dozen commands on the computer keyboard. After a few more keystrokes he looked up.

"I'm afraid you missed him," he informed me. "Someone came earlier this morning and paid his bail."

"What? Who could that have been?" I asked with some surprise. "I came all the way down here, at considerable expense, for this. It couldn't have been anyone authorized by the family."

"It was someone representing your brother legally. His lawyer, I believe," the officer volunteered. "He signed his name, James Hemming."

"Doesn't ring a bell. Did he leave an address?" I asked.

"Just a PO number, but I'm afraid I can't let you see it," he replied.

The description of Mr. Hemming was vaguely familiar.

"Can you tell me what my brother was arrested for?" I asked.

He went back to his terminal screen for a second.

"According to the report, he was arrested for drunk and disorderly conduct, and possession of cocaine. Since this wasn't his first offense, he was held in custody. His bail was set at $5000, which he didn't have. He was in jail awaiting trial at the end of the month. Is there anything else I can help you with?" he asked.

I thanked him and left the building in an acute state of confusion, not a little agitated for coming all this way for nothing. On further reflection, however, considering the state of affairs back home, I decided it wasn't so bad after all. Since my dad was footing the bill, I resigned myself to spending the remaining time I had basking in the sun and forgetting my troubles. Even finding Dick Majerka could wait.

I made my way back to the hotel in rush hour traffic. Going back to my room, I phoned home to explain the situation to my father. He was quite upset when he heard that my brother wasn't where he was supposed to be. He was also peeved he had paid all that money to get me down here for nothing. Although he was pleased that someone else had paid the $5000 bail, he was worried about Billy's well-being. I told him not to worry. There was no cause for alarm.

"It was probably just one of his con-artist friends paying back a favor," I said "I'll check around and see if I can find out anything. I'm sure Billy's OK. He can take care of himself."

That seemed to calm him down.

Before hanging up, I told my father that I would stay down a few extra days to try and find him. However, I couldn't guarantee he'd come back with me if I did. He told me to see what I could do, but if after a couple of days I still hadn't found him, to come home. He also said that if I couldn't locate Billy or get him to come home, to get a refund for the extra ticket he had purchased in advance for his return trip.

It was still hot when I finally got to the beach. The cool breeze off the Gulf felt good. Even though the water was like a warm bath, it was infinitely better than the sweat-soaked clothes I had been swimming in all day. After the hot tub, even the 80-degree water of the bay was refreshing.

I walked along the beach, relishing the feel of the fresh air on my face and the wet sand between my toes. The last rays of the sinking sun warmed my back. The three mile beach was almost empty by this time of day. There were just a few lone couples and a straggling family or two, getting the last bit of sunshine out of their day. I resolved to come out first thing in the morning, stake out a good vantage point, and spend the day girl watching.

When I got back to my room an hour later, there was a message for me from an officer Anderson of the St. Petersburg police. I called from my room and asked for Officer Anderson. When he answered he said we had spoken earlier that day concerning my brother. He then told me they had located him and asked if I would mind coming back down to the station. I asked him if anything was wrong, getting a sinking feeling in the pit of my stomach. He said that my brother had been found dead, apparently suicide.

I hung up the phone and sat on the edge of the bed in a complete state of shock. The room began to close in around me and spin. I was sick to my stomach. A numbing emptiness descended upon me like a black mountain of water.

What was going on? How was I going to tell my dad? It seemed that death was following me around like a starving dog. It was one thing to read about it in your hometown newspaper. To have it happen to your own flesh and blood, and right under your nose, that was just too much! It was one of the most horrible, chilling moments I had ever experienced. Little did I know, it was a feeling I would soon get used to.

Shaking like a man with hypothermia, I drove back to the police station, but it wasn't sorrow I was shaking with but anger. I viewed the body at the morgue in a trance-like state, nodding recognition at Billy's pitiful remains. Mumbling single-syllable responses to their questions, I signed documents blindly.

The only items found on him were an empty wallet full of old family pictures, and a heavy, bronze key-chain. It must have had every key my brother ever owned on it. There were car keys from his last three junk-heaps, house keys from various apartments and rooming houses, keys for cabinets, keys for desks, and keys for which no locks existed. I took them with the idea of going through his things later. They made my pants pocket bulge out. Arrangements were somehow made to take him back the next day.

It was after ten p.m. by the time I got back to the pink castle by the sea. I was numb and exhausted, but too upset to stay in my hotel room and too weak to call my father. I started walking down the beach. The sky was lit with stars, but there was only blackness in my heart. I needed to hide my anger in the dark of the night, and my pain in the roaring surf.

I couldn't shake the feeling that my brother's death was somehow connected with the events taking place back home. I knew how much Billy detested physical pain of any kind. I doubted very much that he would have willingly put a rope around his own neck and slowly strangle himself to death

The whole thing was getting personal. Someone out there was not only messing with people's lives, he had screwed with my family! My rage grew as I walked the beach like an escaped panther from the zoo.

Even though we had never been that close, a good percentage of the scraps I got into when I was a kid were on account of my little brother, Billy. His big mouth and sour disposition often got him into trouble with bigger kids. I'd have to step in to keep him from getting his face bashed in.

Now someone had done the unthinkable to my little brother and I wasn't there to help him. My helplessness in the face of Billy's death made me want to kill all the bullies in the world, kill them with my bare hands. Luckily no one was on the beach that night. Not that I would have hurt anyone, but my visage must have been frightening to behold.

As I walked down the beach in the darkness, I slowly began to realize I was just being paranoid. It was all too farfetched. I was getting worked up over nothing. My brother's death couldn't possibly have anything to do with me or the murders back home. It was just an unhappy coincidence, the logical result of my brother's sordid lifestyle, the bitter fruits of busted dreams and wasted chances, a life too painful to bear. That was, after all, something I could relate to. So I dismissed the whole notion of a personal conspiracy against me, and started to calm down.

My brother's death really was a suicide, I reasoned. I never really knew him or what he was capable of. The thought that my brother was gone, just like my mother, before I ever got to really know him, stung me to tears. Once they started flowing, they were unstoppable.

The silver sliver of moon floated in an endless canopy of stars. The warm Gulf breeze whispered in the clear night air. As I walked along the foaming shoreline, the wet sand beneath my feet, I thought about my brother Billy. How we used to build forts in the trees behind our house. How I'd help him when Tony, our older brother, picked on him. How we would never let him play with us and ran away leaving him stranded and crying. It probably wasn't his fault he dropped out of school and things turned out so badly for him. When mom died Tony was away at college, and I soon followed. Billy was left alone with Dad. It must have been hard to bear.

I walked along, having a good bawl, wishing I had helped him more, or had at least kept in touch. Then through my blurred vision I spotted bright lights up the beach. I continued walking and soon heard some hot music coming from that direction, mingling faintly with the roar of the surf.

As I approached, I saw a low, wind-worn building across the street. It had gray storm-shingles, and was on the boulevard that ran parallel to the beach. It looked like a combination takeout joint and dining room. There was obviously a live band playing somewhere inside. It was the only place around that had any activity. The rest of the street, with private houses and apartments, was dark and deserted. This place was lit up like Times Square on New Year's Eve and jammed with people.

I composed myself. Then I climbed over the low seawall that separated the beach from the boulevard, and crossed the street to the club. The music coming out of the place was sizzling. I could make out a guitar, with piano, bass, and drums, just like my band back home. But these guys were playing real jazz, not the pseudo-stuff mixed with pop we had to play to work. These guys were burning! I felt much better after my walk along the beach, so I decided to go in and have a listen.

Inside there was a colorful interior filled with people and smoke. A large, well-stocked bar stood in the middle of the room. Doors at the far end led to the kitchen. The smell of fried fish and seafood mixed with the acrid smell of cigarettes. Small tables, all taken, covered the floor to the foot of the bandstand. People stood at the bar and along the wall listening to the music. I went into the men's room to straighten up, then to the bar, where I bought a drink and stood listening to the band.

They were playing a fast samba. The kind of tune I was trying to get my band to do. The crowd was appreciative. I felt much better after my second Crown Royal. During the break I talked to the guitar player, a chunky white guy with thick glasses, and complemented him on the sound of his group.

As it turned out, I had happened onto Passe-Grill Beach and a place called the Hurricane Lounge, where topnotch jazz musicians played during the season. Since this was off-season, these guys, from the St. Petersburg area, were filling in. They even let me sit-in for a couple tunes. We had a great session. They liked my playing and asked me to come back the next night. I told them I was flying out that day. I didn't mention it was with my dead brother's casket.

I ended up staying until the last set of the evening. I had just decided to start the long walk back to the hotel, when one of the waitresses, the cute dark-haired one, came by and asked me if I wanted another drink, on the house. I thanked her and said yes, never being one to turn down a free drink from a pretty woman. I started contemplating a long night of pleasure with the long-legged creature.

As I sat musing about the evening's prospects, I saw an unexpected and familiar face. If I hadn't known he was in the area, I might have passed it off as a coincidence. After all, I've been mistaken for someone else enough times. But there was no mistaking this face. Dick Majerka had just walked into the club. He was wearing a loud, red Hawaiian shirt and white pants, and had a male companion on his arm, obviously drunk and young enough to be his son.

They were standing by the door, scanning the room for a table. When his eyes met mine they pretty near popped out of his head. Turning abruptly, he busted through the crowd behind him and ran out of the building, leaving his boyfriend standing there in confusion. I was confused too. The whole last twelve hours had been like a long, bizarre dream. I was afraid I would never wake up.

Chapter 15

Day 11 (p.m.)

I could hardly believe my eyes. Seeing Majerka walk into the club made me think I was home at the Pontiac for a moment. It was so unexpected. I was only stunned for a moment, however.

I followed as quickly as I could without attracting attention. I kept it nonchalant, so not even Dick's bewildered playmate, who was already staggering toward the bar, noticed me as I left. Too bad I had to leave a Crown Royal and a beautiful brunette behind, but I wanted Majerka in the worst way. He knew something about the murders back home. Maybe he knew something about my brother's death as well.

Getting outside, I looked up and down the boulevard in both directions. Cars were parked along each side of the street for blocks. There was no sign of him anywhere. Then, out of the corner of my eye, I saw something drop down beyond the seawall across the street. It was only a blur, just out of my field of vision, but I went after it instinctively.

Jumping down onto the soft sand of the beach, I crouched low and scanned the darkness. I could just make out a figure running along the shadow of the concrete retaining wall. I sprinted after it.

We were heading back in the direction I had come, toward my hotel. I could see Dick moving furtively against the dark-gray seawall. I picked-up speed and ran to cut him off.

I caught him sprawling against the wall, out of breath and gasping for air. He looked like a cornered mouse in a 'Felix the Cat' cartoon. His eyes bugged out through his thick, black-rimmed glasses, which were askew on his head. His hair was messed. The long strands he combed back to hide his bald spot dangled down his temples. He was sweating like a frog and blubbering between breaths.

"What do you want? Leave me alone. Don't hurt me!"

"Hi, Dick," I said jovially. "What brings you to this neck of the woods, heh? What a coincidence finding you here. Why'd you run? What are you up to?"

"Leave me alone," he whined again. "Keep your fucking hands off me!"

He was getting hysterical, screaming in a high-pitched, quivering voice.

I punched him in the stomach to shut him up. It worked. I didn't hit him hard, but he doubled over like a teddy bear with the stuffing knocked out of it. He fell to his knees on the ground, retching and groaning.

"Cut the crap," I said. "What are you doing down here?"

I wondered if he knew something about my brother's death. There was only one way to find out. Without giving him a chance to recover, I grabbed him by the collar, lifted him up, and slammed him back against the concrete wall.

"What's going on? What are you up to? Do you know anything about my brother's death?" My face was inches from his, nose to nose. "Don't fuck with me, Majerka. Your friend, Barry Davids, told me everything. You match the description of the guy who paid Billy's bail this morning and got him out of jail. Then he turns up dead. You're involved in this whole affair up to your shifty eyeballs, so start talking. I'd just as soon kick the crap out of you as look at you. I guess it's just my lucky day."

I slammed him against the wall again. Although I felt a little guilty picking on this defenseless bag of jelly, I wanted to get to the bottom of this thing. I was in no mood to finesse it.

"Wait! Don't!" he protested. "I don't know what you're talking about. I'm here on vacation. I don't know anything about your brother."

"Vacation my ass!" I was losing my patience. I kept my voice low.

"Who called you from the base? Was it Colonel Tunny? Why'd you leave town in such a hurry? Heh? Davids told me everything. He said you knew all about it. If you don't want to talk to me I can take you to the police and let you explain it to them. Or maybe I'll just take you to some quiet spot and beat you until you're brain damaged."

I gave him another quick jab to the ribs, then brought a forearm up to his chest, pinning him like a butterfly against the concrete wall. His glasses fell off into the sand.

"I guarantee, you'll start making things up just to stop the pain. You might as well tell me the truth." As I talked, I cuffed him on the side of the head with the palm of my hand.

I stepped back to let him talk. I could see the rusty gears of his brain moving behind his beady eyes. His pupils moved back and forth nervously. Without warning, he kicked sand in my face and darted toward the stairs leading up to the street. I cornered him against the wall. I had sand in my eyes, but could see just enough to grab him.

Blinded, I started working on him, punching him in the ribs and the side of the head with my free hand, but not hard enough to cause damage.

He bellowed and shrieked as he tried to protect himself from the rain of blows without much success. I kept it up until I could see again, which was some time. As I hit him I tried to make him talk.

"Maybe you think I won't hurt you? Is that it? You don't think I've got it in me, Dick? You sniveling bastard!"

I hit him in areas that I knew would cause discomfort, but not do any real harm.

"Does this feel like I'm fooling? Does it? Does it?"

With each phrase, I hit him again with jabs to the head. Then I struck the side of his neck with the outside edge of my hand. The good old karate chop. Though the blow was only delivered half-power, it cut off the blood bringing oxygen to his brain for a split second. He dropped to the ground on all fours. Then he sat back against the wall like a fat Hawaiian Buddha.

I slapped him back to consciousness, like Len had done when he demonstrated the strike on me.

"Please, please, don't hit me any more!" he moaned, half conscious. "Please. I'll tell you anything you want to know. Just don't hit me again."

"Well," I said as he hesitated to gather his thoughts. I knew he was scared, but was he scared enough to talk? I was ready to start again at a moment's notice.

"What's going on?" I asked again.

"It wasn't my fault," he explained, tears streaming down his eyes. He was shaking like a Chihuahua's hind end. Snot ran down his nose. I didn't feel sorry for him. That would come later.

"I'm just the middle man, you see?" he blubbered on. "I just set up the contacts between the real players. You know, I just put the right people together. I don't have anything to do with all this killing. I don't know what the hell that's about. It's all their doing. Honest, I didn't have anything to do with it. That's why I left. Things were getting out of hand."

"Who? Who are they? Who killed my brother?" I whispered, shaking him violently.

"I don't know, honest."

"What was your connection with Stienman and Dolan?" I asked.

"Can I have my glasses? I need my glasses," he pleaded, standing up and leaning against the wall.

I let him bend down and pick them up, backing off a pace and standing alert. I was ready for any sudden moves this time.

"A few years ago I got into some trouble. Nothing serious, you know, just a small time bust, snorting a little cocaine with an underage girl from the base. Her father was Captain Jack Riley. He called me threatening to press charges for corrupting a minor. That's a joke. That bitch practically set me up. While I was waiting for the ax to drop, I got a call from Colonel Tunny. He told me that if I cooperated with them they would make sure nothing came of the incident. They wanted me to give them the name of my drug connection, Bobby Dolan. Later on I hooked them up with some other people."

"Barry Davids for instance?" I asked.

"Yeah, that's right. How'd you know?"

"I told you, I talked to him. I was the last one to see him alive. In spite of what you think of my investigative abilities, I've broken this case wide open. Davids told me a lot, but got himself killed before I could get him to repeat it to the cops. So, how does my brother figure in all this? Who killed him?"

I bore down on him menacingly.

"Billy was distributing for us. I connected him up when your father asked me to help get him a job. Your dad knew I had connections down here."

"Yeah, he just didn't know what kind of connections they were. You're a regular one man employment agency, aren't you? What happened?"

"Billy was careless. He kept getting into minor scrapes. Not enough to cause any serious trouble, but enough to be a nuisance. This latest thing was the last straw. They sent me down to pay him off and get him out of town. He was more than willing to take the money and disappear. I guess they followed me down and fixed it so there'd be no chance of him changing his mind. Your snooping around probably made them nervous. But you've gotta believe me! I only paid his fine and gave him the money. I didn't have anything to do with his death!"

"Who's calling the shots? Who gives you your orders?"

"I can't tell you. They'd kill me!" he said, terrified.

"You think I won't! Look, they're probably going to kill you anyway. You might as well talk and try to save yourself. Tell me, who is it?" I started shaking him again.

"OK, OK! I get my orders from Ed Tunny. He's a squadron commander at the base. But it goes all the way to the top," he confessed. "They're smuggling drugs into the country using B-52s."

"What? You mean to tell me the base commander is smuggling drugs?"

"Yeah. You gotta believe me. I'm just a bit player. I had nothing to do with the murders. They were blackmailing me. Don't you see? I had no choice but to go along."

"All right, I believe you. I don't know why, but I believe you. You're my only collaborating witness. You're going to repeat your story down at the police station."

I grabbed him by the arm. Locking it at the wrist in an aikido hold, I guided him along the wall.

"No, they'll kill me! Just leave me out of it!"

He tried to pull away, but I had him in a good lock. I used pressure points to cause him pain when he struggled, threatening to break the wrist.

"I'm afraid I can't leave you out of it. You're a very big part of it. If you go and talk now, you can probably make a deal. I hear witness protection pays well."

I could see the odds being calculated in his thick conniving brain as I escorted him up the steps from the beach to the street.

Just when it looked like I was going to get him to go with me and talk to the cops, the door opened on a large black sedan parked on the other side of the boulevard. I don't know if it had been there all along or had just driven up, but suddenly it was there. A few cars had driven by while I confronted Majerka on the beach, but we remained hidden out of sight behind the six-foot sea wall.

Dick looked up, fear plastered all over his face.

"Oh my God, it's him!" he shouted, looking ready to pass out.

A large figure sprang from the car and ran across the street toward us. Reacting instinctively, I pulled Dick along the boulevard back toward the Hurricane Lounge and the lights. The man was big, but ran smoothly like an athlete. Before we had gone ten feet, he was upon us, only a few strides away.

Pushing Dick to the side, I rushed toward our assailant with a sudden, swift, unexpected burst of speed. Dodging to my left as he came in, I caught him in mid-stride with the inside ridge of my hand under his chin, clothes lining him off his feet. He fell hard to the ground on his back, landing on the pavement with the upper part of his arms like a wrestler to break his fall.

He was on his feet in an instant, springing up from his back before I could move in. It was the same move I had tried and failed to do when Barry Davids pushed me. Without missing a beat, he resumed his attack.

It was then that I saw the large knife clenched in his left hand. A chill went down my spine. I was good, but not that good. An unarmed man against a knife only gets one mistake. With the looks of this guy, I'd be lucky to get that.

The best defense I know against a knife is to run and look for a weapon, preferably something bigger than your opponent's. Try to equalize the situation. Only if no other option is possible would I attempt to defend myself bare-handed against a man armed with a blade. And here I was bare-handed, facing a trained man, holding a knife about as big as my arm. More than likely it was the very knife that had carved up all those people back home.

I backpedaled away from him as he advanced toward me. Turning my right to him in a side stance, I continued to edge away. Fear became a tangible thing. I could taste it, like bile in my mouth. It clogged my pores and my mind.

Majerka had finally gotten to his feet after stumbling over the curb. He stood halfway between me and the attacker, next to the railing separating the street from the drop of the seawall. He started yelling with glee.

"Good! Kill 'im! Kill 'im! Finish off the bastard! He knows everything. You've gotta kill 'im!"

Instead of attacking me, the assailant took three quick steps to where Dick stood, and sliced him viciously in the neck. I could hear his life gurgling out of him as he staggered toward the railing and toppled over it onto the sand several feet below.

The killer turned and stared at me triumphantly, an awful glint in his eye. I was past fear now, but my training kicked in. I was able to keep my breathing under control.

All of a sudden, knife pointed forward, he ran at me. I skipped back along the row of parked cars, digging my right hand into my pocket. Just when he was on me, a knife's blade away, ready to lunge, I pulled out my brother's heavy key-ring and threw it hard in his face. It hit him under the left eye and snapped his head back. He stopped dead and held his face.

All I wanted to do at this point was get away in one piece. I turned and ran down the street, yelling for help, for someone to call 911. The boulevard remained dark and empty. I sensed him right behind me. I knew I wouldn't get far like this. I had mere seconds before he'd be on me again with his demon blade. This mother could move!

I ran by a trash barrel next to the wall. Grabbing it, I spun around, and threw it at the killer's legs just as he reached me. He stumbled over it, and looked like he was going to fall headfirst, but at the last minute he ducked and rolled back up to his feet. I hadn't waited to see him crash. I didn't make it far. He was after me again and gaining.

I had to find some sort of weapon, something to equalize the situation and keep him at bay. As I ran, I noticed the antenna of a vehicle parked along the street. Gabbing it, I ripped it from its base with a snap just as my assailant approached.

Spinning around, I whipped the antenna into his face and eyes. The effect was instantaneous. He stopped and grabbed his face, howling with pain and rage. I didn't stand around, but darted out of range as the knife came down in an arcing motion, just missing me by inches.

I continued to whip the antenna in his face, and tried to keep him away with kicks to the legs. They had little effect on him, however, because of his size and conditioning. I was also being cautious due to the large, blood-covered knife he held. Hunching his shoulders, he used his forearms for protection, and loped toward me slashing the knife back and forth like a crazed gorilla.

I dodged the blade and darted away, swinging the antenna across his face and any exposed areas. As we fought, lights were finally starting to come on at the houses across the street. Somebody flashed a light on us and yelled.

"What's going on out there? I've called the police!"

I could hear sirens howling in the distance. They were getting closer.

My assailant gave me one last, long look, then turned and ran quickly back down the street to his car, which sped away with the lights off. I jumped over the seawall and ran down the beach as fast as I could go back toward my hotel. I had the presence of mind to scoop up Billy's key-ring on the way.

I knew there wasn't much I could do for poor old Dickey, and I didn't want to stick around and wait for the police. I'd be lucky if I wasn't implicated as it was. Once more, my only means of collaboration was dead, once again right in front of my eyes.

I made my way back to the hotel and up to my room unobserved. I was shivering with fear and exertion. It felt like I would never get my wind back. Running along the shore, in the surf, I left no tracks.

Day 12

It was almost four in the morning by the time I took a shower and went to bed. I expected the police at my door any moment, or worse, the killer. I lay awake until the sun came up. Then I dropped off for a few hours. I woke at 10:30. The phone was ringing. It was my father.

"Billy's dead," I informed him without preamble.

"What?" he yelled in shock.

"The police found him yesterday. They think he hung himself."

"What?" he yelled again, louder.

"Try not to get upset, Dad." I was worried he'd have a heart attack and tried to calm him down. "There's nothing we can do. Billy's at peace now."

"I don't believe it. It can't be. What the hell are you telling me? Billy? Dead? What happened? How could this be?"

He kept yelling questions in my ear. I didn't know what was worse, telling him my brother had killed himself, or confessing that he had been murdered by an insane hit man. I settled for the more believable lie.

"The police think it was suicide. They're still investigating."

"It's all your fault, Jay," he said. "If you had gone down when I asked you, none of this would have happened. Billy would still be alive."

As much as his accusation stung me, I knew in my heart it was true. When I failed to reply he started yelling at me. I told him he could vent his spleen on me in person.

"I'll be getting in late this evening. I'm flying into the airport across the lake in Burlington so I can fly up non-stop without changing planes with Billy's coffin. I'll need an extra thousand to cover the added expenses."

My father was in shock, obviously devastated by the news. He hung up while I was trying to tell him how sorry I was.

It was almost eleven. I had to be downtown by noon. Then arrange to have my brother's remains picked up at the morgue, and get to the airport by 3:15 - so much for fun in the sun.

The body count was adding up. My brother and Dick Majerka were among them. I had come face to face with the killer and survived, just barely. This guy was your worst nightmare. Obviously highly trained, with a knife to grind, and I had gotten in his way. Majerka must have been on his list. Now I was on it too.

Dick confirmed what Davids' had told me before he died, and shed further light on the situation. He implicated the commanding officer of the base, and the squadron commander that Stienman and Riley reported to. It was a drug smuggling scheme that defied belief. Using B-52s? If only I could find some way to prove it.

I went to the precinct and completed the necessary arrangements. I was mentally and emotionally drained. I kept my mouth shut and offered no additional information or comments to the officials I had to deal with. I was more than a little nervous about being in a police station after the events of earlier that morning.

There seemed to be a lot of commotion at the station. Every cop eyed me with suspicion. I wondered if they had any leads and how close they were to following the trail of evidence to me. I was glad I'd had enough sense to pick up my brother's keys. They would have led them right to me. I hoped Billy was finally at peace, maybe with my mother again at last. Peace is something I could have used a little of about then.

Later that day I boarded the plane to Vermont without further incident. No Federal agents rushed onto the aircraft to haul me off in handcuffs. No maniac tried to disembowel me with a meat cleaver.

The flight home was long and sad. I couldn't help thinking of my brother lying alone in the baggage compartment. Again I thought about our childhood. If I had done things differently, maybe things would have turned out better for him. If we had let him play with us, perhaps he wouldn't have had to do all those stupid things to get attention. If we had thought more of him, he might have thought more of himself. It seemed that all the blame for my brother's broken life could be laid right on my doorstep - his low self-esteem, his craving for attention at any price, his drug problem, his death. I was bathed in guilt, lathered with regret, soaked in remorse. By the time we arrived in Vermont, my mood was as black as the night, which was wet and dark. Thick clouds blanked out the moon and stars.

My father and Mary were waiting for me at the airport. We transported Billy's body back home in Mary's hearse without speaking, just making the last ferry as it left for New York. I stood on the bow of the boat and let the spray splash over me. It mingled with my tears. The lights on the far shore glistened and moved in my wet eyes. How sorrowful to be coming home, to see that shoreline and the shadow of the mountains beyond, shoreline and mountains my brother would never see again.

Chapter 16

Day 14

The next few days were the most depressing I have ever had, except for when my mom died. I was at an all time low point in my life, and that's saying a lot considering my below sea level existence. The events around me took on an unreal hue, like a scene from one of my bizarre dreams. I went through the motions as if watching myself performing them on a stage, detached, isolated within my own wall of self-pity and misery.

The thought of Mary working on my brother drove me to distraction. I wished some other mortician would do the job. Why had my father called her? Wasn't there a taboo against an undertaker working on the brother of an ex-lover?

All the way home that night, the two of them maintained a stony silence. They couldn't hide the accusations in their stares, however. I was too exhausted to utter a word of explanation or defense. I wondered if Mary and my dad had a thing going. That's all I needed for my self-esteem. Perhaps she gave him solace in his old age, but the whole idea mortified me. She was half his age. I had slept with her, for crying out loud! I dismissed the thought as another aberration of my feverish brain, as I sat quietly in the backseat, looking out my window into the darkness.

I had faced my worst nightmare and lived. I had seen him face to face. Would he come after me? The thought gave me chills. A trained fighter with a knife was nothing to take lightly. A few more minutes and he would have had me.

My brother's funeral was short and sweet. Few people attended. It was a stark contrast to Bobby Dolan's media-packed send-off. Only Paul, who was out of the hospital, and Denise and George from the band were there, along with Jerry and his wife. Mary and my dad also attended, of course. A few friends of my father's from his union and politicking days showed up as well. Oh yeah, my brother Tony came with his misbehaved herd of baby goats, three boys ages three through six. They say there's a black sheep in every family. Tony had three of them.

Whatever friends Billy may have had during his brief sojourn on our planet didn't bother coming to his farewell. I suppose it was just as well. I wondered if the common wisdom was true, that a man's worth can be judged by the number of people that show up for his funeral. I realized, with a start, that these were just about all the people that would be coming to mine.

I occupied my thoughts in this morbid, desultory manner, while the priest droned on in a monotone about that other life, the spiritual life. How in actuality it was more real and permanent than this one. Yeah, right. I've heard that old line before. I didn't buy it when my mother died, and I wasn't buying it now. For all the solace I got from the church I might as well have been a pagan. The priest's well-intentioned words sounded hollow, like stalks of corn whistling in the wind, sounds without meaning.

To me, my brother's life was a wasted one, a gift gone bad. But then who was I to judge, with my misbegotten, aimless excuse for an existence, just an endless string of botched chances, repeated mistakes, failures, and barren dreams. Who knows, maybe there really is an afterlife. Or maybe my mother was right about reincarnation, and you keep coming back until you finally get it right. Whatever the case, as far as we the living were concerned, Billy was gone and he wasn't ever coming back. He had gotten himself mixed-up in something deadly and it had turned on him. I tried to console myself with the thought that at least Billy was at peace now, but that didn't ease the hurt and sense of outrage I felt at his murder.

As I walked up the aisle at the end of the little service, I looked up in surprise. There to my delight, in the last row, was Suzie. She smiled a sweet smile and winked at me. I winked and smiled back.

It was as if a ray of sunlight had burst through the clouds. With that single look, she had pierced my impenetrable gloom. Things no longer seemed quite so bad. She wasn't at the reception afterward, but I made a note to call her that evening.

My father blamed the whole thing on me. He didn't come right out and say so in so many words, but I knew what he was thinking. If I hadn't hemmed and hawed, and gone down and gotten Billy sooner, my brother might still be alive. I never got a chance, even if I'd had the nerve, to tell him Billy was murdered because he was dealing drugs. My father responded to most of my attempts at conversation with stony silence. The times he did answer me, it was in single word grunts. Now my own dad wasn't speaking to me.

No matter how I sized it up, things looked grim. The band wasn't working and I had no viable means of support. God knows the few karate students I had wouldn't pay the rent. I'd be lucky if I survived the horror story I had gotten mixed up in. I was embroiled in a nightmarish conspiracy, with no support, no backup, no authority, and no gun, without a paddle, without a corner, without a prayer.

I didn't have the heart to ask my dad for the $250 he owed me for going down, but I kept the $80 left over from the expenses. That and the money I got from him earlier would just pay this month's rent, if I didn't eat.

I had an overpowering urge to skip town, just get in my car and start driving west as fast and as far as possible, not stopping for anybody or anything until I reached the Pacific. There was nothing for me here, nothing except a quick, ugly death. That's if I was lucky. I knew too much, and someone knew I knew. I had seen the killer face to face and lived to tell about it. I had a feeling he wasn't going to let it slide. The only thing keeping me from leaving was the fear that it might throw suspicion on me and make things even worse. That and an almost overwhelming sense of apathy, a listlessness that made even the most mundane decisions seem all but impossible.

I know I should have gone straight to the police with my story, but I couldn't face the prospect of being grilled by that a-hole Eddy McNeil. In any case, I had no evidence. They'd probably have a good laugh and throw me out on the street, if not in jail. I needed some way to collaborate my story before I went to the cops.

The official version of my brother's death from the St. Petersburg police department was suicide by hanging. Majerka's murder had apparently not yet been traced back to town. There was still no news of it in the papers. Who knows, he may have been carrying false identification.

I went home that afternoon after the funeral, and tried to put the pieces of the puzzle together. Two pilots from the base were smuggling drugs into the country using their B-52. Bobby Dolan, a known drug dealer, and the wife of one of the smugglers, killed in the sack together. A teenage girl, the daughter of the other smuggler, murdered and strung on a fence. A boat full of drug dealers apparently recruited with the help of Barry Davids, a counselor at the prison, all butchered on the lake. Two apparent suicides, my brother and Stienman, found hung by the neck. Dick Majerka, the middle man, with his throat cut before my eyes. All dead, murdered by the same person, the man I confronted on the beach in St. Pete. Let's see, have I forgotten anything?

The squadron commander, Ed Tunny, appeared to be implicated. He must be close to the top. Did it stop there or was there more to it?

Both Davids and Majerka said it went all the way to the top. Could that mean the base Commander himself? And the killer, the homicidal maniac, what orders had unleashed his murderous rampage? No wonder no one was talking, they were all too scared or dead. In spite of my skill in the martial arts, I had no interest in confronting that opponent again, unarmed.

What a setup - access to the source of the drugs, the means to transport it completely undetected into the country, and the network to distribute it. It figured that my brother would have gotten mixed up in this. I could have killed Majerka - if he wasn't already dead - for getting him involved.

I sat in my apartment musing in this manner, trying to figure out what to do. I decided to visit Jerry and fill him in on the whole ugly truth. I knew in advance what his response would be. I could also anticipate what Chief McNeil would say, 'That must be good dope you're smoking there, Lawless.'

Jerry lives in an old, refurbished farmhouse that sits on a small hill in the west end of town. Two large oak trees stand sentinel in the front yard, which faces a busy street. I pulled into the driveway, a short, steep dirt track that winds up to the rear of the house, and parked. His wife and kids were away at the mall. Jerry, who was off duty, was mowing the lawn. He stopped the mower and invited me in, grabbing two beers from the fridge on the way down to his basement den. At the bottom of the stairs was a glassed-in wall rack filled with a dozen or so different types of handguns.

"Nice collection you got there, Jer'," I said with envy. "Looks like you've gotten a few new ones since the last time I was here."

"Yeah, the pearl-handled .38-automatic is new. So is the .357-Magnum."

He opened up the case as he said this and took out the 6-inch barreled gun.

"I'd sure love to get the butcher who's been killing people around here in the sights of this baby, whoever it is."

As he said that, he aimed his .357 across the room and sighted-up on his imaginary target.

"Well, that's what I need to talk to you about," I began. "I think I know what's going on."

Jerry didn't disappoint me when I told him my story. He urged me to come in and make a statement before I had gotten five words out. He'd been nosing around, following up the leads I gave him. He didn't know how long he could continue to pursue the matter without informing the chief. He hadn't gotten a warrant to search Davids' squalid dwelling, but on his own initiative he checked the place out. He found plenty of child-porn, but unfortunately, nothing linking Davids to any of the murders.

Jerry confirmed the fact that the late owner of the half-million dollar yacht, twenty-five year old Claude Laplace, had done hard time in the same prison that Barry Davids had worked.

"My story fits the facts," I insisted, not telling him how I learned it. "There's a definite thread connecting all the victims."

The only bit of evidence the police had was the drop of blood from Captain Riley's kitchen, which had been identified as his. There was still no indication of his whereabouts.

"How do you know this?" Jerry asked finally, after I finished. "You didn't mention any of this to me last time we talked."

"I talked to Majerka while I was in St. Pete. He got my brother involved distributing drugs down there," I explained. "That's what got Billy killed."

I didn't bother telling him that Majerka was dead and I had witnessed his murder.

"He confirmed what Davids told me," I continued. "It goes all the way to the top, whatever that means. He's the one who told me they were smuggling the drugs in with B-52s."

"Jesus, Jay!" Jerry replied loudly. "We've got to tell someone."

"I need a few more days."

"OK," he eventually agreed. "I'll probably lose my badge for this, but you're right. Without some hard evidence, they won't believe a word you say. Things are kind of strange down at the station. After hearing you talk, I'm not sure who to trust anymore, but I've known you too long to doubt your word, Jay. Though I have to tell you, what you're saying sounds pretty crazy without some collaboration. We'll need some real proof if we want to convince anyone downtown. What happened to Majerka? Why didn't you bring him in?"

"I wasn't able to. It was after Billy was killed. I was in a state of shock. He got away from me."

I still wasn't ready to tell Jerry the whole story.

"I'll follow up and see if we can track Majerka's whereabouts," he said. "I won't mention your involvement."

"Thanks, Jerry. I can't tell you how much that means to me. You're my only hope of support in this."

"What else do you want me to do?" he asked. I could have kissed him.

"We need an ally on the base, maybe the new Wing Commander, Colonel Fitzgerald. My dad knows him. If we could get to him and tell him our story, somehow convince him to look into the matter, we might be able to get somewhere. It's worth a try."

"It might prove dangerous. If the base commander is in on it, this guy Fitzgerald might be too. But I'll see what I can do."

Jerry said he'd give me another forty-eight hours. Then, if he was going to continue helping me, he'd have to tell the chief everything. He warned me that if certain people knew what I was saying, my life would be in real danger.

I told him I was more than aware of that. We made arrangements to meet later in the week.

"I'll keep you informed if I learn anything more," I said as I was leaving.

I needed a way to confirm my story, some hard evidence or collaboration. I knew that without this, no one would believe me. I also had a little score to settle with the guy who killed my brother. That is, if he didn't settle it first, which was more than likely. I made up my mind to call John Rothburg. If what I thought was true, there had to be a money trail somewhere. If anyone could uncover it, John could.

Talking to Jerry had unburdened my soul. I felt purged. The fact that he didn't haul me down to the station was heartening, but I knew he couldn't hold off doing so indefinitely. In the meantime, there was a deranged killer out there with my dumb image stamped on his brain like a Polaroid picture. There was still hope, however. After all, when all is said and done, what else do we humans have but hope?

Chapter 17

Day 14 (p.m.)

I worked out hard in my dad's basement for the rest of the day. Remembering what little effect my kicks had on the killer, I practically tore my dad's house down working on my power kicks with the heavy bag. Then remembering how quick he was, I spent a couple hours on reflex exercises and quick-reaction drills, using the speed bag to hone and build rapidity and agility.

I normally did a hundred pushups and sit-ups during the day. That day and over the following days, I doubled it, and then doubled it again. I was training as if I had a professional prizefight coming up. I did - the heavyweight fight for my life. During the training sessions later that day, I worked on aikido locks and throws, since these were especially effective against knife attacks.

My students were all fairly advanced by this time. I decided to introduce them to the bats, hard red plastic wiffle ball bats used to add a sense of realism to our training. Even though they are made of plastic, and no strikes to the head were permitted, those bats get whipping good and fast. They sting like wasp bites when struck against bare skin, leaving nice ugly red welts.

I had them strip down to the waist, and got them familiar with the bats in a light, easy fashion. As we worked, I reminded them of the defense techniques they had learned in class. They then took turns defending against each other with the bat. All of them were sporting good welts by the end of the workout. The theory goes that after defending against a trained man whipping one of these light plastic bats at you, some 'stroker' on the street with a real baseball bat will seem like a joke. Except of course, instead of welts you get broken bones if you get hit.

At the end of the night, I defended against each one of them in turn, showing them different techniques in the process. I went through them like a badger in a hen house, until they got tired and bowed out, one by one. I imagined each opponent was the guy that night on the beach, slashing at me with his giant blade. Not one of them was able to lay a bat on me. I dodged and threw them. I blocked and punched them. I locked and hawked and kicked and swept them. Flipping and slipping, chopping and hacking, I guess I put on quite an exhibition. They seemed to like it. The harder I worked them the more they responded. Yet, despite the skill I demonstrated, I didn't feel confident enough to face that opponent from the beach again.

After the lesson, I practiced with my samurai sword. I kept it razor sharp. Made in Japan, it was crafted by the Suburo blade masters, makers of traditional samurai swords since the late Middle Ages. The tempered steel, two and a half foot blade flashed in the setting sun as I slashed it this way and that. Forward and backward, I sliced the air as I simulated multiple attack scenarios in my mind, dancing around my father's back yard.

My father made a point not to be home. He seemed to have an uncanny sixth sense that told him in advance when I was coming. He had hardly spoken a dozen words to me since I brought my brother home.

Later that evening I went back to my apartment, where I sat alone in the dark, contemplating my bleak future. Around nine o'clock there was a knock on the door. I wasn't expecting company, and wondered who it could be. As usual, my sink was full of dirty glasses and dishes.

"Hello, who is it?" I asked through the door, not a little nervous. I scanned the room for a weapon, and grabbed a dirty kitchen knife from the sink.

"It's me, Suzie. You going to let me in or what?" she yelled back, banging the door again with the palm of her hand impatiently.

"Oh, I'm sorry. I wasn't expecting company," I said, relaxing and opening the door.

"Yeah, I can see that," she said, coming into the kitchen with a cardboard box of food in her hands. "I figured you probably haven't had a chance to shop, so I brought you some provisions. Nothing special, some sauce and pasta, bread and stuff." She looked around the room disdainfully. "Boy, this place is a mess. When was the last time you had company, when Howard Hughes stopped by?"

She looked at the knife and back at me with a quizzical expression.

"Ah, I've been away," I said, putting it back in the sink. "I was just about to do the dishes," I lied. "Why don't we go into the other room."

I led her out of the kitchen area to a couch. My drums were in their cases, stacked in a corner.

"So, to what do I owe this pleasant surprise?" I asked, trying to tidy up as inconspicuously as possible.

"Oh, I just wanted to see how you were doing. You looked so sad at the funeral this morning." She said this with a warm, sympathetic smile. She smelled of the fragrant perfume she wore around the office. I liked it immensely. It almost made breathing a pleasure again.

"I'm doing fine. The band will be working at the Holiday Inn in a couple of weeks, now that Paul's feeling better. I may get some more karate students. I'll get by," I said with false bravado.

"Don't you believe in lights? It's like a mausoleum in here. Oops, I'm sorry, Jay," she said, turning red with embarrassment.

"I'm having trouble with the electric company. It's only temporary, I assure you. So, how you been?"

I went over to the table and lit two candles. They gave off a sweet scent. The soft glow of the candles accentuated her blue eyes, and made them seem even larger. They were a striking contrast to her soft red hair.

"Not too good," she admitted. "I still haven't heard from Mr. Majerka. It's been almost a week since he left town. I don't know what to do. I talked to his wife and she told me to run the place as best I could, but there's so much I don't know. If Mr. Majerka doesn't show up soon, I don't know what I'm going to do."

"Well, his wife doesn't sound too worried about him. Have you talked to the police yet?" I asked innocently.

"No, not yet. Do you think I should?"

"Yeah, it's probably not a bad idea," I advised. "Talk to Jerry LaGrand."

She asked me if I knew anything. I hadn't planned on telling her Majerka was dead, but I realized it was important for her to know. I didn't have to tell her how he died or that I saw it happen. I decided I'd take a chance. If I couldn't trust Suzie, who could I trust?

"I'm afraid he's dead," I said to her.

"What! Oh, no! Poor Mister Majerka."

"You can't tell anyone, not even Jerry LaGrand. Just say he's missing. They'll find out on their own soon enough. Jerry will take care of things. I can't get involved. I'd be implicated."

"What happened?" she asked.

"The same thing that happened to Billy. Dick got him involved dealing drugs and it got them killed. I think it's the same people who are killing folks here in town."

"Oh, no, that's terrible. What are you going to do?"

"Jerry and I are gathering evidence so we have some proof. We don't know how high it goes in the base command, or the city, for that matter. These people are very dangerous."

"I hear Dan Dolan has left town. No one knows where he and his family went."

"That's strange. At my request, John Rothburg hacked our company's computers. He didn't find any record of Dolan's policy. I think it was a scam he and Majerka dreamed up. Who knows, that may have started the whole thing."

"I'm scared, Jay. I don't want to go home tonight."

"You can stay here if you want, although you're probably safer at your place."

"I have to tell Mrs. Majerka," she said. "That poor woman."

"No, you can't do that. Just go on as you've been doing at the agency. Jerry will make sure she's notified."

"I really need help at the office. You couldn't come by, could you? I need an assistant. I'll pay you."

"I'll have to think about it," I replied, although I really needed the money. "I have some things I need to do first. I'm not sure I can commit to anything right now. How can you pay me with Dick gone?"

"I have my ways," she said with a mischievous grin.

"Oh, how is that?" I asked. "What? Have you found a sugar-daddy or something?"

"Nope, just a checkbook and some credit cards," she confided.

"Suzie, you're not forging Majerka's signature are you?"

"I don't see where that's any concern of yours. You have enough to worry about with your own affairs."

"Yeah, I guess you're right, but you can't blame me for asking."

"Are you hungry," she asked.

"Famished," I replied.

"Then why don't I cook up some spaghetti and meatballs."

"Sounds good. It's my favorite dish," I replied. "I'll pick up some vino."

"Yes, but do the dishes first," she ordered.

"Yes, ma'am."

We had a lovely evening. It was just what the doctor ordered, the first real home cooked meal I'd had in years. Suzie turned out to be an exceptional chef. The food was delicious. We washed it down with my father's expensive imported wine.

After dinner we listened to records and sipped more wine. Her taste in music was similar to mine. A smooth tenor solo served as a backdrop to our stimulating conversation.

Something had changed, something imperceptible. Things seemed brighter, although my situation was the same. For once, things were finally starting to go my way.

Suzie spent the night.

I lay in bed next to her, bathed in the glow of her presence. I could smell her sweet scent and hear her soft, rhythmic breathing. I no longer felt the suffocating loneliness and isolation that had plagued my nights and sapped my strength for so long. I felt at peace with the world. In actuality, it was only the calm before the storm.

Interlude

Lake Shore, North End of Town, Midnight

The killer watched his quarry drive up to the motel in his red BMW. The 'Studebaker', as it was called, featured single, two-room cabins nestled in a wooded setting. Each cottage had a picture window view of the lake. Selected rooms featured hot tubs, ceiling mirrors, and oversized beds, with pay-per-view porno piped in via cable TV hookup. They were private, swank, and suited Tech Sergeant Joe Adams' needs to a 'T'. Tonight he wanted to make a big impression.

Joe had plenty of dough to fuel his hedonistic pursuits, more than your normal Air Force technical sergeant could acquire. Joe had connections. Born and bred on the streets of Harlem, he joined the Air Force at nineteen to escape a pregnant and underage girlfriend, the gang he ratted on, and a prison term for possession of narcotics with intent to sell. In the hard merciless streets of New York, Joe was one of the luckier ones.

He did well in the Air Force. He applied himself and learned a trade. After six years he became a master aircraft mechanic, with five stripes and twelve airmen working under him. But his street instincts and appetite for the good life eventually got the better of him. The hicks in this burgh were such easy marks, and the authorities so clueless, that Joe soon found himself hustling, pimping, and dealing his way to easy street. All was not well, however. The recent murders had put a damper on things. Everything was in danger of coming unglued. He should have been more wary, but he had other things on his mind.

The killer smiled as his target ran around to the passenger side door like an eager Eagle Scout, and opened it with a flourish. Extending his hand courteously, he helped the two beautiful women out of the low-slung automobile. Then he escorted them into the luxury cottage, wrapping his arms around their slim waists. The killer grinned broadly in anticipation. They would pay for their sins.

He was observing them from a long hedge, which separated the Studebaker from another motel next door. He was unseen in the dark shadow of the thick green leaves. His cold, bullet eyes stared out at the cottage with grim satisfaction. Waiting, he gave his victims time to get comfortable. He wanted them fully engaged when he busted in.

As he waited, his mind flashed back to that special day, the day that had changed his life.

He was fourteen. Alone on his vision quest, he was in the middle of a vast mountain range. His grandfather had dropped him off days before. Now he was in a bad way, lost, and suffering from dehydration, hypothermia, and exhaustion. Long past being hungry, his stomach felt like it was being squeezed from the inside. He had been chased by a bear, fallen off a cliff, and almost drowned in the river. On the verge of death, he had crawled into a hole to die. That's when he saw it.

All this was necessary if he were to become a warrior. That was his fate, what his grandfather demanded. He had no choice and did as he was told so that he did not get beaten or put in the hole. If he'd had known how harrowing and terrifying it was going to be, however, he would have defied the devil himself to avoid it. Now all his fear and pain had vanished.

There before his blurred vision was a gigantic bear, larger than a prize bull. Its head and paws were as big as the boy's entire torso. The youth lay transfixed as the huge animal stood up on its hind legs and spread its arms wide. As it stood, the skin of the animal pulled back. Under the fur was a large giant of a man, naked and covered with blood.

He had long flowing, raven-black hair. Blood dripped off his forehead, from his chest and hips. It was smeared over his arms and legs. His eyes blazed forth like two solid chunks of red-hot coal. A necklace of human ears and fingers, from long ago dead enemies, hung around his neck.

Shimmering shapes and incandescent forms swam before the boy's vision. Grids, zigzags, dots, and wavy lines, turned into honey combs, mountains, rivers, and hills. They shot from the being's outstretched fingertips, entopic images from the youth's frazzled nervous system and the mushrooms he had nibbled in his hunger. It felt as if he were in a dark, swirling vortex, a rotating tunnel, where the ground kept slipping out from under him, making him nauseous and dizzy.

The apparition made no sound, but silently pointed behind the young warrior, back in the direction he had come. The boy turned to look, and when he turned back the vision was gone. His grandfather had told him how he would encounter his personal spirit-guide on his rite of manhood. And how that being would succor him and bring him to safety, and thereafter give him power over other men.

He stood up and walked unsteadily in the direction indicated by his vision. He would survive. The supplies of the young couple he found camping in the woods saved him. Following his spirit guide's silent orders he killed them with their own hatchet. Their blood, which he smeared over his body, sealed his pact, his promise with the devil.

An hour had passed. The killer slowly returned from his daydream. Leaving his hiding place, he walked down the edge of the trees toward the lake. No one was about at this late time, only a few hours before sunrise. At the end of the hedge line was a small sand beach that continued onto the next property, where the Studebaker cabins were located. He walked across the beach toward Tech Sergeant Joe Adams' cottage.

Quickly surveying the area, he saw it was perfect for his plans. He couldn't have found a better spot if he had picked it himself. Shielded from view by the surrounding trees, separated from the other cabins, it was the ideal death trap.

"Time for retribution," he whispered to the night.

Creeping up to the bathroom window, he peered in. A light was on in the adjoining room. It spilled across the linoleum floor to illuminate the large hot tub that dominated the center of the room. There were three naked people in it. Music played on a boom box sitting on the floor. No one would hear him enter.

He examined the window. It was partially opened and screened to let in the cool evening breeze. He took his knife from its leather sheath and with a few deft strokes, quietly removed the screen. Being blocked from view by the shower stall, he had no trouble slipping through the window unobserved.

No one heard him until it was too late.

Tech Sergeant Joe Adams was having about as much fun as a New York City boy could have, pleasure you only fantasize about. He was about to climax when he looked up and froze in fear.

Not a sound came from the cabin. No one had time to scream.

Chapter 18

Day 15

Suzie left early the next morning before dawn. The apartment had no AC, and it was already getting hot. The room was stifling. Even though Suzie and I didn't get much sleep, I couldn't lay in bed another minute.

I left the room and walked down the beach to watch the sunrise over the lake and catch a few rays. I figured I'd have just as much luck sleeping on a towel in the sand as I would in my stuffy apartment.

I sat on a driftwood log. The early morning sun flooded over the mountains of Vermont and poured into the lake valley. The light sparkled on the water like living things, darting this way and that over the surface. Another dawn, the last of a chain of sunrises stretching back to the beginning of our world, the first of those to come. What would it bring?

I sat thinking about Suzie. Was it a dream? She seemed the only real thing in my life. Everything else was illusory, as if it wasn't actually there. Had I really slept with her, made love to her? I felt an intense affection for this girl. I was haunted by her image.

As the sun got higher in the eastern sky, I cleared a little spot amongst the rocks and driftwood, and placed my beach towel in the sand. Stripping down to my trunks, I lay down.

I must have fallen asleep because when I woke up the sun stood high in the sky. I felt the telltale prick of a sunburn. A family had pitched themselves a little distance down the beach from me. Other than that, I still had the place to myself.

It took awhile before I was able rise. I staggered into the water, unsteady on the sharp rocks that cluttered the shoreline. Diving in, I let the cold water splash over me, washing the weariness from my brain. I floated on my back like a dead man, bobbing in the waves limply, letting the sun broil my brow. Finally, I swam to shore, dressed, and managed to drag myself back to the apartment.

I tried catching up on some shut-eye, but as tired as I was I couldn't sleep. I never was one to catnap. There's something about losing consciousness during the day when the rest of the world is awake that bothers me. I guess I'm not very trusting. At that moment I pretty near distrusted the world.

I was lying in bed, contemplating a day of drowning my troubles in cheap booze, with maybe some chess with John Rothburg. I was getting out of bed to call him when there was a knock on the door.

Throwing on a robe, I went to see who it was, half expecting to see Suzie, back for more loving. I flung open the door with a big grin on my face. To my immense mortification, Chief McNeil was standing there with another crew-cut detective by his side.

"Sleeping late, Lawless?" he sneered. "What's a matter, have a big night last night?"

"What can I do for you gentlemen?" I asked, closing the door in front of me a little for cover. I felt underdressed in just my robe and undies.

"What you can do is put your clothes on and come with us down to the station," McNeil said.

"Am I under arrest?" I asked. "What am I supposed to have done now?"

"No, smart ass, you're not under arrest," he said through the crack in the door. "We just want to ask you some questions. There was another murder last night. Where were you yesterday evening and early this morning?"

"Are you going to ask me the questions here or downtown? Make up my mind."

"Don't give me any of your smart-ass sarcastic crap, Lawless," McNeil growled. "I came here in person to make sure you don't give us any trouble. I'm in no mood for your bullshit. Let's go! Get dressed."

"I know my rights," I said. "Unless I'm under arrest or you have some sort of warrant, I don't have to go anywhere with you. Where do you think you are, Nazi Germany?"

"OK, wise-ass, if you wanna be arrested, we can arrest you. Phil, why don't you read mister attitude here his rights." He looked over at the other cone-head.

"Mr. Lawless, sir, we only want to ask you a few questions," said the other detective. "You can appreciate the pressure we're under to solve these brutal murders. Would you please accompany us downtown?"

"Well, why didn't you ask me like that in the first place? I'll be right with you, officer."

I didn't ask them in, but shut the door in their faces. They could wait outside. I got dressed, called Jerry and left a message, then joined two of the city's finest in the parking lot. As I followed them to the station I wondered about the newest homicide. Who had bought it this time, and why were they bringing *me* in for questioning?

At the station, they led me into one of the interrogation rooms. McNeil was there with his partner, along with another goon named Sergeant Clark. Jerry was nowhere to be seen. I hoped he'd get my message.

They started off by asking me again where I had been the previous night. It already sounded like they considered me a suspect. I told them I had worked out with my students at my dad's house and then went home to my apartment, where I spent the night. I didn't mention I had company. He asked at what time. I told him around nine.

McNeil next asked if I had been home from then until the time they came to pick me up this morning. I told them that I had woken up early and gone to the beach to watch the sunrise and do some swimming. Clark and McNeil looked at each other with knowing glances.

Suddenly changing the subject, Clark spoke.

"You were in Florida last week, weren't you?" He rustled through some papers, pointing vaguely to the middle of a page of text. "You went down last Sunday to get your brother, William Lawless, out of jail. Is that right?"

"That's correct. I went down for two days. He wasn't at the police station when I got there. Someone else had been there before me and paid his bail. Then they called me later that day and told me he'd been found dead, apparently suicide. It's all on the record. You can check it out," I answered. I had a hunch they knew about Majerka. I resolved to deny everything.

"Oh, we've checked it out, Mr. Lawless," said the detective. "Did you happen to meet Richard Majerka when you were down there?"

"Strange coincidence, wouldn't you say?" chimed in McNeil before I could answer. "Your boss fires you. You both turn up in the same South Florida city. Then he turns up dead, the victim of a vicious knife attack. Yes sir, that's a mighty interesting coincidence, if you ask me."

"Well, that's all it is, a coincidence." I lied. "I had no idea he was in Florida. I certainly didn't see him when I was there."

"Where'd you stay in St. Pete?" asked Sergeant Clark.

I hesitated to answer. I knew that if I told them it would only add fuel to their suspicions, but also that they probably knew the answer already.

"Out at St. Pete Beach," I said finally. "I forget the name of the place, but I can look it up for you if you want."

"Wasn't Majerka found on St. Pete Beach?" asked McNeil, right on cue.

I was getting nervous, but didn't want to show it. I was determined to keep my cool, but felt like a fly in a spider's web. I would have asked to call my lawyer if I had one, but I couldn't bear the thought of enduring my brother, Tony's, patronizing drivel.

Clark returned the subject neatly to the previous evening.

"Mr. Lawless, did you happen to stop by the Studebaker Motel any time late last night or early this morning? Say between three a.m. and six this morning?"

"No," I answered curtly.

"Do you know a Sergeant Joe Adams?" he asked. "He lived on the base."

"No," I answered again. "Why?"

"Because some time this morning between the hours of two and six, he along with two of his companions, were murdered in one of the cabins at the Studebaker. They were killed with a large knife or knifelike object, maybe a sword."

"They were brutally mutilated," added McNeil "It was similar to the previous murders, but worse. Real sick. Do you own a knife, Lawless?"

"I may have some throwing knives on my father's basement wall, but they couldn't be used to do anything like that."

"How about swords?" asked McNeil. "You own any swords?"

"Sure, but they're mostly ceremonial, for display. You're welcome to examine any of my martial art equipment."

"Phil," said McNeil. "Make sure all Mr. Lawless's knives and swords are confiscated for analysis."

"You know the martial arts?" asked Clark, before I could object. "Is that what you used on those kids on the yacht? How did you handle all four of them?"

"Yeah, you sick bastard," goaded McNeil. "You can't get it up in the normal way, can you? So you use a knife."

"You don't think I did this, do you?" I objected finally. "That's crazy. Why would I do a thing like that?"

"You still smoke dope, Lawless?" asked McNeil. "There was a large quantity of cocaine found at the scene, just like some of the other murders. You snort coke once in awhile, Jay?"

"No, that stuff will kill you, McNeil, but I wouldn't put it past you. You're just the type of fucked-up jerk that would do something like that. You guys better watch the evidence room," I said to the others.

"Watch your mouth, you little punk," said McNeil. "Your disregard of the law is going to land you in big trouble. It already has."

Despite the grilling and rude remarks, I knew they were just grasping at straws, hoping to get me riled enough to say something incriminating. I knew McNeil was just looking for an excuse to lock me up and throw away the key. I tried to control my temper, and sat quietly waiting for the next barrage.

They took turns questioning me, round robin. It was much like sparring with my students, defending each attack as it came. They asked me about Stienman again, and the Riley girl, about Bobby Dolan and the gang on the yacht. I repeated my story of how I had found Stienman. I added that I couldn't possibly have killed Bobby Dolan or the Riley girl because I was working those nights in front of a dozen witnesses. That alone should have proved I wasn't the killer. I didn't need to get Suzie involved.

Without telling them what I really knew about the case, I suggested it was drug related and had something to do with the base. I told them that in the process of investigating the Dolan insurance claim, I had found a connection between some of the murdered people on the yacht and a counselor at the prison. But before I could follow it up, he had been killed in a highway accident. They wanted to know how I obtained this information. I claimed client confidentiality. The fact that I was neither a lawyer nor a doctor nor a priest, and didn't have a client, didn't help.

They weren't interested in my theory, just in busting my ass. McNeil went so far as to insult my parents' intelligence. He had the nerve to tell me to keep my nose out of police business. I told them they needed all the help they could get.

Not only did they not believe my theory, they treated me as if I had already confessed to the killings. I was in a room with a bunch of pea-brained airheads, and they held my balls in their fat, grubby little hands.

I told them they should get a search warrant for Davids' phone records, and check if there was any link between him and the murdered owner of the yacht. I didn't mention I had reason to believe they were using bombers to smuggle drugs into the country. Nor that someone high up in the base command was involved. For all I knew, these cone-heads were in on it.

"I've got a good mind to lock you up, Lawless," said Chief McNeil. "You got off lucky last time. Those Air Force flunkies didn't want me to press charges for assault. But you're on my turf now. You're a menace to society."

"You're full of it, McNeil. If you weren't such a pig-headed ignoramus, you would've figured it out by now, unless you don't want to for some reason."

This got Eddie a bit upset. I guess it wasn't the first time such an idea had come up. He all but exploded, his face inches from mine and beet-red.

"You fuck-up! Who do you think you're talking to? Show some respect. I'm sick of finding dead bodies everywhere you happen to show your ugly face."

"Bite me," I replied. "That'll be the day when I show respect to a sniveling little mama's boy like you. You fucking stiff! You're so inept and gutless you don't deserve any respect."

My resolve to sit there and swallow the insults spewing from this eternal fool's mouth gave way to total incautious disdain. He was either the world's greatest incompetent or in on it, one or the other.

"Why, I have more respect for a wart on a fat man's ass than I do for you, you puke!" I added.

His face turned scarlet. He blustered and sputtered.

"You wise-mouth little bastard!" he screamed in rage. "I'll..."

Unable to continue, he bellowed, "Get him out of here!"

Clark quickly escorted me out of the room. I think he was afraid the chief was going to shoot me. I reached the door. McNeil had followed me out and down the corridor. I was sure he was going to have me arrested for verbally assaulting him.

I turned and waited for his onslaught. Clark looked worried. At least there were witnesses now. I saw Jerry out of the corner of my eye, coming to my rescue from behind his desk.

"If I so much as glimpse another stiff anywhere near you," McNeil threatened. "I'll personally put enough lead in you to sink a battleship. Got that?"

"Are you threatening me in front of all these witnesses, Chief?" I answered coolly.

"Get him out of here!" he screamed again, slamming his fist into a nearby cabinet. His face had turned a violent purple. His neck veins bulged out. It looked like his head was about to pop off. Jerry escorted me speedily out of the building, while Clark tried to calm McNeil down.

As I left, I could still hear him yelling after me like a gangster.

"If I see his stinking face around here again, I'll kill him. So help me God, I'll kill him!"

All in all, the whole episode left a bad taste in my mouth. I was quickly plunged back into my habitual mode of self-doubt, self-pity, and remorse.

Chapter 19

Day 15 (p.m.)

I talked Jerry into meeting me for a drink later that evening. I wanted to see if he had found out anything since our last meeting. As a favor to him, we met at his favorite bar, the Rainbow Lounge. It's a little place down by the paper mill frequented by assorted cow-kickers, cops, and mill workers. They came for the live country music and the cheap booze. A little guy in a large cowboy hat fiddled away on the bandstand. We took a booth at the rear and ordered a couple drinks.

"What the hell did you say to McNeil to set him off?" Jerry asked as we sat down.

"Nothing he didn't have coming," I answered indignantly. "I don't mind going down and answering some questions, but the abuse he put me through wasn't called for. They're trying to pin the whole damn thing on me! I'm surprised they didn't arrest me."

"The chief is the only one who thinks you have anything to do with the murders, and he has nothing on you."

"Yeah, nothing but intense dislike."

Jerry filled me in on what he had found. He had done some nosing around at the base. The base commander, Colonel Michael Dene, had been there for over ten years. Recently passed over for promotion to one star general, he had a reputation for being a rather gruff individual.

"He pretty much runs the base like a sailing ship of old, a real disciplinarian," Jerry informed me. "He's expected to retire at the end of the year. Lieutenant-Colonel Tunny, the commander of the bomber squadron Stienman and Riley belonged to, has been there almost as long."

"That's what John said," I confirmed.

Jerry continued.

"Colonel Fitzgerald is a relative newcomer, an up and coming rising star, at the zenith of his career. He's currently the wing commander, but is expected to be taking over command of the base when Dene retires. There's reported to be little love lost between Dene and Fitzgerald, his future replacement."

"He sounds like a good prospect to approach with our story," I observed.

"I'll try and talk to him," Jerry said. "I'll make it seem like routine questioning regarding the homicide case. Maybe we can get him to help."

"Don't tell him what we suspect," I warned. "See if he knows anything. It's a chance, but I think it's worth taking."

"The trick will be keeping it from the chief," Jerry replied.

Jerry told me that they had contacted the Florida police and asked them to trace Dick Majerka, who they had reason to believe was in their city. They tracked him to a John Doe from a recent unsolved homicide. When the chief heard I had been down there at the same time, he put two and two together, and came up with me as a suspect.

"That explains it," I said. "That dimwit. The guy must really hate me. I have an alibi for last night. I was with Suzie. She brought me dinner and spent the night, but I wasn't going to tell McNeil. The less he knows about my love life the better. The funny thing is I must have been sitting on the beach not far from the Studebaker when the murder took place early this morning. For some reason I had a strange urge to head to the beach and take in the sunrise. I haven't done something like that since I was a kid. I don't know what got into me. I just had to go out there."

"Hmm, that is strange," Jerry agreed.

I started humming the theme from the Twilight Zone.

"Did you tell the chief that?" he asked.

"Yeah, no wonder they looked at each other and smirked."

"This guy is getting worse, Jay. He really mutilated this last group, two women and a man. Worst thing I've ever seen or heard about."

"You said that last time," I reminded him.

"Well, it was so bad that Irene Fiddler, the owner of the motel, had a heart attack on the spot. And one of the first officers on the scene, some snot-nosed rookie, fainted dead away at the sight of it."

"But it looks like the same guy, right? Multiple stab wounds, sexual mutilation?"

"Yeah, but worse. He seems to be getting sicker, if such a thing is possible."

"Who were they?" I asked.

"A Sergeant from the base, named Joe Adams. They haven't identified the two women yet."

"Yeah, they asked me if I knew him."

"Did you?" he asked.

"No, but let me guess, he was in Stienman' bomber squadron?"

"I don't know, but you can bet I'm going to find out," he said with determination.

"Good!"

Again the police were baffled. Another murder in a grisly string of homicides, and they still had no clues. The lab boys were shifting through the crime scene, but so far had found nothing. There were no fingerprints, either in the room or on the bodies, other than the victims'. The killer must have worn gloves. There had been plenty of blood and body fluids at the scene, but it had all been irretrievably confused in the pandemonium following the discovery of the bodies.

The killer had broken in through the bathroom window. There were a few scattered footprints under a stand of trees near the cabin. The trees would have concealed him from view. But there were no footprints leading to or away from the spot, and no trail of blood, though whoever did it must have been covered with it.

"The St. Pete police said Majerka's throat had been cut," Jerry informed me, changing the subject. He was probably beginning to have doubts about me himself. "Do you know anything about that?"

I decided to tell him everything. He was committed. There was no turning back now.

"I saw Majerka get killed," I informed him, looking around to make sure no one would overhear us. "I saw the killer. He almost killed me, too."

"What?" shouted Jerry. Everyone looked over to our table as if there was about to be a fight, something that happed quite frequently in the Rainbow Lounge. "Why didn't you tell me?"

"And implicate myself in a murder, no thanks."

"Jesus, Jay!"

"This guy is your worst nightmare, Jerry. I'll never forget his face. He was big, about six foot five or six, 250, 260 pounds. He had a thick neck and a broad chest, and was strong. Built like a bull, but moved like a cat. My kicks had almost no effect on him. He slit Dick's throat with a large Bowie knife without batting an eye. He almost slit mine, too. Only quick thinking and the sirens of the police saved my ass."

"You think this is the same guy killing people up here."

"It's a good bet," I replied. "He probably killed those last three too."

"You saw him face to face?"

"As close as I am to you now."

"Then you're probably one of the few people who can identify him."

"Don't remind me."

"Jay, you've got to come in. We can protect you. You might be able to ID him. We've got mug shots and computers. We can plaster his picture all over the media, smoke him out."

"I'll doubt you'll find any mug shots of this guy. Like you said, he's a professional"

"You're probably right, but you can't hide this kind of information. You might be able to tell us something that would help us solve the case."

"I'm telling you everything I know. All I'd be doing is putting a noose around my neck while the real killer goes free."

"Hey, there are a lot smarter people than you and me downtown. We need help, Jay."

"Yeah, and there are a lot less honest people than us downtown. Who do you think you can trust?"

"I don't know, but you're a witness to a murder. This is obstruction of justice."

He stopped abruptly, stared at me helplessly, and sighed.

"What do you want me to do?" he asked.

"Just what you're doing. Talk to Fitzgerald, find out what you can."

"Well, you better watch yourself," Jerry warned. "This guy's not your average murderer. He's a sadistic butcher. You should have seen how he left them, all laid out in obscene poses. The coroner said it looked as if the blood had been squeezed out of them, almost like a ritual sacrifice."

"Please Jerry, not on an empty stomach," I objected, feeling sick. I'd had enough madness and mayhem for one day.

It was almost ten p.m. by the time I left Jerry at the Rainbow. He told me he was going to try and see Colonel Fitzgerald the following afternoon. I told him I hoped his association with me wasn't going to be detrimental to his career. He responded that he had picked his path and was going to see it through to the end. He hadn't gotten where he was by being afraid to take a few calculated risks now and then. He could handle McNeil.

I hadn't eaten yet and was a bit tipsy from the drinks. I drove out to the Depot on the west end of town and tempted fate with a couple hotdogs doused in Michigan sauce. I guess I had been tempting fate quite a bit lately, and we all know it's not wise to tempt her too often.

Chapter 20

Day 16

The next afternoon I went to see John Rothburg at the college. His office is in the new science wing. Several pretty young co-eds were leaving just as I got there.

"Hey, John. How's it going?" I said walking into his office. "What a racket. Don't you have any male students?"

"Yeah, a few, but more and more women are getting into math and science these days."

"And here I thought you were doing all this for astronomy. Hey, did you get a chance to look into that matter for me, about finding a money trail between those names I gave you?"

"No, I haven't had an opportunity to do anything yet," he admitted. "Actually, it's a good thing you came by. I'm leaving on a ten-day trip tomorrow morning, a scientific conference in Israel. I won't have a chance to look into it until I get back."

"Oh, well, if I'm still alive when you get back we'll do that," I said, not a little disappointed. This was the last chance I would most likely have to establish a hard connection between the drug-related murders and the base.

"I'm sorry, Jay. Is it that serious?" he asked with concern.

"Yeah, it's that serious. You wouldn't believe what I've been through since I saw you last."

"Yeah, I was sorry to hear about your brother. I wanted to attend the funeral, but the damn jeep broke down up at the mountain. I was stranded there for three days."

"Don't worry about it, John, as long as you come to mine."

"Hey man, don't be so morbid. It can't be that bad."

"Oh yeah? What if I told you I met the killer face to face in Florida? You were right, John. Majerka was in St. Pete. He was in the process of confirming what Davids told me, when this big freak came out of nowhere and sliced his throat. He tried to make it two for one, but I was lucky and managed to get away. He was one scary mother!"

"Fuck!" he exclaimed.

"Not only that, there was another murder and the police suspect me of being the killer. Can you believe that?"

"Shit," he added.

"I've told the cops more or less what I know, but they won't buy it without more evidence. I was thinking that if we could find a money trail between any of the drug dealers and the top brass at the base, we might have enough to get them to investigate. I was hoping with the new names I gave you something solid might turn up."

"OK, Jay," he said. "I was going to try and get some sleep before the trip. It's a long flight and we leave early. I can never fall asleep on a plane and the jet lag really gets to me. But this sounds serious. Why don't I see what I can do and call you later this evening, say in about four or five hours."

"I'll call you," I told him. "I'm not sure where I'll be. John, you're a life saver. Just for that, I'll let you win next time we play chess."

"You maggot!" he answered. "That'll be the day you have to let me win. Remind me to kick your ass next time I see you."

After talking to John, I decided to stop by the agency and see Suzie.

"Hi, kid," I said walking in. "How you doing?"

"Hi Jay, good. What brings you here?" she asked.

"I just came by to tell you how much I enjoyed seeing you the other night. I wanted to thank you for dinner. I owe you one."

"You bought the wine. You don't owe me anything. I'm glad you came by. I was just thinking about you."

"Me too," I replied. "I mean I was thinking about you too."

"Have you seen this morning's papers?" she inquired.

"No, but I don't tell me. There was a murder early this morning. They brought me in for questioning."

"I know. It's in the paper. It sounded horrible."

"Great, just what I need, another nail in my reputation. Don't leave town," I told her.

"Why?" she asked.

"Because you're my alibi, I was with you when the murders at the motel were committed. Don't worry, I didn't tell anyone. I doubt it will come to that. McNeil's just grasping at straws. The guy hates me."

"Why?"

"It's a long story. What are you going to do about the agency now that you know Dick's not coming back?"

"I talked to Mrs. Majerka this morning. They're bringing his body back for the funeral and burial. She wants me to run the place for her. I'd be a partner."

"Good, you won't have to forge any more checks. Hey, I was wondering if we could get together again sometime."

"Sure, why don't you come over tomorrow night? We can have dinner. I want to talk to you about your old job. I'd like to have you come back."

"I'll have to think about it. Now might not be a good time."

"We can talk about it over dinner. Does seven sound good?"

"Perfect!"

Finally, I had something to look forward to.

Later that day, after the karate class, I went upstairs to see if my dad was home. I hadn't seen him or spoken to him since the funeral, and was determined to clear the air between us once and for all.

"Hi, Dad. How you been?" I asked, finding him on his recliner watching a baseball game on the tube. "Haven't seen you in awhile. It was getting so I thought you were avoiding me."

"I was," he said grumpily.

"What did I do?" I replied. "It's not my fault Billy got himself killed."

"If you had gone down when I asked you in the first place, none of this would have happened," he said, getting up from his chair.

"How do you know?" I asked. "If I had gone down earlier, I would have probably ended up dead like Billy. He didn't kill himself. He was murdered. Dad, I saw the guy that killed him. He killed Dick Majerka right in front of my eyes. He would have killed me, too, if I hadn't been trained and kept my head. As it was I was lucky to come away alive. It's all a conspiracy, a drug smuggling ring using B-52s, and the commander of the base is in on it. Majerka was in on it too."

I was talking as fast as an auctioneer, spilling my guts in motor-mouth overdrive, unable to apply the brakes.

"If that's true you should tell the police," he said skeptically.

"What do you mean, if it's true?" I said, raising my voice.

"Don't yell at me!" he barked back indignantly.

"I don't like being called a liar by my own father. And I did tell the cops my story, at least most of it. They don't believe me either. So you're in good company."

"Yeah, I heard about that," he said in disgust. "Now our family name has been associated with this ghastly murder business again. I told you to mind your own business and drop the whole thing. But no, you had to go and stick your nose in it like some mongrel."

155

"Dad, I'm on to something. If I crack this case, I'll be able to write my own ticket in the criminal investigating business, police record and all."

"Ah, you're dreaming, Jay. All you're going to do is get yourself in trouble," he answered, with a get-out-of-here hand gesture. "But then you're too smart to listen to anybody else, especially your father. Mary was right. You *are* an arrogant, know-it-all. You have no respect for anything or anybody."

"Been talking to Mary about me have you? That's nice," I said, simmering a slow burn. "It must be nice living in your own little world, with your preconceived idea of reality. You wouldn't know the truth if it bit you on the nose!"

I stood there glaring at him.

"Go ahead, hit me!" he yelled. "Hit your old man, you good for nothing ingrate."

"What do I have to do to get though to you?" I yelled. "What do I have to say to get through that thick skull of yours?"

He pulled his arm back as if to slug me. I put up my arm in a hand-sword block.

"You have no respect!" he said in a broken voice. "After all I've done for you."

Suddenly, the realization of how hard he must have been affected by my brother's death hit me. I realized, at that moment, how much he blamed himself for Billy's failures. After all, my dad had brought him up by himself through the formative teenage years. Billy's death must have also brought back all the pain of losing my mother, like running warm water over your hand after you've burned it.

"Dad," I said, softly. "I'm sorry. I could never repay you for all the things you've done for me, never. I do respect you. Of all the men I know, I respect you more than anyone. I've looked up to you for as long as I can remember. I'm sorry. I'm sorry for Billy. It wasn't your fault. There's nothing any of us could have done."

I flung my arms around him and hugged him tight. Tears welled up in my eyes.

"I know, Jay. It wasn't your fault. Poor Billy. Poor, poor Billy."

He put his arms around me and hugged me back, tears streaming from his eyes.

We stood like that for awhile, bawling like old ladies at a funeral. Then I led him to the couch. As we sat down, I laid my arm on his shoulder.

"Dad, the thing I admire most about you is that you speak your mind and follow your own heart. You never let anybody tell you what to do or think. You'd listen and weigh the facts, but God help anyone who tried to force you to do something against your will. I swore I wanted to be just like you. I admit I haven't exactly done that great with my life, but at least I tried. Dad, you've got to believe me, Majerka told me everything before he died. He was the one who got Billy involved selling drugs down there in the first place. Dad, I've seen the killer in action with my own eyes!"

"Then you've got to tell the police, Jay," he said solemnly. "This is serious."

"If they knew I was anywhere near Majerka at the time of his death, they'd haul me into jail so fast it'd make your head spin. Then where would I be?"

"If what you say is true, and I'm not doubting you, then you need help. You can't handle it alone." He got up and retrieved some Kleenex from the top of the TV.

"Jerry LaGrand is working with me on this."

"Say, that little sister of his, what's her name, Judy or Joy?"

"Jackie," I volunteered.

"That's it, Jackie. What a cutie she turned out to be. Why didn't you ever go out with her? If I remember right, you had a crush on practically all his sisters."

"Her sisters were too old for me and she was too young," I replied, not wanting to tell him the real reason she had turned me down for a date - my lousy reputation.

"Two or three years younger? She's the perfect age for you."

"Well, it seemed like more when I was twenty and she was only seventeen and jail bait."

"Want to go to the Depot and get something to eat?" he asked.

"Sure," I answered. Then I remembered something he had said earlier.

"So, since when have you and Mary been talking about me? How's she doing?"

"Oh, fine. We went out to dinner last week. Had a nice time," he informed me.

"What?" I exclaimed. "You went out with Mary?"

"Sure. What's the problem? Since when do I need your approval to take someone out to dinner? She's too old for you anyway."

"She is not," I insisted. "She's only a few years older than I am. She's definitely too young for you! How's it going to look, you dating my ex-girlfriend?"

"Like I've got something you don't," he said with a sly gleam in his eye. "Since when do you care what people think?"

I just stared at him, shaking my head back and forth dumfounded. I couldn't believe it. It was bad enough that she dumped me, but to go out with my old man? That was really hitting below the belt.

"I don't feel much like eating," I said, feeling slightly nauseous at the thought of my father sleeping with my ex-lover.

"Oh, don't be like that, Jay. Grow up for Christ's sake."

"That's easy for you to say. Your father hasn't taken up with your old girlfriend. Really, I've got some local calls to make. I don't want to hold you up. I'm not that hungry, honest. Maybe I'll grab a sandwich or something. Why don't you go along without me, OK? Call Mary. I'm sure she'd be delighted to join you."

"Fine, suit yourself. Just make sure you don't charge up a lot of calls. I happen to know you have no means of support at the moment. That reminds me. I may be able to get you an interview at the Howard Johnson's Motor Inn. Your mother's Uncle Tony is the manager up there now. Interested?"

"Sure. maybe," I said without conviction. "Suzie might give me my old job back."

"Hey, this would be a big opportunity for you," he said. "Tony is looking for someone to head up their new security department. Get your foot in the door and make a good impression, and you'd have a good career there."

"Don't worry, I'll call him."

"Good," he said, putting on his sweater and opening the door to leave. "You sure you don't want to join me for dinner?"

"No," I said. "You go on. I've really got an important call to make."

I didn't want to admit that after hearing about him and Mary, sitting and eating food with him would have been out of the question. I had definitely lost my appetite.

As soon as he left, I called John Rothburg. He answered with a wide-awake voice. In fact, he sounded wired.

"How's it hanging, Lawless?" he said on hearing my voice.

"Great, John. What do you have for me?"

"That's just like you, Lawless. Don't waste any time with the small talk. Get right down to business, right down to brass tacks. No beating around the bush with you. No beating dead horses. No beating the meat. Just the facts, ma'am, nothing but the facts. Don't ask how I've been, how's the job, how's the family. No, just, 'what d'ya got for me, Rothburg?' Have I ever called you a fair-weather friend?"

"Yeah, that and a few other choice things, fur ball," I replied. "What have you got for me, Rothburg?"

"A lot," he said, "most of it with my little PC here at home. I started with the easy stuff, checking those systems I already have backdoor access to. The Registry and Telephone Company, you know, looking through the data and correlations we obtained previously. Nothing really new or striking turned up.

"I wasn't getting anywhere," he continued. "To pick up a money trail you have to go to a bank. So I tried nosing around some of the local banking system networks. This isn't so easy. Most banks, because of the nature of their business, have elaborate computer security measures in place. You know, things like extra long passwords and special break-in detection software. They even have stuff so sophisticated now it can notice when someone is using the computer differently than normal. Like they can notice that the backspace key is being used more than usual, or that activities not normally done under the current user are being performed."

"I'm glad this isn't a long distance call," I quipped.

"Hey, do you wanna hear this or not?" he said in a hurt voice. "If you don't, I can go back to bed, which is where I should've been long ago if I hadn't been out on a wild goose chase, taken on out of the goodness of my heart for a friend in his hour of need. I could've been well rested for my trip, instead of strung out on caffeine. I probably won't be able to sleep tonight. I know I'll be unable to sleep on the plane. I'll arrive zonked out at the conference from lack of sleep, blow my talk, lose my standing in the scientific community, and lose my job. Then I'd probably go postal and shoot all those scientists who laughed at me. Of course, I'd get caught and executed, and all because I did a favor for someone who didn't even wanna listen!" He finished with a crescendo.

"I'm listening! I'm listening!" I said. "Please go on."

"As I was saying before I was so rudely interrupted. What was I saying?"

"You tried breaking into some bank computers," I volunteered.

"Oh, yeah," he said absentmindedly. "I wanted to see if I could pick up any information on the financial activity of the people on our list, but I had no luck. The banking systems really have their security act together. Too risky, you know. I was stumped. I had no idea what to do next. Then it hit me. The college library has loads of reference material at the Resource Center, computer based registers of all the businesses and corporations in the state, together with the names of the principle owners and executives. I decided to search these directories for references to names on our list. I could easily access this information from my PC here at home. I finished just before you called."

"And?" I said expectantly after he paused uncharacteristically long.

"And bingo!" he announced triumphantly. "Claude Laplace's name came up as the owner and operator of a chain of Laundromats, 'North Country Cleaners'. They're located across this part of the state and worth several million dollars. Not bad for someone who was in prison just two years ago. Regular rags to riches success story, wouldn't you say?"

"Yeah, the guy was a regular George Jefferson," I quipped. "It must have been a front."

"Exactly, and get this, there appears to be another partner, a company called NSR Corp. They're the ones who put up the initial capital and own the controlling interest in Laplace's business. Funny, NSR Corp is not in any of the directories. I have no idea what they do or who's involved. A dead end, right? Wrong," he said, answering himself smugly. "The information on Laplace's Laundromats listed 'Lake Valley Community Bank' as his business's chief financial institution. I wasn't able to access their systems, but I was able to look them up in the university register and pull some information."

"John, you blow my mind," I said in admiration. "Just when I think you've outdone yourself, you do one better."

"Wait, I'm not through," he said. "One of the owners of the bank is none other than Dan Dolan. Isn't he the father of the first murder victim?"

"None other," I confirmed. "Are you telling me that Dan Dolan is part owner of the bank where Claude Laplace, ex-con Laundromat king, kept his money? Ain't that a kick in the head. Small world, isn't it?"

"Ayep, even smaller than you think. I looked up Dan Dolan in the directory of local businessmen, and under the long list of establishments and businesses owned and operated by him, nestled inconspicuously between 'Apple Valley Development Company' and 'Golden Gate Apartments', was little ol' NSR Corp. And get this. Our Colonel Tunny is a part owner."

"You're fooling me?" I said. This was just the link I needed to unravel this nightmarish puzzle.

"Are you going to the police?"

"Yeah, eventually," I said. There was a long silence over the phone as we were both lost in thought. "Dan Dolan," I mused out loud. "He's behind all this?"

"I don't know, little buddy," he said humbly. "I just give you the facts. You're the one who sifts through them and ties it all together to solve the crime, Sherlock."

"Right," I responded doubtfully.

"If you want, I'll leave a copy of the printouts in my mailbox. You can come by tonight or tomorrow morning and pick them up. Just don't knock or wake me up late tonight. I need to try and get some sleep. I hope I'm not too keyed up with all that caffeine I drank."

"Don't worry, John. You'll be fine. You'll sleep like a baby knowing how much you've helped a friend in need. Not only that, you'll be helping all of us if we can put an end to this madness. There's nothing like a good deed to overcome insomnia."

I knew from past experience that John would not sleep. Excited by the challenge of the chase, he had fueled himself with pot and caffeine until his brain was buzzing 9600 baud. He'd be way too 'hepped-up' to sleep. The facts of the case would be swirling around his brain like horses on a merry go round. His overactive mind would go on processing information, crunching through data, searching and synthesizing, long after his will had tried demanding sleep. He'd probably get to sleep some time around five a.m. But I had confidence John could get through his talk with his eyes closed, which as it turned out, is practically what he did.

It was eleven-twenty p.m. I tried calling Jerry at home. There was no answer, so I decided to call it a night and go back to my room.

As I drove up to the entrance of the motel, I saw a half-dozen police cars sitting in the lot with their lights flashing. People were standing around in their bathrobes staring at my apartment. The place was obviously being searched. I drove by slowly and took the thruway back into town.

It was obvious I was still suspect number one. It was also certain that I couldn't drive around all night or sleep in the car. Who knows what they would find or plant? They were liable to pick me up as soon as they saw me. I had to find a place to lay low. I thought of Suzie.

Chapter 21

Day 17

I spent the night at Suzie's. She lived in a nice second-story flat in a quiet section of town, on a street named for some French Catholic saint. My car was parked behind the house, hidden from sight. She made me a turkey sandwich. I woke up on the couch where she left me after providing a pillow and blanket. She was sorry to hear the police were looking for me, but not surprised.

"Don't worry," she told me. "I'll be your alibi."

I thought we were going to have sex again, but it was not to be. I contemplated knocking on the bedroom door and walking in, but fell asleep before I got the nerve.

That morning at breakfast, I thanked her again for helping me, and asked her about the previous night.

"I don't want you to think what happened back at my apartment the other night makes me think I have any hold over you," I told her. "I don't expect anything, although I really enjoyed being with you and hope we can do it again sometime. I really like you."

"I like you, too, Jay," she replied. "I just want to take things slow. Things can get strange sometimes. Some guys think they own you if you go to bed with them."

"Not me. You owned me after that night!"

She laughed and patted my hand.

I leaned over and softly kissed her neck. She moaned and reached up to caress my hair. I kissed her lips. She kissed me back passionately.

"If I knew you felt like that, I would have come to you last night," I told her.

"I was waiting for you," she replied.

The rest of the morning went by fast.

I was still trying to integrate John's latest piece of information into the scheme of things. Dolan seemed so upset over the death of his son. Could he have actually been involved in his murder? It seemed unlikely, unless he knew about it but had no power to stop it. And how did NSR Corp fit into all this? Was Dolan's bank being used to launder drug money from Laplace's Laundromat front? Like I didn't have enough to worry about already. John had greatly expanded the scope of possibilities.

After Suzie left for the agency, I called Jerry from a payphone down the street. The first thing I asked him was why they were searching my pad.

"Did they find anything? What's going on, Jer'?"

"McNeil still suspects you of Majerka's murder," he answered. "He's looking for evidence. I don't think they found anything, but they sent several items to the lab. They also grabbed the weapons in your dad's basement."

"Great, I'll never get that stuff back. Good thing I've got my swords in the car."

"They could bring you in at any time, so don't tell me where you are."

"Don't worry, I won't. Did you see Fitzgerald?" I asked, changing the subject to what I really wanted to talk about.

"Sure did."

"How'd it go?"

"OK. I played it low-key. I told him it was a simple follow-up to the homicide investigation," he explained, getting into gear. "I said I was investigating the murder of Kathy Riley and the disappearance of her father, as well as the suspicious death of John Stienman. I also asked him about the recently murdered aircraft mechanic. I knew I liked him when he told me he never believed that bull-crap about Stienman's suicide. A bomber pilot like the major would never do such a thing. He also confirmed that the most recent victim, Sergeant Joe Adams, was a member of Stienman and Riley's bomber squadron. He said he thought at first there was no connection between the murders and the base. After the police reports were published pointing to a serial killer, he didn't think it warranted any concern."

"No concern, my eye," I commented.

"No," Jerry insisted. "This guy's on the level. He admitted this most recent murder raises the odds that there's some connection between the deaths and the base. He's no dummy. You'd like him, Jay."

"Yeah, my dad said he was a good guy."

"Real sharp, and down to earth too. He agreed that since several of the murder victims were involved with drugs, including one from the base, it's not unreasonable to suspect that what's going on might involve narcotics."

"Talk about your understatements," I commented.

"He told me he was recommending a full-scale, but secret investigation of the base and its possible participation in illegal drug-related activities to his superiors in Washington. Although he didn't come right out and say so, it sounded like he had to go over the base commander's head."

"Yeah, that's not surprising, considering what Majerka and Davids told me about it going all the way to the top."

Jerry continued.

"Fitzgerald said he'd be in Washington at a military conference for the next three days, at which time he would bring the matter up. He also mentioned that the base was slated for major cutbacks, including a lot of early retirements. His job when he takes over next year will be to implement these reductions in materiel and personnel. He expected quite a bit of fat would be cut away at that time. I got the impression from the look on his face and the tone of his voice that he wasn't kidding around. I wouldn't want to be the target at the end of that flyboy's sights."

"That sounds encouraging, Jerry." I let out a sigh of relief. "That's the first good news I've heard since I heard about Bobby Dolan's murder. Good work!"

I told him about the information John had garnered, legally this time, mentioning the mysterious NSR Corp. I also told him about Dolan's connection to Laplace's Laundromat front, and Tunny's involvement with NSR. He said he'd see what he could find out on his end. Again, he asked me if I wanted to try and get a police artist to sketch the murderer.

"We might be able to get the state boys to have a go at it," he said.

"Thanks, Jerry. I'll let you know," I told him. "They're probably all busy drawing my picture. After all, I'm a fugitive from the law."

.

Interlude

Lyon Mountain, New York, Same Day and Time

Deep in the woods, in a solitary hunting camp, the killer sat alone. He had been there since his last assignment several days ago. His task had been completed. Besides the well-publicized murders around the city, there was a string of disappearances that baffled the authorities throughout the area. All of them were due to the silent work of the man sitting at the table in the half-light of the waning day, Daniel Tunny. He had been called and he had responded. The sinful had been scourged. The world would never be the same.

Anyone connected to the drug ring had been brutally eliminated. This included Dan Dolan and his wife and daughter, whose private plane had recently crashed mysteriously on the side of Mount Katahdin in Baxter State Forest, Maine, killing all aboard. It had been a terrible task, but one Daniel had been quite willing to do. This is what he had been born and bred for. Still, he was vaguely disturbed. Things had not gone well in Florida.

That one had gotten away. It was for this reason that his superiors had asked for this meeting. He had never met the leader, only communicating through drop points and phone. The other one was his father, Ed Tunny, a father in name only. He hadn't seen the man since his mother died when he was ten. His mother's death changed his life.

He replayed that moment, like he did other moments, continuously through his life.

He had come home from school that afternoon. The street in front of his upper Queens apartment was crowded with police cars and ambulances. Entering the building, he saw her crumpled body lying at the foot of the stairwell. She lay half covered with an old army blanket, being pawed at and examined by strange men. They told him she had fallen and broken her neck. He watched in silence as they wheeled her out of the building on a gurney. Her arm dangled limply from underneath the starched white sheet. He would never forget the sound the creaking gurney made as they wheeled it past him. It was the sound of death.

His father was flying his bomber across the Atlantic, and didn't come home that evening. He was never questioned about his wife's death. Apparently, he had an impeccable alibi. Daniel could have told them the truth, however, if he had wanted. He was surprised the man hadn't killed her long before this, the way he continually knocked her across the room. His father was a big, important person, untouchable. Unfortunately, Daniel was not. Soon after the 'accident', he was sent to live with his grandfather. He stayed there until his eighteenth birthday. Everyday was a living hell. Then he learned the terrible, exhilarating truth.

Daniel wondered what he would do when he saw his father again, the man who had killed his mother. Would he squeeze his neck until his tongue popped out, or gut him like a fish? No, he would do neither. Not yet. Revenge would come with time. For now, he'd do as he was told and see what happened. Things were about to change and he wanted to be around to enjoy the fruits of their victory.

While he sat reminiscing in this way, a car drove up to the cabin in a cloud of dust. In an instant, he was out of his chair, his knife in his hand. Slipping out the back of the cabin, he circled to the side and carefully peered around the corner. Two men dressed in green military fatigues with Air Force insignias got out of the car.

The taller man was silver-haired but young looking, with a boyish face and an upright bearing, Daniel's father.

Daniel's grandfather had trained him well, not only physically, but mentally too. Like the Khmer Rouge in Cambodia, his training was designed to make the boy a sadistic killer. It also made him malleable and obedient to his trainers, like a half-wild animal who will obey any command to avoid being caged again.

Daniel looked at his father with a combination of fear and hatred.

The other man was Colonel Michael Dene, the leader of their group. He was short, with dark, graying hair. A sour man, the corners of his mouth were turned down in a perpetual scowl.

As the three men walked back to the cabin, Tunny, stopped and sniffed the air.

"What's that smell," he asked his son. "It smells like decaying flesh."

Daniel said nothing.

"Is that a body? You're not burying bodies around here, are you?"

"It's that Riley guy, the teenage girl's father," Daniel admitted. "I had to do *something* with him. He was in the trunk of the car. I forgot about it. I dug a pit behind the cabin and threw him in. You said to make sure no one found him, so I did."

"Not around here! The least you could have done is bury him deeper. Are you stupid or something?"

Daniel hung his head.

"Don't worry about that," said Dene. "Daniel will dig a deeper hole a little farther from the cabin and throw in some quicklime, won't you Daniel?"

Daniel nodded his head sullenly.

"We've got more important things to discuss," Dean continued.

They sat around a rugged pine table in the middle of the room.

"Tell us what happened in St. Petersburg, Daniel."

Daniel reiterated what had occurred in Florida. His father reprimanded him again.

"You were too cautious. You failed miserably."

His father's words stung him. Daniel said nothing and glared at the floor.

"We've got to do something about that guy, Lawless.," observed Dene. "He knows too much. We can't allow anything to disrupt our plans. It is too important. We are the only ones left. The other groups have all been discovered or disbanded with this fucking glasnost business. We alone have survived to be activated in this time of need, at the last minute. We have been planning this for years. How long has it been now, Ed, since you and I were implanted into our host families in this country? We were mere boys, barely out of puberty, but we had been trained well. We have succeeded against all odds, both of us. We have gained high ranks in the U.S. military, and have access to everything we need to cripple this country. We have made it! All that's needed is to take the next bold step. This is for the Mother Land!"

"I'll take care of the snoop," Daniel said, ignoring Dene's rant and staring at his father. "I'll kill him like I should have in Florida."

Tunny didn't like the way his stepson was looking at him. He was about to say something when Dene interrupted.

"No, I have a better idea," he said. "Ed, your drug smuggling scheme worked well, and brought in a considerable amount of cash. The murders not only eliminated anyone who had knowledge of our activities, but caused a significant diversion. Better yet, thanks to Daniel's methods it spread terror, which is just what I hoped it would do. Maybe we can pin the whole thing on this guy, Lawless, make him look like the sex murderer."

Dene thought for a moment. "Ed, you know that little cock-teaser you've been balling. She may be just what we need."

"You said we wouldn't have to hurt her. She's loyal. She'll do anything I say," Tunny replied.

"That's the idea. It will be just the distraction we need. Here's what I want you to do."

Chapter 22

Day 17 (p.m.)

Later that evening, after having dinner at Suzie's, I went to check out my pad. I was curious how much the police had trashed it, although I didn't have much to toss around. To my surprise the place looked neater than I'd left it. Who knows, maybe the cops tidied up for me.

I was collecting some things to take over to Suzie's, where I had been invited to stay, when there was a knock on the door. It was one of my neighbors - one of the few still talking to me. She said I had a call on the motel payphone. I walked down to the office and picked up the dangling receiver.

"Hello, Mister Lawless. I've got some information for you," a male voice said.

"Who's this?" I asked suspiciously.

"Never mind that. I'm just a concerned citizen. A good friend of yours told me you were working on the Bobby Dolan case. I saw him just before he was murdered. He told me something that might be very helpful, but I can't tell you over the phone. Do you know where the Paradise Club is, in town?"

"Sure, down by the river, under the bridge," I replied.

"Good, meet me there in half an hour."

"Who is this? I'll need more time."

"A half an hour," insisted the voice, and hung up.

The 'Paradise' is a small dance club catering to the college crowd. It's located downtown behind the main street, where the river flows beneath a stone bridge leading to the railroad station and the docks beyond.

I called Suzie and told her I was following up a lead, then headed to the club.

I got there ten minutes early and cased the joint. The place was mobbed. As I watched the college girls wiggling their asses on the dance floor, I kept an eye on the door, looking for the person I was there to meet. I also scanned the room for anyone resembling a 250 pound knife-wielding maniac.

I ordered a drink from the waitress. I had just finished paying for it when a young blonde wearing pink short-shorts and a halter-top approached me. She had high-heels and legs that looked like they went on forever.

"Could you please help me?" she asked quickly. "Just pretend you're my husband. There's a couple of creeps who've been bothering me all night and I told them I was meeting my husband to get rid of them. Just pretend we're married, OK?" she pleaded.

"I don't have a ring," I answered.

"It doesn't matter," she replied

"Don't you think I'm kind of old for you?" I asked. "They won't believe a young chick like you is married to an older guy like me. Why don't you find someone your own age to play with?"

"You don't look that old," she observed. "And anyway, to scare them I said you were a mafia guy, and you look just like one."

"Gee, thanks," I said, uncertain whether I liked the comparison or not. "Well, dear, nice to meet you. Want a drink?" I asked, getting into my role. Perhaps she was the one who had called me, although the voice on the phone was male.

"No, dear," she said playfully. "I know where there's a party. Want to go? Come on."

Thinking she might be taking me to the person that called me, I followed her outside.

"Where's your car?" she asked.

Pointing it out, I followed her over and opened the passenger door for her. The plastic seat cover made a pleasant squeaking sound as she slipped into the front seat.

I got behind the wheel wondering where this was going to lead. As I did, I noticed two rather seedy looking individuals eyeing us with hostile glances. They were lounging against the side of a building on the other side of the street. I suspected they might be the ones who had been bothering her.

"Do you have information for me?" I inquired.

"There's a big party going on at the base. I live there. We can talk there. Let's go."

"I don't think so. I'm afraid they won't let me onto the base. I'm, eh, not exactly liked around there. Why can't we talk here? Are you with the one who called me?"

"Don't worry, I know a way to get in," she cooed cheerfully, wiggling around in her seat to face me and ignoring my question for a second time. "Come on. let's go."

I figured I'd play along to see if I could find anything out. My instincts told me it was probably a set-up. There was a chance, however, she might take me to the informant. Pulling out of the parking space, I headed through town toward the base living quarters.

After a short while, she directed me to turn left off the main highway, onto a little used lane, then along a dirt road that ran up a bluff overlooking the lake. This was several miles below the area where Mary and I had entered, on a part of the base reserved for the top brass and their families.

She had me park the car in a bare spot on the side of the road near the top of the bluff. The night was brightly lit by an almost full moon. It shimmered off the water thirty feet below. It was warm, with a cool breeze from the lake. I almost expected some guy to jump out of the bushes and attack me. I'd be ready for him. I had my swords in the back seat.

"Are you with the guy who called me?" I asked. "Do you have information about Bobby Dolan? He told you something?"

She looked at me quizzically.

"Heh?" she said finally. "I don't know what you're talking about."

"You and your friend didn't call me earlier?"

"No, I just met you."

"OK, I'm sorry. Why don't you let me take you home?"

"I live here. I know a way to slip in. We can walk from here."

She slurred her words slightly. Her breath smelled heavy of rum and cokes.

"I don't think so," I said. "Why don't you go? I'm getting too old to sneak into military bases. Next time they catch me they're liable to shoot me on the spot. Anyway, I don't like parties."

"Ah, come on, no one's going to shoot you as long as you're with me. We'll have fun," she promised. She sat pouting. Her long, tanned legs stretched out before her. "I lied," she confessed finally. "There's no party. I have a friend who lives in one of the houses up here. When he's away, he lets me take care of the place for him. Sometimes, when I meet someone I really like, I let them come and keep me company. It's so dark and lonely up there."

"I bet someone could get into a lot of trouble with a little girl like you," I observed.

"Yes, but its very nice trouble," she replied, with a seductive smile.

If I played my cards right, I thought to myself, this could be my lucky night. From all accounts, this was where Tunny and Dene lived.

Then again, I could end up in the brig for trespassing on government property for a second time, not to mention corrupting a minor. For all I knew, she could have been the base commander's daughter.

"How old are you, anyway?" I inquired.

"How old do you think I am?" she asked back.

"Oh, about fifteen."

She looked insulted and got out of the car.

"I'm almost twenty," she informed me indignantly, slamming the door shut with a bang.

"Oh, excuse me! I wasn't that far off than, was I?".

"How old are you," she asked.

"Twenty-six," I answered, as if I was old enough to be her father.

"That's not that old," she said. "My boyfriend's way older than that."

She sauntered to the front of the car and threw her sweater on the hood. Laying on it, she stretched across it like a hunting trophy. The moonlight peeking through the treetops splashed on her body like pale, filtered rays of sun. Her long blonde hair spilled across the faded maroon of the car like silken honey.

"Imagine how it would look if you drove through town with me on your hood," she said from the front of the car.

"I don't think we'd get very far," I replied.

I couldn't take my eyes off her. She certainly was uninhibited, probably horny to boot. I guess if I looked like that I'd be horny too.

I got out of the car and walked across the road to look at the view. She slid off the hood and joined me.

"Whose house did you say this was?" I asked. "You're not the general's daughter are you?"

"No, silly. This base doesn't have a general, just a colonel, and the old goat doesn't have any kids. His wife died a few years ago. If you ask me, he probably poisoned her," she confided. "It's my boyfriend's house. He's a colonel, too. His name is Ed. Come on."

Taking my hand, she pulled me back across the road and onto a small path, which led further up through the trees to the top of the ridge. I followed, much against my better judgment. After hearing the name, I wondered if it was Ed Tunny she was talking about. I knew I had to go and find out.

She walked quickly up the dark, sloping path to a gate in the chain-link fence. It was padlocked. To my amazement she took out a key and unlocked it.

"Come on!" she squealed. "Hurry up!"

"Nifty," I said, following slowly. "How'd you get the key?"

"I told you, I have friends in high places."

She continued up the path, through a patch of leafy green willow trees with silver bark, to the top of the hill. I followed like a mongrel in heat.

We were in a large field of long, yellow grass, with a spectacular view of the lake below. A well-kept lawn bordered the field. The yard swept down a slope to a spacious two-story brick house, with a colonial entrance. The yard was interrupted briefly by an Olympic-size swimming pool. It was obviously the home of someone with wealth. It didn't look like your typical military style dwelling. It was more like the custom-built mansion of a mafia boss.

"Wow!" I said in surprise. "That's some spread. Are you sure we should be doing this?"

"Trust me," she said disarmingly. "I come here all the time. And anyway, Ed, the guy who owns the place, is away on official business. He's away all the time."

Was she talking about Colonel Ed Tunny? I wondered.

I followed her across the lawn and over the tiled patio that ran along the pool, to the house. We came to a sliding glass door that led to a stone-floored inner patio. She unlocked the door with another key, slid it open, and walked in.

"There, scaredy-pants, does that make you feel better? Would I have a key if I wasn't supposed to be here?"

"I guess not," I conceded. "Now who are you, anyway? I'd at least like to know who I'm married to. And you'd better be nice to me. Remember, I'm a Mafia guy, and you know how we treat our women."

"Ooh! I'm really scared of the big bad handsome man," she cooed, putting her hands up in mock terror and leaning toward me with her tongue sticking out.

"You should be," I said sternly, turning serious. This is where the lecture comes in. "For all you know I could be the guy that's been going around killing all those people. He murdered a young girl right here on this base not that long ago. You should be more careful."

She laughed.

"Oh, I knew you were OK. I know who you are. I've seen you around town. You're the one who found Major Stienman. Your name was in the paper. They questioned you and let you go. That kind of clears you, doesn't it?"

"You seem to know a lot about me. You have me at a disadvantage, young lady."

"Good," she giggled. "I like having the advantage over older men, though you're only six years older than me. That's not that bad."

"I'm too told for you.

"You're just right. I like them just about your age, especially when they're strong looking and well preserved."

"You think I'm well preserved, do you? I'll show you something well preserved," I said under my breath.

"What?" she asked, opening the inner door to an elegantly-furnished living area.

"Never mind," I responded, surveying the room.

She walked across the plush carpet as if she owned the place. Standing at a wet bar, she switched on the lights and opened the liquor cabinet. An expensive Italian cupboard with rose-tinted, curved-glass doors stood against the opposite wall. Next to it was a large, ornate fireplace. If this was Tunny's house, he sure lived well, too well for a government employee, no matter what the rank.

"So whose house is this?" I asked, standing at the entranceway.

"Let's just say a friend's, and leave it at that."

She poured herself a snifter full of very expensive Cognac.

"The least you can do is tell me whose whiskey we're drinking. Your father isn't Colonel Ed Tunny is he?"

"No, my father's a sergeant. We live on the other side of the base. Ed is my boyfriend. He's rich. He had this place especially built just for him. He's kinda old, but he's not that bad for someone his age, and he's very nice to me."

"I bet. How nice for you both." I was starting to get the picture. "So Tunny's your sugar-daddy, eh?"

"Yeah, why, are you jealous?" she asked coyly.

"Hardly," I lied, taking the glass of deep brown liquid she handed me.

"Why?" she asked in a hurt tone of voice. "Don't you find me attractive?"

"Sure, in a lollipop sort of way."

"What's that supposed to mean?" she inquired, with a frown wrinkling her brow.

"Nothing, just that I'd as soon lick you as talk to you."

I couldn't tell if she was offended or turned on. Neither could she. She shrugged and walked into one of the rooms that opened off the spacious, high-ceilinged living area.

"Come on in!" she called. "Maybe you can lick this off me."

I went to the door and looked in, the glass of Cognac in my hand. I was getting more nervous the deeper I got into the house, but that didn't stop me.

She knelt over a low, round, mirror-topped table, on which she had emptied a packet of white powder. Cocaine, insidious Cocaine!

I didn't want any part of this scene. It was bad enough being here like this, but the presence of illegal drugs was another matter entirely. I had already had enough bad experiences with the stuff to last me a lifetime. As much as I was intrigued at the opportunity of checking Tunny's place out, I thought it was about time to leave.

"Come on, try some," she encouraged, taking a snoot full up her cute turned-up nose with a whoosh. "This stuff is great."

"No thanks! That shit'll mess up your brain and I haven't got any to spare."

She just laughed at me and did up the remaining lines of white death.

"I'd better be going. It's getting late," I said nervously, turning and walking back into the living room.

Putting my glass on the bar, I started to leave the way I came in.

"Wait! Don't be such an old fuddy-duddy," she protested. "The fun's just beginning."

"I can see that. That's why I'm leaving," I told her, going out through the glassed-in, jungle-like patio.

She followed me out.

"Does your sugar-daddy get drugs for you?" I asked casually.

She ignored my question and asked one of her own.

"Want to go swimming?"

"I didn't bring my suit," I replied.

"Who needs a suit," she said, abruptly pulling her halter-top over her head. "I always go skinny-dipping here at night. No one can see."

I looked around nervously, noticing the high, well-kept hemlock hedge surrounding the spacious yard.

"Yeah, famous last words," I said.

She walked over to a lounge chair and slipped out of her tiny pink shorts. She had nothing on underneath.

"You coming?" she asked, as she dove into the pool and swam across it on her back, giving new meaning to the phrase 'skinny dipping'.

I stood there like a fool and watched her swim back and forth. She obviously enjoyed showing off her body as much as I enjoyed watching it. Finally climbing out of the pool, she shook her hair back and forth like a movie queen. I obediently brought her a towel and wrapped it around her shoulders.

"Thanks," she said gratefully, shivering slightly in the chilly night air. "I need my drink."

She rapped the towel around herself and we went back into the house.

"So, where do you get the drugs?" I asked again, joining her. "I wouldn't mind having a good connection like that."

She ignored me and went into the side room again to do more coke. I sipped my drink at the bar and tried to get her to spill the beans on Tunny. I was getting more paranoid by the second. This situation was sure to lead to trouble. I felt things closing in on me. Information or no, I had a strong impulse to leave while the going was still good.

She sat on a sofa in the small side room getting high, wearing nothing but the towel. Between the booze, which she drank like water, and the drugs, which she sucked up her nose like a Hoover, she was getting bombed out of her gourd. I was finally getting up to leave, when she stood and went over to the stereo system. Putting on a loud, rhythmic rock tune, she flung off her towel and started dancing to the music.

Well, maybe I won't leave quite yet, I thought as she twisted and twirled provocatively in front of me to the wild beat.

"Come on!" she shouted over the music. "Don't you know how to dance?"

She started twirling in front of me like a whirling Dervish, arms over her head, hair flying back and forth. Then she slowly sank to the floor and passed out. I stared at her serpentine form for a few seconds as she lay there. Then my fatherly instincts took over and I gently tried to rouse her.

"Hey, cutie, time to call it a night. What do you say? Why don't you let me put you to bed?"

I nudged her gently and tried to pull her to a sitting position.

"Mmm," she moaned, opening her eyes. She looked at me blankly with a faint smile on her lips.

"Come on, honey," I said, raising her to her feet. She tried to stand, groaned, then keeled over and threw-up. I moved out of the way just in time to avoid getting splattered and almost got sick myself.

Managing to get her to the bathroom, I stuck her head over the john until she was done emptying the contents of her stomach. Then I laid her on the sofa in the side room. The smell of booze and barf on her breath made her less than appealing. I threw a blanket over her to protect her from the chill night air and left the room.

As I walked toward the exit, I passed a stairway leading to the second floor. Being in Tunny's house presented an opportunity I couldn't pass up, despite the risk. In for a penny, in for a pound, I always say. I might never get this chance again.

I bounded up the stairs two at a time to explore the upstairs rooms. I wasn't sure what I was looking for, but I had a vague hope I'd find a piece of evidence linking Tunny to one of the recent drug related murders.

I searched the master bedroom and what appeared to be guestrooms, through drawers and closets, without finding anything of interest. Lastly, I examined the room at the top of the stairs, a small den or office.

A desk sat against the wall facing a window looking toward the rear of the house. Switching on a desk lamp, I started looking through the contents of the desk. It contained personal papers, bills, receipts, and bank statements, but nothing out of the ordinary. I studied the bank statements in more detail.

Then I found it, a bank deposit slip for $25,000 from NSR Corporation. Bingo! I almost jumped for joy. Here it was, my hard evidence linking someone from the base with Dolan and Laplace, and the whole drug smuggling operation.

Hearing something downstairs, I shut off the light and listened. Everything was quiet. It was time to go. I stuck the slip into my pocket. I knew it probably wouldn't be admissible in a court of law, since it had been obtained illegally. However, if I left it, it might be gone by the time the authorities could search the place. That is if I could even convince someone to believe me and get a warrant.

I tiptoed back downstairs, listening for any sound. Perhaps the girl had woken up. All was silent. Walking toward the rear entrance, I glanced at a wall clock. It was half-past twelve midnight. Passing the side room where I had left the girl, I looked in and gasped.

I couldn't believe my eyes. I doubted my senses as well as my sanity. There, hanging by her ankles like a dead deer, was the young girl who had been skinny-dipping and dancing in front of me only moments before. She was naked and covered with blood. A large Bowie knife protruded from her chest.

Chapter 23

Day 18 (early a.m.)

For a moment after spotting the girl I stood in shock, frozen in my tracks. Then I panicked. Turning abruptly, I ran blindly, smack into someone who had been sneaking up behind me. We went crashing to the floor in a heap. He was a tall individual in an air force blue uniform. The gun he had been carrying flew across the hardwood floor of the hallway.

Landing on top of him, I reacted quickly. Before he could move, I hit him with a vicious forearm to the forehead, shoving the back of his skull into the floor with a crack. His head bounced up like a basketball and I hit him again. He was out for the count.

Before I could get off him, I was lifted from behind and thrown head first, hard against the opposite wall. I felt like I'd just dived into two inches of water head first. I hit the wall with a teeth-jarring thud, pile-driven into the hard plasterboard. I landed on the floor, stunned and dazed.

I had just enough senses intact to see my attacker's feet coming at me as I lay scrunched up on the floor. As he stepped toward me to finish me off, I tangled his legs up in mine. Putting pressure on opposite sides of his knee and ankle, I twisted. His legs were strong, but he was unprepared for my move. All his weight was on the forward knee. It buckled and he went down.

Before he could recover, I stiffened a heel into his down turned jaw. The kick had power. His head snapped back, but it only stunned him, giving me just enough time to get to my feet. As I did, I recognized, with a sinking feeling, that it was the same opponent I had faced on the beach in St. Petersburg. He must have killed the girl while I was upstairs.

I glanced around, looking for the gun, but there was no time to go for it, even if I had spotted it. The good news was that as long as the knife was stuck in that poor unfortunate girl, it wouldn't be stuck in me. The bad news was he was on his feet and coming at me.

Crouching down like a football player at the line of scrimmage, he ran up the hallway, arms outstretched as if he was blitzing the quarterback. I had the distinct impression that once this guy tackled me, I'd be out of the game for keeps. With his size and bulk, he looked like a charging bull coming at me. With no place to run and no place to hide, I did the only thing I could think of.

As he reached me, I stepped back and grabbed his arms. Then sitting on my heel, I rolled back and shoved my other foot straight up into his gut. Using his forward momentum, I threw him up and over my head like an acrobat. He was driven across the room and into the antique Italian cabinet, where he landed with a tremendous crash, shattering the rose-tinted glass.

As he got to his feet, apparently unhurt, I attacked, going straight at him, hard. Accelerating with a burst of speed, I delivered several well-aimed blows. I hit him in rapid succession - nose, eyes, temple, neck, throat - with punches, hand-swords, and leopard's paws. These are strikes designed for maximum stopping power to weak areas of the body, no matter how big and strong the opponent, but I was barely able to halt his forward motion.

He countered with surprising speed, throwing a powerful right-hook that sent me flying down the hall on my back. The punch split my left cheek like a cracked egg, and pretty near knocked me senseless. I wasn't seeing stars. I was seeing entire constellations.

I managed to wobble to my feet just as he was on me again. I met his attack staggering like a drunk, ducking under a whistling left that brushed my ear. I was reeling with pain, unable to breathe normally. I couldn't see straight and in a bad way. To add injury to insult, he picked me up and slammed me against the hearth, where I crashed amongst the various fireplace tools.

Even though I had slapped hard when I hit, and absorbed most of the impact along my arms, I was dazed when I landed. I could barely make him out through my blurred vision as he moved in on me. He hit me with a shoulder block as I tried to stand, and knocked me back against the wall. I kiei'd and kicked his knees. As he tried to grab me again, I kicked him in the groin. He let go and circled away to let his gonads settle, throwing a hard left in retaliation, which I ducked.

Bending my knees, I breathed deeply through my nose, drawing the air down to my diaphragm. Remembering my training, I called on the inner strength of the body, the chi, that internal force that all of us have, but few know how to control. The chi doesn't grow tired or weak. It cannot be touched or hurt. It does not dim with age. Strong and powerful, it is the eternal life-energy, only waiting within us to be tapped.

Keeping my knees bent, I relaxed almost to the point of closing my eyes. I cleared my mind even as he was upon me again. Stopping all thought, I remained focused in the moment. I became the reaction to his action, the emptiness to his force, the recoil to his fury. Using a combination of sticky-palm, aikido, and tai chi chuan techniques, I moved with him as if I was his shadow. I became the invisible opponent, there one minute, gone the next, avoiding his punches and kicks. I anticipated his slightest movement, instinctively, without thought. In this way, I kept him off balance and made myself difficult to handle, while I regained my wind and strength

He fought expertly, and was tossing me about pretty much at will. But I was faster than he was, and made him pay when he grabbed me. Although he hadn't been able to land a good punch after that first right-hook, I was still reeling from it. I couldn't take being flung against the wall much more.

His strength and agility was impressive. Using my speed, I went for his eyes, trying to jab my fingers into them and pluck them out. I stomped and kicked his ankles and knees as he attempted to grapple with me. Try as I might, however, I couldn't hurt him. He countered my moves expertly and seemed impervious to pain, his body hardened like tempered steel.

His powerful fists whipped through the air, missing my head by fractions of an inch. Straight hard hand strikes delivered to his head hardly dazed him, although I had cut him in places. My kicks had little effect against his well-muscled body.

He grunted with frustration and came at me again, fists swinging. I blocked and countered. He grabbed me, and before I could break the hold, lifted me up and slammed me to the floor again. I kiei'd loudly and slapped the ground. I thought he had broken my back. As he reached down to finish me off, I saw the poker from the fireplace lying nearby, where I had knocked it over in one of my nose dives. As he grabbed me, I swung it up and hit him square on the side of the head. Without stopping, I hit him again, harder, right on the temple. Then I hit him a third time, full force, cracking the side of his skull.

He fell backward stiffly and crumbled to the ground. Unbelievably, he was still conscious. Even more incredibly, he was getting to his feet. As he rose, I stepped in and stomped my heel into his face. My foot glanced off his chin and struck his exposed throat, full power. I wasn't trying to kill him, but I felt my heel crush his windpipe. I'll never forget the look on his face at that moment, when he realized what was happening. Then he laid still, his dead eyes staring at me, full of surprise.

I stood over him, ready to stomp him again, but he didn't move. It didn't look like he was breathing – how could he? That suited me just fine.

Turning, I looked about the room. Somewhere behind me there was a gun. What I didn't expect to see was someone pointing it at my head.

"Don't move!" the man yelled. "Hold it right there!"

I dropped the poker and put up my hands. I was staring at the seeming huge black muzzle of a luger. It stared back at me unblinking.

"Don't shoot!" I pleaded. "He's the killer! He did it!"

I was breathing hard, my left knee shaking wildly.

"Shut-up and don't move!" the man barked. I didn't like the way he was looking at me. He had Colonel's insignias on his shoulders. The hair on the back of my neck stood to attention.

"Is he alive?" he asked, jabbing the gun in the direction of the motionless figure on the floor.

It seemed like a direct order. I knelt over the unconscious form and checked for a pulse.

"I think so," I said, standing up and sliding imperceptibly closer to the man with the gun.

"Don't move!" he shouted again. "I'd just as soon blow your head off as look at you."

I wondered how my opponent could still be breathing after his trachea had been crushed. His skull should have been cracked, the brain seriously damaged from the poker strike to the temple. He should have been in a coma, suffocating, his trachea swollen and closed. Yet he was breathing evenly, although with shallow, short breaths. As I pondered these things, the uniformed man ordered me to help carry my unconscious adversary out of the house.

We carried him back across the yard in the pitch-darkness toward the gate. The moon, which had been bright when I arrived, had disappeared behind dark storm clouds. The wind, which had been nothing but a breeze as I stood on the bluffs, was blowing cold and damp. It whipped the uncut yellow grass of the field like a blanket. I could hear sirens in the distance coming in our direction.

Carrying the killer down a path to the beach, we came to a landing. There was a small boat anchored near the shore. Everything was a blur. Then something hit the back of my skull and all went black.

Interlude

Small Boat Landing, Lake Champlain, That Morning

Each breath was a battle. The air came in small, burning gasps. He lay on a cushion in the small boat's cabin, covered with a thin blanket. Concentrating on his breathing, he forced air into his lungs, pushing it out the same way. He should have been dead. Only his exceptional conditioning and superior training saved him. He had clenched his jaw at the moment of impact, pulling in his neck and pushing his tongue to the roof of his mouth. In this way, he was able to draw his windpipe in behind a thick sheave of muscle. As it was, the blow had caused serious damage. Yet, he lived.

If we had 'Jim', he thought, things would have been different. Then we'd see who would die. Yes, then we'd see.

Chapter 24

Day 18 (Noon)

I woke sometime later that day to the swaying of the boat and the creaking of mooring lines. My skull felt like it had been cracked in twelve places from the butt of the pistol they hit me with when they got me onboard.

My mouth felt like a little furry creature had spent the night in it. When I tried to open my eyes, I was blinded by excruciating pain. The room spun violently. I almost passed out again. Suppressing the urge to vomit, I looked around. It took a few moments to remember where I was and how I had gotten here.

I was lying on my stomach, with my arms tied behind me. When I tried to move my legs, I discovered they were bound as well. I calmed myself, taking long deep breaths and letting the air out slowly, relaxing my muscles as I did so. Concentrating on my breathing, I ignored the pain in my head, which was agonizing. I tried to counter the waves of terror that swept over me and dispel the fear of impending death. I worried that some irreparable damage had already been done, and had to pee so bad I could taste the bile in my throat.

Slowly taking damage control, I felt a little better when I determined that I was all right. Both eyes were still working. My limbs were intact. And all my faculties were more or less functioning. After making sure I wasn't bleeding, at least not badly, I began to relax. The smell of coffee and toast coming from the ship's tiny galley made my dry mouth water.

Just when I succeeded in recovering my composure, my captor paid me a visit. He was the same one I had fought earlier, the one who had butchered all those people. His head was bandaged. How could he still be alive? Had he come for revenge? I felt an instant revulsion, like some reptilian carnivore had just slipped into the room. I stilled my fear. Playing possum, I lay still.

He prodded and probed me roughly, trying to rouse me. I continued to play dead, hoping he would get bored and go away. Just as he was turning me over onto my back, someone came into the boat's cabin. My tormentor left, kicking me in the ribs for spite on his way out.

He should have been dead. The stomp to the throat should have crushed his windpipe. I hit him with a poker on the temple, for God's

185

sake. He at least should have been permanently incapacitated. What was he, some sort of robot?

As I lay recovering from the latest ordeal, I heard their muffled conversation through the thin wall of the bulkhead. From what I could make out, it didn't sound good, especially the part they had planned for me. Whatever their reasons for wanting to bring me back onto the base, it couldn't be very healthy for my future. It appeared they were going to blame me for the girl's death. My wallet and watch were missing. They were probably at the scene of the crime. And what was this about a day of reckoning and destruction? What was going on now?

None of that mattered. All that was important now was staying alive, survival, and it didn't look like it was going to be that easy.

I must have passed out, because the next thing I remember is waking up. The lake was completely calm. By the temperature of the room and the light filtering through the small portholes, it appeared to be late in the afternoon.

I rolled over onto my back and called out. I was sick and thirsty.

"Help! Is anybody there?" I yelled, hoping someone would hear me and call the cops. I'd take my chances with them. I didn't have many options. "Help, anybody. Help! Call the police."

I heard someone stir in the ship's cabin. The hatch door leading to my prison cell slid open with a snap, revealing my abductor.

"Shut up in here," he snarled at me. In the light of day I saw he was about six-six or seven, in his mid-twenties like me. He must have weighed at least 250 pounds. He looked like a professional wrestler, a very disturbed one. There was a weird maniacal glint in his eyes. One of them was higher than the other, as if his face had been hit by a bus. His head looked dented where I had struck him with the poker. I felt sick to my stomach at the sight of him, but ignored the feeling.

"How about a drink of water? It's about a hundred degrees in here," I said, trying to sound in control.

"How about I p-p-piss down your throat," he said in a raspy, menacing tone. The thought made my skin crawl, but I laughed loudly in defiance.

"Well, if it isn't the big, tough killer of little girls and helpless women. Yeah, you mother-fucking fairy, you're really brave when people are tied up and defenseless." I said this with all the venom I could muster, which, given the circumstances, was considerable.

He looked at me with surprise. He probably wasn't used to getting abuse from his helpless, hog-tied victims.

"I whipped your ass good," I continued. "That's twice by my count."

"S-s-s-shut up!" he blurted finally.

"OK-K-K, dimwit," I taunted. "I'll tell you what. You untie me and I'll let you try again. What d'ya say, tough guy? Three out of five."

"S-s-shut up!" he yelled again, kicking me sharply in the side.

I could see this tack was getting me nowhere, but I could think of nothing better to do, so I charged on.

"Yeah, you're good when your opponents can't fight back, but you're nothing but a punk. I kicked your ass. You suck. You can't beat me." I crowed.

"S-s-shut up!" he repeated, repeating the kick, as well, this time to my face. I dodged my head to the left, just avoiding the heel of his boot, which brushed my ear.

I thought perhaps I could get him riled enough to untie me and continue where we left off the previous night. I may have gone too far. Suddenly, he knelt over me, digging his knee into my groin. His breath reeked like dead flesh. I expected to be throttled or worse at any moment. Instead of ringing my neck, he deftly proceeded to gag me with a wide strip of packaging tape, which he applied unsparingly to my big mouth.

He then turned abruptly and went out of the room, slamming the sliding door shut behind him.

The seed had been sown. Doubt, frustration, anger, guilt, only time would tell if it would bear fruit. I didn't have very much of it left. My own emotions were overwhelming me.

I panicked. Fear overcame me. I struggled against the unyielding ropes that bound me. I twisted and jerked like a bulldogged steer, all to no avail. Soon I lay spent and exhausted, panting and puffing through my gag, on the floor of the tiny cabin cruiser.

I fought to regain my composure and retain my sanity. The ropes, tied tightly, cut off the circulation in my arms and legs. My mouth was taped, which made breathing difficult and yelling for help impossible. I could feel the fear coiled beneath the surface of my mind, serpent-like, ready to squeeze me in its grip.

I tried to control my breathing again and clear my mind. It helped. I was able to calm myself and concentrate on the situation at hand, neither anticipating nor imagining the bad things that could happen to me. In this way, I remained centered in the moment.

Examining my surroundings for the first time in detail, I looked for anything I could use to facilitate my escape, but found nothing. I was on the floor of a small area at the bow of the boat, wedged between two sleeping platforms, barely able to move.

The boat bobbed up and down in the gently undulating lake. The sounds of the world came dimly to my ears. It mingled with the splashing of the waves against the hull, and the cries of the seagulls, a constant humming that threatened to lull me back to oblivion.

Panic threatened to return with each labored breath. In my predicament, I tried to recall all I had learned on controlling one's fear, on overcoming one's weaknesses and self-imposed limits.

I visualized the various forms and kata I knew, trying to simulate the hand and foot moves as much as possible, while hog-tied on the floor. I twisted and turned my ankles and wrists, and was able to keep the blood flowing in my arms and legs. Straining at intervals, isometrically, on the ropes that bound me, I was able to generate heat in my muscles.

Even the creature that killed all those people had a mother and a father. What did they do to him? I thought about the recent conversation I had overheard earlier that day between my captors. Maybe there was something there I could use. I had to find a weak point, a crack in my adversary's obviously brittle sanity. Either that or I would soon be food for the arthropods. The only consolation I had was that they must have needed me for something. Otherwise I'd already be dead, but I wasn't looking forward to whatever that something was.

My thoughts drifted, despite my efforts to control them, like slow moving clouds, to the valley of my own life. Looking at it now as it passed before me, it seemed so empty and meaningless. I bequeathed nothing to anyone, nothing but pain. My mind drifted to my mother and how I had never really mourned her death, but instead carried it around inside me like a burr. I was overwhelmed with sorrow. As I fought to regain my composure, I was bombarded with fits of dizziness and nausea. I oscillated between hope and despair in this way until my captor came back.

He stood over me gloating. The last thing I remember is his big fist coming down on my head.

Chapter 25

Day 18 (p.m.)

I woke with a start. It was dark outside. The whole left side of my face was swollen and racked with pain, where my assailant had split my cheek open. The lumps on the side of my head, one for each of his large, bony knuckles, throbbed and pulsated. My ribs hurt where he had kicked them. I ached all over from being tied-up for hours on the floor. At some point while I was out, my hands had been tied in front of me. I had also relieved myself. Now besides being uncomfortable and in pain, I was wet and smelled like urine. Shaking with fits of nausea, I could barely breathe. On top of it all, I was overcome with guilt. That young girl would still be alive if it hadn't been for me.

It looked like I had messed up for the last time. Maybe it was just as well, but this was not exactly the kind of ending I had in mind. If I was going to die violently, I wanted to die while making love to a beautiful woman, not tied up on the floor of some stinking boat, slit open like a hog. I really did it this time. Death was bearing down on me like a locomotive, the huge wheels about to crush my empty skull, and I had done just about everything in my power to put myself right smack in front of it.

I fought the panic, the pain, and the fatigue. I knew my only hope of staying alive was to keep my head. Somehow I had to gain an advantage, play on this guy's weaknesses. He must have had plenty of them to be such a sick puppy.

Speak of the devil. My captor came in at that moment armed with a nasty looking machete. Bending down over me, he raised the wide blade over his head. For a moment I thought he was going to behead me right there on the spot. Instead, he swiftly cut the ropes binding my legs and ripped the tape from my mouth. Lifting me effortlessly to my feet, he looped the end of a short rope around my neck. Then he proceeded to pull me violently through the small 'head' and galley, out onto the rear deck of the boat.

Without stopping, he yanked me forward. Swinging me around by the neck, he threw me over the stern of the boat. I thought I was going in the drink, but I landed on a small dinghy instead, where I fell forward onto the front of the boat. The killer jumped in behind me, still holding the rope and the machete.

"Sit," he ordered as I turned around and faced him.

I did as I was told, and managed to sit on the small seat at the bow of the dinghy. I briefly contemplated diving into the water, but realized I wouldn't have a chance with a rope around my neck.

The murderer tucked the machete into his belt. Then he started pulling at the oars, moving us away from the boat. As we rowed ashore in the gathering darkness, I realized time was running out. Once they got me on the base again, it would be over. The only chance I had was to somehow take care of this guy while we were still alone.

"Hey, you must have had it pretty rough," I said. "What did they do to you, anyway?"

"Shut up!" he snarled.

"Don't you know they're just using you?" I replied. "Once they get what they want and no longer need you, you'll be discarded like the others."

"I t-t-told you to s-s-shut up!" he said ominously. "It's n-n-not going to make a b-b-bit of difference where you're g-g-going."

"I heard the way he talked to you," I continued. "Are you going to let him treat you like that? What kind of sniveling coward are you?"

He stopped rowing and pulled the machete from his belt, staring at me with a weird half-smile. The look froze my blood. My throat contracted like a cartoon character's. I could see this line of attack was getting me nowhere, yet I pressed on.

As he resumed rowing us ashore, I taunted him, forcing bravado into my voice I didn't in the least bit feel. Remembering the conversation I had overheard earlier, I told him that Tunny was right.

"You failed. I beat you."

I paused for a moment waiting for him to do something, hoping he would make a mistake. He said nothing, but continued to glare at me. I went on.

"Don't you want to know if you could beat me?" I asked him. "Now's your chance. Just you and me."

"You think you're so g-g-g-good," he retorted. "My training was for real, n-n-not some yuppie bullshit. You t-t-think you're t-t-t-tough? You just got l-l-lucky. If I had had Jim, t-t-things would have been d-different."

"You mean your knife? You gave it a name. You really are a sick fuck."

As I said this, the dinghy lurched ashore, grating to a stop on the smooth wet sand. He looked at me malevolently and picked up the machete.

"Get out," he ordered.

I remained sitting and continued taunting him.

Standing up, he pulled me out of the boat. I grabbed the rope to take the pressure off my neck, but could not resist his strength. I was being led like a sheep to the slaughter. I had to gain the initiative, make my opponent react to my moves, rather than allow him to follow out his own plans unhindered.

We were at the small beach area that served as a boat landing. He told me to start walking up the dirt road where my car was still parked. The sky was overcast and inky black.

Suddenly, there was a glimmer of hope. It was almost too good to be true. The previous morning I had worked out with my swords in the park as usual. I had left them in the back seat of my car. Could they still be there? I might still get out of this yet.

It was my last chance. It was now or never.

We were walking up the road to the bluffs and the base above. I was in the lead. He guided me by nudging my back with the sharp tip of the machete. We were not far from where my car was parked. I stopped abruptly and turned. Holding the rope with both hands, I started pulling away from him as hard as I could. He yanked me back toward him. As he did, I leaped forward with a burst of speed. He pulled me right into him, hard. I hit him square with a flying thrust kick to the chest. He wasn't expecting the move.

He took a few steps back, but didn't fall. Instead, he swung the machete down at my head. I darted out of range, pulling the line taunt. The sharp blade slashed through the rope, missing my neck by a fraction of an inch. Without stopping, I ran toward my car.

I didn't get far. He caught me before I was halfway there. I turned to face him, back peddling rapidly and dodging the machete as it slashed at me from all angles. The sword made a whooshing sound as it cut through the thick night air, a hair's breath from my head.

I dived away from one strike and ducked another as I ran. Trying to avoid the blade, I circled around toward the parked car, where I hoped to find my sword. He had already cut me in several places, my arm, side, and thigh. Only flesh wounds, scratches really, which I didn't even feel until later. But the sight of my own blood and the knowledge of how much more of it there was to spill almost made me lose my senses.

My opponent's strokes were expertly delivered. He used minimum arm motion, slashing the machete with just his wrist in a twirling fashion. He didn't telegraph his strikes or leave himself open to counterattack. He wasn't making many mistakes, and with my hands bound in front of me, I was limited in what I could do. I had to get to the car. Even with my hands tied, I'd be able to handle the two-handed sword. Getting there, however, was not going to be easy.

He missed with a down stroke. I grabbed his arm with both hands as he reached the bottom of his downward motion, and tried to lock it. He was too strong and fast, however, and swept me aside with a powerful backhand. Then the twirling blade swept down again, missing my nose by a fraction of an inch as I arched backward out of the way.

I tried kicking his arm with a reverse crescent kick as it passed by me, hoping to knock the machete out of his hand. The kick landed square and hard on his wrist but had no effect. His arms were like steel bars.

The wide flat blade kept up its incessant whirling movement, like an out of control buzz saw, as it came toward me. Things were getting bleak. It was only a matter of time before I was chopped liver.

The machete whisked by my head. I was starting to learn his pattern. Timing was critical.

He was getting careless, probably overconfident. He came in with another downward stroke, with all his weight on his forward foot. Using an aikido technique, I stepped in, catching his arm by the wrist with both hands. Then I pivoted sharply, swinging his arm out and down, using his momentum to throw him foreword much faster and farther than he intended to go. The lock I had on his wrist threatened to break it if he resisted. Instead, he went with it and flipped head over heels over my shoulder, landing hard on his back.

My luck had held. I had the initiative, but I wouldn't have it for long. He was getting to his feet. I tried kicking him to keep him from rising, but he used the machete to good effect to keep me at bay.

Deciding it was now or never, I made a mad dash for my car. I had about a five-foot lead on him. I wasn't sure if that was going to be enough.

Reaching the car, I threw open the driver's side door and dove in and over the front seat into the back. As I did, the machete came down, slicing the seat-back upholstery where my leg had just been.

I grabbed frantically for my sword. It was still there. I got it up just in time to block another slashing stroke from the machete. Leaning over the front seat, my assailant stabbed and hacked at me in the confined space like a crazed wind-up toy. There was a dull, mechanical look in his eyes.

I blocked another blow, then another. Somehow I managed to open the rear door and slither out. At the same time, I pulled the blade sharply from its sheath. It sang with a metallic ring as it came out.

On standing, I noticed that the heel of my right boot had been hacked off. Another half inch and it would have been my foot.

The killer backed out of the car and ran around the front with a hideous yell. I met him beside the car with a double-handed attack of my own. Metal clanged on metal as the blades clashed. The lone street lamp was the only witness to our deadly duel.

Attack and parry, thrust and counter-thrust, we circled each other looking for an opening. Using both hands, I wielded the long samurai sword like a piece of balsam. Whirling and stabbing with lightning strokes, I made the blade quiver. He held the machete in one hand, slashing the flat sword at me with wide, windmill-like motions so fast it looked like a propeller.

As big and strong and fast as he was, he didn't have a very wide variety of moves. He was limited in the ways he came at me with the weapon. This made him predictable. I was able to frustrate him, countering his attacks while striking him with mine. I was slowly backing him up, the advantage of the longer blade starting imperceptibly to tell.

I could read the doubt beginning to show in his eyes at the surprise of finding himself fighting an armed man. I attacked harder. Throwing caution to the wind, I flew at him with a loud kiai. Blocking his strike with the blade of my sword, I cut his upper arm. He stepped back, but showed no sign of pain, only annoyance. Blood spurted from the wound. I came in instantly with a double strike to his opposite side, high then low, hitting him on the outside of the thigh. Blood began to seep out of his leg as well. He stopped his attack, as if considering his next move.

In his uncertainty, I started to taunt him again.

"How's it feel? Weren't expecting a fair fight, were you?"

As I said this, I slashed at him with a downward stroke aimed at the top of his head. He sprang back and blocked it with his machete.

"You're just the loser I thought you were," I said.

I laughed at him. My insults affected him like blows. I could see him back up as if slapped by the words. Perhaps it reminded him of something from his past. He appeared confused and unsure of himself.

Then, without warning, he bellowed like an enraged bull, and charged me with a hard driving attack. Instead of trying to stop it, I stepped back and leaned away into a low side-stance, ducking under his blade. Then I sprang back in, extending my sword forward. He ran right onto it. Without hesitating, I thrust the blade all the way into his belly. It made a sickening sucking sound as it entered.

He screamed. It was a bone-chilling sound that I never want to hear again. Blood spurted from his mouth. I pulled the sword out quickly and stepped away, poised ready to strike again. I didn't have the stomach to jerk the blade across his abdomen to disembowel him as I'd been trained.

It was fortunate I moved out of the way because the killer still had the machete gripped tight in his hand. In a last desperate move, he swung the blade wildly, cutting the damp air twice with a wind-whipping sound, right where my neck had been only a second before. Then his legs buckled and he dropped to his hands and knees with a guttural sound, clutching his stomach. He looked like a sick three-legged dog. His black-handled weapon skidded across the sand to rest at my feet.

Looking up at me with anguish, he bellowed in rage and mortal pain. It sounded like a dying dog, howling its final, agonizing protest by the side of the road.

It looked for a moment as if he were going to try and come at me on all fours. Instead, he collapsed on his face with a muted grunt.

I kicked the machete out of reach and crouched ready, waiting for him to move again. He lay on his face, still as the grave, with not so much as a twitch. It didn't look like he was breathing, but I didn't care to get close enough to find out.

It was pitch-black outside the meager glow of the single forlorn street lamp, shining as if against its will. A low fog had come in from the water. It was rising up the wooded bluff that was the lakeshore at this point. It was starting to drizzle, small soft misty droplets like the light spray from a nozzle opened wide.

I was soaked to the bone. Wet sand stuck to me like tar. I wheezed like an old asthmatic, fighting for breath and shaking. Taking a silent inventory, I determined that all original body parts were still intact. No major arteries had been severed. I'd live to fight another day.

The realization of what I had just done hit me, causing me to shudder involuntarily with dry heaves in revulsion. I looked at my sword in disgust and threw it away into the darkness. I kept reminding myself that the guy was a cold-blooded killer. It was either him or me. I had no choice. I was lucky I wasn't the one lying there with his guts spilling out.

Suddenly, my adversary groaned and pushed himself up in a half pushup position. His knees were on the ground, arms extended in front of him. The earth beneath him was black with gore. With considerable effort, he managed to turn over onto his back. Then he collapsed again holding his belly. His mouth opened and closed like a dying fish. His eyes stared at the sky. The misty rain spattered on his dirt-covered face. He was trying to speak. I edged toward him cautiously, and leaned forward to listen.

"You won," he whispered. "You are a worthy opponent. It was meant to be."

"OK, just take it easy," I said sympathetically. "We'll get you some help. You'll be all right."

I knew it was a lie. The blood pouring between his fingers as they clutched at his dirt-spattered shirt told the truth.

"No," he gasped hoarsely. "You can still stop him. It's not too late. It was all a lie. It's over."

Dying had cured his stutter. He spoke clearly but softly.

"Don't try to talk," I told him, kneeling in the wet sand by his side.

"No. You must put an end to it. He killed my mother. You must stop him!"

"What do you mean? Stop what? What are you talking about?" I shook him urgently. It looked like he was succumbing to delirium from loss of blood.

"My Father...going to...bomb...Washington. Stop him!" He coughed up a glob of plasma-tinted phlegm as the blood and air seeped out of him.

I stared at him hardly believing my ears, but after the last few weeks, anything seemed possible. Or was he just delirious?

"Who? Who's going to do this? Where?" I asked.

I was still breathing hard from my exertions. My filthy cotton shirt clung to my wet skin like a cold plaster. I was sweating even though I felt chilled to the bone.

It was obvious he didn't have much time left. He'd lost enough blood to fill a carton of milk bottles and was losing more by the second.

His eyes glazed over. He started shivering violently. I couldn't feel sorry for him, not after what he had done. I didn't exactly feel elated either, kneeling there watching his life seep out of him. I looked around desperately for some means to summon assistance, but found nothing. We could have been on an uninhabited beach on the other side of nowhere. I felt so entirely alone.

For some reason I didn't want to leave him. I stayed there and held his hand. At least he didn't die alone, I gave him that. It was good that I did, for as he breathed his last breaths he told me more about what was transpiring. Then his voice faded away into a long, drawn out rattle and he was silent.

I stared at the inert figure for some time, losing all track of the passing minutes. I half expected him to start up again. I wondered what to do. It was late, probably after eleven, though I had no way of knowing. My watch and wallet were at the scene of the murder.

If what he told me was true - and pieced together with the scraps of conversation I had overheard on the boat, I had every reason to believe it was - I didn't have much time.

There was no one I could go to. My fingerprints and personal effects were all over the murder scene. In the eyes of the authorities, I was as good as convicted of the gruesome murder. By the time I got anyone to listen to me, whatever was supposed to happen would have occurred. I was sure I'd be shot on sight if found on the base.

It all seemed so hopeless. What was I to do? I had no will. My frazzled brain refused to order my weary limbs to move. I just sat there as immobile as the dead man lying before me in the drizzle.

At that moment the night woke up with the blare of sirens and flood lights. It sounded like the entire base was coming down the beach road. All I wanted to do was curl up in a hole and go to sleep. Instead, I was forced to take action, but how do you escape madness?

Chapter 26

Day 19 (12:00 a.m.)

Running up the path, back to the scene of the murder, I had a flash of déjà vu. This was the last place I wanted to go, but I didn't have many options. I hoped I'd find a place to hide. I was moving on pure instinct and adrenaline alone.

I had thrown my samurai sword away in a wave of disgust as I squatted in the sand next to my fallen opponent. The sight of the blood and gore on the blade made me retch. As I was about to run up the road to the path leading to the bluffs, I stopped at the last minute remembering that I still had my short sword in the car's backseat. It's the one traditionally reserved for ritual self-disembowelment, seppuku. I thought it might come in handy, for one thing or another. If all else failed, I could commit hari-kari.

Taking it from the car, I used the sageo of the scabbard to tie the short sword over my shoulder, handle up. The light one-and-a-half foot blade gave me an extra sense of security.

I walked rapidly up the trail in the darkness, feeling my way along cautiously. There were sirens behind me and dogs barking somewhere ahead. It sounded as if the entire base was on alert and converging on the area. I was trapped like a rat, which was fitting. I was born in the 'Year of the Rat' in the Chinese calendar. Those born in that year are said to have a knack for survival. I hoped it was true.

As I neared the fence a dog barked. The gate was just a short distance away. It was no longer padlocked and slightly ajar. Recalling what the killer told me, I stopped and listened. I could sense more than see someone crouched behind the bushes on the other side of the barrier. I waited as the dogs got closer. The illumination from the flashlights of the searchers came nearer. Time was running out. It sounded like a company of men were crashing up the path behind me. I had no place to go but forward.

Just when I thought I was about to be caught, a figure stood up from the shadows and abruptly moved away from the gate toward the rapidly approaching search party. The guards and dog concentrated on the lone figure that had materialized out of nowhere. While they did, I crawled on my hands and knees through the opened gate and across the field of tall, uncut grass. As I slipped through the gate, I heard the challenge of the guard and the sharp barking of a large dog.

"Halt! Who goes there?"

My blood turned to ice. I thought I was dead, but soon realized it was the figure from behind the bush they were talking to, not me. I was still safe and unseen.

Scurrying across the yard in the drizzle, I headed toward the rear of the house. Whatever was going on back at the fence had given me the opportunity I needed, as if it were all planned. I aimed to make the most of it.

As I reached the house, I saw the lights of patrol cars cruising the streets. The area was crawling with armed men and guard dogs. I was in the very place they wanted me to be, without a clue what to do.

My mind worked at quarter speed, as if I was in a trance. My head felt like it weighed half a ton. Fear gripped my throat like a vice, but I forced myself on and concentrated on my breathing.

Sneaking along the rear of the house, I crawled under some bushes to the first door I came to. It was the same one I had entered the previous night, or was it two nights ago. I had lost all track of time. The door was locked.

Continuing around the side of the dwelling, I came to another door. This one was open and led to the garage. I entered warily. It was pitch dark inside. I edged along the wall, feeling my way blindly as I went. My eyes soon adjusted to the half-light enough to make out a large sedan parked in the center of the floor. Everything was silent. The house appeared to be empty. I tried the door leading to the interior and found it locked from the inside.

From what I could put together, I was supposed to have been brought into the base and disposed of as the murderer. The guy hiding at the gate was probably waiting for us. He almost got caught himself and had to go confront the search party. It was a lucky break for me.

I made my way around to the rear of the parked vehicle, to the trunk. It was slightly ajar. I opened it and crawled in, closing it part way. I left it just wide enough to allow me to breathe and get out when I wanted to. I figured this was as good a place as any to hide. If I was lucky, I might be able to crawl out in a few hours and get away.

Despite what the killer had told me before he died, I didn't think there was anything I could do. First of all, I didn't quite believe him. It was too crazy. Even if it were true, how could I stop them on my own?

Who could I have gone to for help? Even Jerry would have been unable to come to my aid in time.

I closed my eyes and soon drifted off to a fitful, restless half-slumber, like the sleep of a war-weary soldier on the field of battle. Not so much sleep, as dropping from sheer exhaustion and the need to escape the horror of my life.

.

Interlude

The Boat Landing, Same Time

Daniel saw himself lying as if dead in the sand below him. No air passed his lungs. His heart had no beat. No blood flowed through his veins. His brain registered no activity. But he was there looking down, cocooned in forgetfulness, a soul without identity. He felt nothing. He floated in nothingness.

Then something disturbed his peace. At first it was just a vague annoyance, but it grew until it drove his mind to awareness. Someone was kicking him. His consciousness jumped back into his body.

"You stupid fool!" his father shouted on finding Daniel on the beach. His son hadn't shown up at the appointed time. After dealing with the search party, Tunny had gone down the path to see what had happened to him. Finding him lying there lifeless and the prisoner gone, he had flown into a rage.

Kicking his son in the ribs again, he swore at him loudly.

"You couldn't even do a simple thing like bring him up the hill! What's the matter with you? You stupid bastard! You make me sick!"

He kicked the body again, but this time, instead of laying inertly, Daniel caught his father's foot between his ribcage and the crook of his arm. With a sudden twisting motion and strength born of madness, he took his father swiftly off his feet.

Daniel was no longer recognizably human. All those characteristics that distinguish us from dumb animals - speech, intelligence, rational thought, self-conscious awareness - were gone. No thoughts went through his brain. No feelings crossed the threshold of his mind. For all practical purposes he was a dead thing, moved not by normal bodily functions, but by hatred, not by conscious will, but by some inner supernatural drive to destroy the cause of all his misery.

Tunny shrank back at the sight of his son, who was drenched in his own gore. His blood-red eyes showed with an intense coldness, lifeless, yet full of hate. His lips were pulled back to bare gnashing teeth. The sound of their grinding was the only sound he made.

He crawled and clawed his way up his father's leg. All he wanted was to get that smooth, white neck in his hands and squeeze the Adam's apple until it popped like a plastic bag.

Tunny pulled the revolver from his holster, and pointed it at Daniel's head as it inched toward him. Closer and closer it came, like a slithering snake. Then just before Tunny pulled the trigger, his son stopped moving once and for all. A mighty spasm shook his whole frame, and he was still.

Tunny lay panting for several minutes. Then he kicked the dead body away, leaving him face down in the mud.

He realized that the patsy must be miles from there by now, but it didn't matter. No one would believe his story. Daniel would be just another victim of this guy's handiwork. It wouldn't make any difference one way or the other. There was nothing anyone could do to stop them now.

He followed the path back to his house, where his private Mercedes was parked in the garage. They would have to carry on without Daniel and hope for the best. Not that they had any more need for him. From here on he would only have been a liability. This guy Lawless had actually done them a favor. Tunny hoped to return it.

Entering the garage, he got in the car and backed it out. Then he drove to the maximum security area on other side of the base, where the strategic bombers were kept, along with their nuclear ordnance. He had a date with destiny. Time was running out - for everyone.

Chapter 27

Day 19 (1:00 a.m.)

I woke up feeling the car moving. It took me a few minutes to orient myself and remember where I was and how I got there. There was nothing to do now but wait for it to stop. The good news was I hadn't been discovered yet. The bad news was I didn't know where I was headed, but there was a good bet it was someplace I didn't want to be.

I couldn't get the killer's words out of my mind as he lay dying in the sand whispering his confession. I found it hard to believe, but why would he make up something like that with his last breath? Incredible as it seemed, I had to assume it was true. But what was I to do, hiding helplessly in the trunk of a car? I figured I'd most likely get caught and shot. I felt cornered.

We came to a halt after about ten minutes. I laid there in silence, straining to hear what was happening outside the car. After awhile, hearing nothing but the rain beating on the trunk hood, I slowly eased it open a crack to peek out.

I don't know what I expected to see, but it certainly wasn't what greeted my eyes. I blinked twice in disbelief as I gazed upon the two-story high tail section of a giant B-52 bomber, sticking out of a massive gray hanger.

It all had an air of unreality to it, like a dream or a scene from some spy thriller. I was apparently on the flight strip of the air base, where the bombers and fighters were kept, a no-man's land, where they shot first and asked questions later.

I had actually done the impossible. I had gotten into the high security area of a SAC Air Force Base, an area even Rambo couldn't have broken into in a million sequels. The story the killer had told me was true. It looked like I was smack in the middle of it, a pretty grim predicament, if you ask me.

I lay there trying to decide what to do for some time. I was just about to jump out and run for it, when I heard the whine of an engine. Peeking out, I saw the massive hanger doors open and the large plane slowly being backed out, pulled by a couple small tractors.

What now?

I huddled in the trunk of the car. Peering out through the small crack, I watched a crew of four fuel and ready the giant aircraft for flight. Was this it? Were they really going to bomb Washington? It sure looked like it. I wondered how I would handle all four men, when they abruptly went back into the hanger and shut the doors.

Shortly after that I heard a faint rattling, like the sound of a muffled jackhammer. I had no idea what was going on, or what I was going to do. Being the chicken that I am, I decided to stay hidden in the car trunk until I was driven back out of the base again to safety.

As I looked out at the big bomber sitting on the airstrip, the hanger doors reopened. Two men in green fatigues came out riding on a small tractor. Piled on the cart behind it were the bodies of the four airmen who had just readied the plane. They were covered with blood and looked quite dead. Those sounds I heard suddenly made sense. It was gunfire. They had bumped off the whole ground crew in cold blood! These guys weren't messing around. But then I already knew that.

The sight of the dead men piled up like so much refuse sent a chill through my spine. It only reinforced my resolve to lie low until the killers had gone and the danger was past.

I watched as they loaded the bodies into the plane. When they finished, they disappeared into the hanger again. A short time later one of them emerged dressed in a gray flight suit and climbed into the pilot's hatch. I could see him sitting at the controls in the warm glow of the cabin lights. I couldn't see the other one and assumed he was still inside the hanger. I heard the whine of machine engines closing the huge hanger doors.

I lay in the darkness and waited, peeking out of the crack every now and then to ascertain the situation. The rain pounded incessantly on the metal hood of the trunk. I just wanted the plane to take off so that I could get the hell out of there. After that, I wasn't sure what I would do, probably try and call Jerry, which is what I should have done in the first place.

I heard footsteps clicking on the wet pavement nearby, but could see no one. I shut the trunk door gently and waited in the blackened compartment, listening.

Then, without warning, the door of the trunk swung open. For a moment we looked at each other in surprise. Then, before I could move, the man brought up the snub-nosed machine-gun he had strapped around his shoulder. For the second time in two days, he pointed the barrel of a gun at my head.

"So here you are!" he said in recognition. "Nice of you to join us. Get out of there! Move! Get your hands up!"

I slowly complied and got out of the trunk, blinking dumbly and putting my hands up.

"OK, get moving. Toward the plane, stupid," he ordered, not letting the gun waver from my gut.

I couldn't believe it. I cursed my luck. I'd been caught. I was a dead man. I tried to clear my mind as I walked slowly toward the giant bomber. I fought to dispel the fear clouding my brain, which made it hard to think.

We reached a hatch next to the oversized landing gear. He told me to climb the short metal ladder and get into the plane. I tried to judge how close he was to me from his voice. It didn't sound close enough for me to reach him before he shot me. He must have noticed the short sword tied to my back, but said nothing.

As I entered the compartment I noticed the bodies of the unfortunate ground crew lying in a pile on the corrugated metal floor. My hand accidentally touched one of the still forms. I thought I saw him move, but it must have been my imagination. Nobody could have looked like that and still be breathing.

I couldn't help thinking that in a few moments I would be just like them, full of holes, covered with blood, and dead. My captor, who was right behind me, but out of kicking range, told me to lie down on the floor on my stomach with my hands over my head.

As I lay there on the cold hard floor, I hoped the end would be quick and painless. There was nothing I could do. My sword was useless. This guy wasn't taking any chances.

I felt bad that my friends, Suzie, my Dad, everyone who I really cared for, would never know what had happened to me. I hoped my name would somehow be cleared. I was thinking of going for my sword. At least I wouldn't go without a fight. But the slim chance that I might still have some time left if I did nothing stopped my hand.

The man suddenly pulled my sword from its scabbard. I was sure I was about to be skewered with it. Instead, he brought the hilt down on the back of my skull, sending lightning bolts flashing through my nervous system. Then all was darkness.

Interlude

Flight Strip, SAC Air Force Base, Minutes Later

Tunny and Dene sat in the cockpit, readying the plane for take-off. The B-52 they were flying had been modified with all the latest avionics - radar and communication gear, landing and navigational aids, terrain correlators and computers. Not to mention the advanced Electro-optical Viewing System.

Cruise missiles hung in pylons under the wings. They would be used to neutralize bases on the return route if necessary. The two Douglas Quail decoy missiles would deceive radar tracking after the takeoff and bombing.

Dene smiled with satisfaction when Tunny told him how the 'patsy' had turned up in the trunk of his car. They laughed and toasted their good fortune with coffee.

"The gods must be with us," he said, clapping Tunny on the back.

What gods he had in mind is hard to know. Maybe the gods of death and destruction - Baal, Kali, Loki, Huitzilopochtli - would not be too far off the mark.

"Are you sure we can handle this thing ourselves?" Tunny asked nervously, still shaken from the sight of the airmen jumping like frogs as the high-powered bullets ripped into their bodies.

"Yes, I'm sure," said the commander confidently. "The flight pattern has been programmed into the plane's computers. The bombs' arming systems have also been preprogrammed. This baby'll pretty near fly herself. Just like the good old days, eh Ed?"

Tunny didn't answer, but prepared for takeoff. Their men were in the control tower. Their flight was logged as a top secret training mission to Greenland.

As Dene taxied the plane down the runway, his face took on a frightful visage, a ghastly expression of unbridled, malignant intent.

Taking off, they headed north toward the Canadian border, gaining altitude to their specified flight path of 47,000 feet. Tunny checked the flight data entered earlier into the Quail decoy missile's autopilot mechanism. Just before reaching the Canadian border, he opened the doors of the internal weapons bay and activated switches controlling the decoy's release mechanism.

Dene banked the aircraft sharply to the right and downward as the decoy was released. The missile ejected from the weapons bay and the doors closed back up. Tunny, acting as weapon's officer, ignited the decoy's rocket engine by remote control. It climbed to 47,000 feet, their bomber's original altitude, where the onboard autopilot took over to control flight. It fired the decoy toward the St. Lawrence Seaway, in the northeasterly direction they had been logged to follow.

Dean headed the aircraft south, over the lake. Their tear-drop flight pattern would take them over western New York and central Pennsylvania, toward DC. They flew low to avoid radar detection by the bases that lay along their route, which were few. Dene knew the flight patterns of all aircraft in the area. So they would not be spotted from the air.

They skimmed the ground at 400 miles per hour. The rain splashed on the blacked-out cockpit windscreen. Using EVS displays to guide them, they flew blind.

In an hour, they were less than ten minutes from their target. Flying low, they were only a few hundred feet above the treetops, the altimeter reading under 1000.

Tunny made a last minute check of the target-guidance computer, while Dene went over in his mind the difficult toss-bombing approach. At over half the speed of sound, they drew inexorably on toward the drop-point.

The effects of the two 22.4 megaton detonations would be devastating. One on DC, the other on New York City, would virtually paralyze the entire northeastern and Atlantic seaboards. The government would be wiped out. The country would be overwhelmed. No one would know who had done it, or what to do about it. Chaos would reign.

To prevent possible interference on their return flight from planes dispatched from New York or New England, his supporters in Washington - who by the way had left the city - had been able to influence emergency response plans for just such an incident. These ensured that no one would observe Dene's final escape route except his own squadrons, which had been assigned to cover the area. Those squadrons would never receive the emergency alert signal. Dene and Tunny's flight recorder would be replaced with a prerecorded one indicating an aborted flight to Greenland, not that there would be anyone left around to check.

"Estimated arrival at destination red-A is 5.15 minutes," observed Tunny, looking up from his calculations.

Dene reached down and opened the bomb bay doors.

The giant aircraft hugged the ground. All the plane's transmitting devices had been switched off. They had virtually disappeared off the face of the earth. There was no turning back now. Armageddon was about to be unleashed.

Chapter 28

Day 19 (2:30 a.m.)

I woke to find myself sitting on the grated metal floor of the aircraft, which vibrated violently against my buttocks. My hands were tied to something behind me. I had no idea how long I had been unconscious. I could feel what must have been blood trickling down the back of my neck from where I had been hit on the head with the hilt of my long samurai dagger. The fuselage swirled around in my blurred vision. I would have given anything just to hold my aching head.

I tested the knots, but was not able to loosen them. The plane bumped along at considerable speed as I continued to struggle against the rope binding me, to no avail.

I turned my head to survey the situation. The bodies of the dead ground crew lay in a heap only a few feet away. Their blood seeped in all directions down the grooves in the corrugated metal floor. Then I spotted it, the short, gleaming steel blade. It was lying next to the outstretched hand of one of the dead airmen. It looked incongruous against the dull, battleship-gray of the fuselage.

Try as I might, I was unable to reach it. It might as well have been miles from me instead of only a few measly feet. The situation was hopeless. I was about to give up, slumping back in resignation, when I heard a low moan coming from the pile of bodies. I strained at my bonds.

"Is someone alive there?" I yelled hoarsely over the din. "Can you hear me? Can you move?"

Again, another low moan, the sound of pain mingled with fear. It was coming from the airman whose hand lay near my sword.

"Can you move?" I asked again frantically, hoping against hope. "Can you hear me? Try to move your hand. Throw me the sword!" I yelled.

I could see him respond to my entreaties. His whole frame shuddered with the effort to move his hand.

"Throw me the sword!" I screamed again over the noise of the aircraft. "It's right by your arm. Throw it to me. You've got to try. They're going to bomb Washington, the President. We've got to stop them! You're the only one who can help me. Throw me the sword.

Please, throw me the sword! Help me get the bastards that did that to you!"

He went still, crushing my hopes.

Then, when all seemed lost, his hand jerked with a start. The man's entire frame lifted off the floor at once. With a sweeping motion that was his last on earth, he scooped up the short sword and tossed it at my feet. It landed with a clatter on the grating.

Stretching out my legs, which were bound at the ankles, I hooked the hilt with my feet, and edged it closer until it was directly under me. From there I was able to reach the hilt. Bracing it against the bulkhead behind me with the sharp edge pointed up, I slid my hands back and forth. As I worked the ropes in this way, I heard the whine of the engines. The aircraft abruptly rose, ascending rapidly, nose to the sky.

The rope binding my hands finally snapped apart. I worked at the one around my ankles and had it untied in no time.

At that moment, the bomb-bay doors opened.

The sound of the wind and the jet engines became deafening. The plane shook beneath me. Standing uncertainly in the swaying fuselage, I started to creep forward up the confined body of the plane.

I stopped and checked the miracle working airman to see if by any chance he might still be alive. He wasn't. There was nothing I could have done for him, in any case. He had done his part. Now I had to do mine.

The sound was deafening. The plane shook as if it would fall apart. I was still seeing double from the knock on the head. I moved as if possessed. Perhaps I was. Keeping low and to the side of the aircraft, I used the outcroppings and bulkheads to pull myself forward.

Climbing a short ladder to the cabin, I yanked open the hatch in a blind rage. I was no longer Jay Lawless, a down on his luck ex-insurance investigator. I had become that murderous animal hidden deep inside me, a holdover from some primitive past. I saw nothing but red fiery death for everyone. They didn't hear me over the din of the engines.

Both men had helmets on and were engrossed with what they were doing. They sat side by side in the cramped cockpit, in front of a narrow windshield. There were panels of dials and controls in front of them. Neither had noticed my dramatic entrance. By the time they looked up in astonishment, it was too late. I was on them like a half-mad cougar.

"Stop this plane!" I yelled, shaking with terror and rage. "Bring it down and land it or I'll kill us all!"

I stood in a wide stance, the short sword tight in my right hand and pointed at the pilot's neck. I had all intentions of crashing the plane. I figured my life wasn't worth much at this point. If I could stop these guys and avenge the victims, I would be selling it at a good price. After all, it seemed to be my destiny.

The pilot jerked the controls to the left, banking sharply. The other man grabbed for the small black machine-gun at his side.

Knocked momentarily off balance, I was thrown against the bulkhead. I was still able to deliver a cross-handed blow with the back of the sword to the co-pilot's face. His head snapped back, his forehead cut deeply. He dropped the gun with a scream and grabbed his head. Instinctively, without thought, I stabbed the short blade into his throat. It sliced through his neck like a melon. The knife came out the other side and dug into the seatback.

His eyes bulged. His mouth gaped. Warm blood gushed out like a fountain. His hands grasped the blade as his head jerked back and forth violently. In the back of my mind, in some hidden compartment where it still functioned, I wondered grimly at how easy killing had become. I hoped it wouldn't become a habit.

In the meantime, the pilot was grappling with me while he flew the plane. Unable to extract the blade from the still shaking co-pilot's neck, I let it go and concentrated on the other man.

To avoid crashing, the pilot had been gaining altitude and circling the aircraft. He was desperately trying to fly the plane and fend me off. So far, he had managed to keep the thing in the air despite my attack.

I screamed and jumped on him, hitting him with forearms, punches, elbows, and chops. Buckled in his seat, he had nowhere to go, but the helmet protected him and my blows had minimal effect.

"Land this thing now!" I demanded, jarring his skull with an elbow. "Land us now or I'll kill us both!"

In spite of my savage assault, the pilot managed to get the plane in a tight, ascending turn. We were slowly gaining altitude as it circled ever higher over the lights of the capital.

Getting weaker by the minute, I was out of breath, in danger of passing out. In desperation, I grabbed his helmet and tried to pull it off. Yanking it violently, first in one direction, I snapped it back in the other. His neck cracked. He started jerking spastically. I let go and his head lolled back limply.

Falling forward in his seat, he pushed the control wheel into the panel and took the plane into a nosedive. I was thrown forward as well, into the mass of dials and lights.

We were losing altitude rapidly. I could feel the dark earth spinning up at us. I struggled to regain my balance in the plummeting aircraft. Looking around the cockpit wildly, I spotted two things, the emergency escape latch, and the parachute built into the pilot's seat.

I took hold of the pilot, unbuckled his harness, and pulled him out of the seat. Jumping in, I strapped myself in his place and put on the helmet. Then, saying a silent prayer, I grabbed the emergency ejection lever and pulled.

It blew with a loud explosion. I shot out of the belly of the plane like a man shot from a cannon, straight down. The air rushed at me like a tornado. It took my breath away and filled my eyes with dust. Blinded, with tears and prayers, I plunged through the air.

I couldn't have been more than a few thousand feet above the earth. I felt myself falling toward the dark ground at an incredible speed. I don't remember pulling any ripcord. The parachute must have opened by itself. I passed out waiting for something terrible to happen to me. My eyes were shut so tight I'm surprised they weren't squeezed shut for good.

As I fell into oblivion, I thought about my life, the lost chances, the missed opportunities, the failures and disappointments. It didn't seem so bad now. I would have given anything to have it all back. I thought of the friends I would never see again and hoped somehow they would find out the truth. I thought about my father and how proud he would have been, if he only knew what had really happened. I thought about Suzie and all the things we might have done together. Now I would never get to share my life with her.

I was comforted knowing that it had not all been in vain. I had done something with my measly life. Even though no one else would more than likely ever know, it couldn't negate the fact that I, Jay Lawless, an obscure loser from nowhere-ville, living a dead-end life, a man without a future and too much of a past, had saved countless lives from untold misery. And maybe, just maybe, one day, historians would discover and write about me, and my fame would live on far beyond the span of my miserable existence. I accepted my fate. These thoughts and the fact I had taken three of them with me, gave me some solace as I sank into the darkness and the cold embrace of oncoming death.

Chapter 29

Day 164

I have no memory of hitting the water or swimming to shore. Somehow, in a state of semi-consciousness, I managed to survive. Lucky for me, I had the help of two motorists, who happened to see the bomber crash into the Potomac River. They saw my parachute come down only a hundred yards from the shore, through the dark misty sky. It was silhouetted against the red glow of the fireball that ignited as the bomber hit the surface of the water.

It crashed into the river as if it were cement. The plane's fuselage ripped apart and spilled jet fuel into the hot engine exhausts. Flames spewed across the liquid surface of the water like wood chips. One of the motorists swam out and rescued me as I was going down for the third and possibly last time. Now there's a hero! They brought me to their car and called an ambulance. I was taken to a nearby hospital.

The plane went down in the lower Potomac, below Washington, near Potomac Heights in Maryland. And so here I am, in a Maryland hospital writing down my story for posterity.

The next few days were rather vague. As soon as it was determined who I was and what had happened, things got rather intense. An endless procession of military personnel, law enforcement officers, and government officials paraded through my room to ask me questions. This was despite my doctor's strenuous objections and my half-unconscious, doped-up state. I answered all the questions the best I could. I had a story to tell.

Needless to say, not too many people believed it. In fact, a good number still don't, even after all the facts have come out. I can't say I blame them. I hardly believe it myself and I lived through it.

That whole previous forty-eight hours had an unmistakable air of unreality to it. It was like one of those nightmares you keep waking up from only to find you're still dreaming. I lay in the hospital recuperating, trying to come to grips with what had happened to me. Nothing seemed real, not the doctors or the nurses, not the surroundings, certainly not the idiots interrogating me. I had lost the ability to distinguish reality from fantasy, if in fact I ever had it in the first place.

Most of the details of the incident are being withheld from the public. The two military police guards outside my room guarantee no one, including newspaper reporters, will be visiting me. I have not been able to see my family or friends, although they've been informed I'm alive and in custody. The authorities have hatched a suitable story to cover-up the appearance of the B-52 in the Potomac River. I was never there. Oh, that I wish it was true.

The newspapers reported that a plane from an unspecified SAC air force base, flying a special training mission, crashed into the Potomac. No immediate mention was made of the nuclear ordnance aboard. That came out later, when the expensive and difficult retrieval operations began. No mention was made of the plot to nuke the Capital, though it was eventually confirmed by the data on the in-flight computers and target systems found in the river by navy divers.

The two spies were listed as the distinguished pilots of the ill-fated special training mission. None of the crew of six were reported to have survived the crash. Ironically, Dene and Tunny were hailed as heroes for going down with the aircraft and making sure it crashed away from any densely population centers. My name was not mentioned at all or linked in any way with the incident. This despite the two eyewitnesses who pulled me out of the drink and saved my life.

There are still some pinheads who suspect me of being responsible for the series of murders that have plagued my hometown for two and a half weeks. Chief McNeil is one of them. As the facts have slowly emerged, however, it has become clear that the murders were related to a drug smuggling ring involving the base. These facts also show that I could not possibly have been the killer, having iron-tight alibis for at least three of the murders.

With the help of Jerry LaGrand, the base commander has been connected to the drug smuggling ring. It didn't hurt that I still had the bank statement recording the deposit of $25,000 to Ed Tunny from NCR Corp. I had forgotten all about it. They found it in the back pocket of my wet, dirt-stained suit pants when they searched my clothes. It clearly tied him to the money laundering Laundromats owned by Claude Laplace. Never mind that this evidence was obtained illegally. It collaborated my story.

Unfortunately, they never recovered the killer's body from the boat landing. Someone must have moved it, but it makes one wonder.

The plane had crashed and sunk in deep water. Once the news got out that there were enough nuclear explosives in the bottom of the

Potomac to separate Maryland and Virginia permanently from the union, all hell broke loose. It became nationwide news, carried on all the network stations and CNN for five consecutive days. The plane and bombs were finally recovered, but only after the most difficult process and several million dollars.

As usual, the government has tried to turn the whole situation to their advantage. They claimed the incident as proof that the accidental detonation of a nuclear bomb from a freefall drop is impossible. With the complex and foolproof safety arming systems in use today, nothing can implode the core of a nuclear bomb or warhead to the point of thermonuclear explosion, except the arming system itself.

I'm being kept in detention under lock and key, watched day and night by an armed guard who doesn't let me out of his sight. They call it protective custody, but it's more like they are trying to protect the public from me. I'm not allowed any visitors or phone calls. They're trying to make me sign an agreement promising not to talk about the incident to anyone. But I don't trust anybody in uniform after my latest experience, and refuse to sign it.

Just to be safe, I'm writing the entire thing down and smuggling it out of here in case something happens to me. After a while they'll probably realize that no one will believe my story. Further efforts on their part to silence me will only add to my credibility. They'll eventually have let me go home. At least that's my hope. Still, I imagine it will take awhile for things to settle down and get back to normal, if that's what you want to call it.

I've recovered from the physical effects of my trauma. The psychological and emotional damage, however, is another matter. It's lasted long after the physical wounds have healed. For weeks after my ordeal I went through a period of severe depression. I spent days in mental anguish over the guilt of killing three human beings and causing the deaths of at least two others. Even when, with considerable mental ingenuity, I'm able to persuade myself that I saved countless lives. I still feel guilty for the fact that I'm alive while so many better people have died. I often wake with a start, just as I'm falling asleep, feeling as if I'm falling through the air and plunging to the ground far below.

Recently I've begun to feel better, like a survivor. I actually did it. I beat the odds. I conquered my fear and overcame adversity. I no longer feel like a loser. Somehow, deep within me, I found the strength I needed to endure. Maybe it's just an almost insane inability to give up and admit defeat. Whatever it was, it gave me a new perspective. My personal problems don't seem so important anymore.

In spite of all the thoughts clamoring for attention in my frazzled brain, the one thing that dominates my thinking the most is Suzie. I long to see her again. I'm thinking of asking her to marry me, that is if she'll have me. I'm determined to put more effort into my relationship with Suzie than into any of my other pursuits.

I realize now that in the scheme of things, when life comes to its end, that love is the only thing that matters, and love is something that has to be worked at to succeed. Not sometime, not almost, but all the time. Not a very romantic notion, but one I hope to build a lasting and long relationship out of.

With the recent reduction in defense spending and subsequent consolidations, the base is being closed. I'm sure the events that I've described in this small narrative had more than a little to do with it, although no one will admit it. The closing might hurt the town, but we'll survive. My main concern, when I lie awake at night waiting for sleep that lingers just out of reach, is how close they came to succeeding in their plan and unleashing a nuclear holocaust. The thought still sends a shiver down my spine and makes me break out in a cold sweat.

Several of the experts still don't believe the plot was feasible. They doubt the two terrorists could have pulled it off and gotten away with it, two lone spies, flying an antiquated 1960's bomber. They may have succeeded with the initial strike, but an armada of defensive counterattack aircraft would have destroyed them long before they ever got near New York City. The fact is they almost pulled it off. With their knowledge of the disposition of defensive forces, the pilots' skill and experience, and given the element of surprise, they had as good a chance as anyone of succeeding.

In any case, all the experts agree on one thing. Even partial success, the dropping of a nuclear bomb on the capital at that particular time, would have had a devastating affect on the nation and the world.

Newly commissioned Brigadier General Fitzgerald visited me personally to thank me for my part in preventing the nuclear disaster. He even gave me a medal I wasn't allowed to keep. He informed me that since the near holocaust, certain security and defense arrangements, as well as SAC protocols, have been modified to prevent such events occurring in the future. Hey, live and learn I always say.

Epilogue

Deep in a mountain solitude, nestled amidst tall silent pines, inside a rustic log cabin, dust particles dance in the rays of the sun. They slant through a skylight window and splash on a page of newspaper. The front page picture shows two Air Force officers, with a story about a B-52 training mission gone bad. Another story tells about a grisly string of murders.

'Jim' glints in the dying light and flips the page. One by one he turns them, with a twisting, mechanical motion. The light reflects glaringly off his smooth, steel skin. It focuses on a picture on the second page, an old college photo that triggers a vague sense of recognition. It quickly turns to hatred. A caption under the picture reads, 'Police solve string of gruesome murders with the help of local insurance investigator, Mr. Jason Lawless, pictured above'.

One by one, 'Jim' flips the crinkled pages, back and forth, forth and back, long after the faint twilight of the day fades into darkness, long after the dim glimmer of thought flitters like a butterfly out of conscious reach.

The End?

About the Author

Joe was born in upstate, New York, where he grew up and went to school. He holds a Bachlor's Degree in music composition from Berklee College of Music, and a Master's Degree in Computer Science from Boston University. Joe lives in Hudson, Massachusetts with his wife Kathy. Until his retirement a few years ago, he programmed computers for a living. Joe studied Chinese Kenpo karate in Acton MA, obtaining his black belt in 1977. He took over the school (Acton Academy of Self-Defense) when his instructor left for the west coast. Joe ran the school for several years, obtaining the rank of nidan in the process. He has won first place in kata and second place in sparring in local tournaments. Joe also studied aikido and thi-chi over the years. Although he no longer goes to the dojo, he still does all his forms (fifteen of them) and continues to teach from time to time. As Joe used to tell his students, "Martial Arts are a way of life."

ALSO BY JOSEPH BEBO

Lake, Land, and Liberty

Family Legends – The Charbonneau Letter

Lamp of the Gods

Bach Again

In the Back of the Van

Stricken: Quantum of Revenge

The Shivering

My Terrible Mistress

The Shot

Altered Realities

Alex – A Lesson in Courage

Waiting to Take Off

www.ingramcontent.com/pod-product-compliance
Lightning Source LLC
Chambersburg PA
CBHW071310200626
46813CB00015B/1323